Thomas Dekker, Alexander Balloch Grosart

The non-dramatic works of Thomas Dekker

In five volumes. Vol. 1

Thomas Dekker, Alexander Balloch Grosart

The non-dramatic works of Thomas Dekker
In five volumes. Vol. 1

ISBN/EAN: 9783337304485

Printed in Europe, USA, Canada, Australia, Japan

Cover: Foto ©Andreas Hilbeck / pixelio.de

More available books at **www.hansebooks.com**

The Huth Library.

THE NON-DRAMATIC WORKS

OF

THOMAS DEKKER.

IN FIVE VOLUMES.

FOR THE FIRST TIME COLLECTED AND EDITED,
WITH MEMORIAL-INTRODUCTION, NOTES AND ILLUSTRATIONS, ETC.

BY THE REV.
ALEXANDER B. GROSART, D.D., LL.D. (Edin.), F.S.A. (Scot.).
St. George's, Blackburn, Lancashire.

VOL. I.

CANAAN'S CALAMITIE, JERUSALEM'S MISERIE, AND
ENGLAND'S MIRROR.

THE WONDERFULL YEARE (1603), AND
THE BATCHELARS BANQUET ; OR, A BANQUET
FOR BATCHELARS.

1598—1603.

PRINTED FOR PRIVATE CIRCULATION ONLY.
1884.

50 *Copies.*]

CONTENTS.

Fair is the mark of Good, and foul, of Ill,
Although not so infallibly, but still
The proof depends most on the mind and will.

As Good yet rarely in the Foul is met,
So 'twould as little by its union get,
As a rich jewel that were poorly set.

For since Good first did at the Fair begin,
Foul being but a punishment for sin,
Fair's the true outside to the Good within.

In these the Supreme Pow'r then so doth guide
Nature's weak hand, as he doth add beside
All by which creatures can be dignified,

While you in them see so exact a line,
That through each sev'ral parts a glimpse doth shine,
Of their original and form divine.

The Idea, by LORD HERBERT of Cherbury.

TO

A. H. BULLEN, Esq.,

EDITOR OF "OLD PLAYS," ETC., ETC.,

THIS FIRST COLLECTION OF

DEKKER'S NON-DRAMATIC WORKS

IS DEDICATED

WITH MUCH ADMIRATION AND THANKS.

———

IN FAR-BACK JACOBEAN DAYS, THE NAME
  OF DEKKER SEEN ON ANY TITLE-PAGE,
  DREW, MAGNET-LIKE, MEN'S EYES; HE WAS THE RAGE;
NOR, HOWE'ER SWIFTLY HIS ROUGH PAMPHLETS CAME,
DID GENTLE OR COMMON MURMUR OF BLAME.
  HE CLAIM'D NOT, TRULY, TO BE SAINT OR SAGE;
  CHALLENG'D FOR POET, HE'D SCARCE TA'EN THE GAGE;
BUT HE HAD THAT FORCE IN HIM WHICH DID TAME
EVEN "RARE BEN"; OR CALL IT MOTHER-WIT
OR GENIUS, HIS LIGHTEST WORKS LIVE STILL.
  MANY A MANNERS-PAINTING BOOK HE WRIT,
  PACK'D FULL OF QUAINTEST WIT AND PLAY OF WILL;
    BULLEN, ACCEPT THESE WORKS; TOUCHES IMMORTAL
    WILL GLEAM UPON YOU FROM THEIR LOWLY PORTAL.

ALEXANDER B. GROSART.

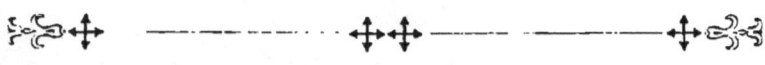

CANAAN'S CALAMITIE.

1598—1618.

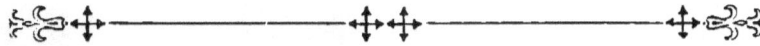

NOTE.

No perfect exemplar of the original (1598) edition of 'Canaans Calamitie' is known. Hazlitt (*s.n.* in 'Hand-Book.' vol. i.) describes an imperfect copy. For our text we are under obligation to the British Museum. See Memorial-Introduction on other editions; and related Notes and Illustrations.—G.

CANAANS
CALAMITIE

Ieruſalems Miſery,

OR

The dolefull deſtruction of faire Ie-
ruſalem by TYTVS, the Sonne of *Vaſpaſian*
Emperour of Rome, *in the yeare of* Chriſts
Incarnation 74.

Wherein is ſhewed the woonderfull miſeries which
God brought vpon that Citty for ſinne, being vtterly
ouer-throwne and deſtroyed by Sword,
peſtilence and famine.

AT LONDON,

¶ Printed for *Thomas Bayly*, and are to be ſould at
the corner-ſhop in the middle rowe in Holborne,
neere adioyning vnto *Staple Inne.*
1618.

TO THE RIGHT WORSHIPFVLL

M. Richard Kingſmill Eſquier, Iuſtice of peace
*and Quorum in the Countie of Southampton, and
Surueyer of her Maieſties Courtes of Wardes
and Liueries. All proſperitie and happines.*

Auing (Right worſhipfull) often heard
of your extraordinary fauour, ſhewed
in the depth of extremitie, to ſome
poore friendes of mine, remayning in your
pleaſant Lordſhip of *High-cleere* : by meanes
whereof, they haue had no ſmall comfort for
the recouerie of their wiſhed deſire : I haue
been ſtudious how I might in ſome meaſure
declare both their thankfulneſſe and mine owne
for ſo great a good. But ſuch is our weake
abillity that we cannot requite the leaſt poynt
of that life prolonging kindnes, which the riches
of your courteſie did yeeld : neuertheleſſe to
make apparent, that our poore eſtates ſhall not
obſcure, or clowd with ingratitude, the well
intending thoughts of our hearts : I haue pre-

fumed to prefent to your worfhip this little
booke, an vnfaigned token of our good affection,
hoping that like the Princely *Pertian* you will
more refpect the good will then the gift, which
I confeffe farre vnworthy fo worthy a Patron in
refpect of the fimple handling of fo excellent a
matter : But a playne ftile doth beft become
plaine truth, for a trifling fable hath moft neede
of a pleafant pen. Wherefore if it fhall pleafe
your Worfhip to efteeme of my fimple labour,
and to let this paffe vnder your fauorable pro-
tection, I fhall haue the end of my defire. And
refting thus in hope of your worfhips courtefie
I ceafe wifhing you all hearts content
in this life, and in the world to
come eternall felicitie.

Your worfhips moft humblie affectionate :
T. D.

To the Gentlemen Readers health.

Entlemen, I prefent you heere with the mourning fong of Ierufalems *forrow : whofe deftruction was Prophefied by our Lord Iefus Chrift, while he lived among them : notwithftanding they neither regarded, nor beleeved his words. And after they had in the mallice of their hearts, compact his death, and that the Iudge fought to cleare himfelfe of fo foule a crime : The curffed Iewes cryed with one confent faying :* his blood be on vs and one our children. *Which wicked wifh of theirs the Lord brought to paffe within a fhort time after, as in this following Hiftorie you fhall perceiue. At what time both Cittie and Temple was brought to vtter confufion : the mifery whereof was fo extreame as the like was never before, nor fince : And you fhall perceiue that this deftruction came vpon them in the time of their greateft profperitie, when their gould and Treafure moft abounded, when pride excelled, and that the people were bent to all*

*wantonnes.   Such was their daintineſſe and deli-
caſie, that they could not deviſe, with what meate
they might beſt pleaſe their nice ſtomacks, wiſhing
for better bread then could be made of Wheate:
abuſing in ſuch ſort, the bleſſings of God (which
was in great abundance beſtowed vpon them) that
being glutted with to much wealth and plentie,
they loathed every thing that bore not an high
price ; caſting ſcornefull eyes vpon Gods great
bleſſings: but in reading this Hiſtorie, you ſhall
ſee how ſoone their ſtate was changed, and the great
plaugs that followed their peuyſh and hatefull
pride : by whoſe wofull fall, God graunt vs
and all Chriſtians to take example leaſt
following them in the like ſinne, we
feele the like ſmart.   Vale.*

Yours in all courteſie.   T. D.

A description of Ierusalem *and the Riches thereof.*

Ike to a Mourner clad in dolefull
　　black,
　　That sadly sits to heare a heauie
　　　tale :
　　So must my pen proceed to shew
　　　the wrack,
That did with terror *Syon* hill assaile.
　What time *Ierusalem* that Cittie faire,
　Was sieg'd and sackt by great *Vespatians* heire.

A noble Iew *Iosephus* writes the storie.
Of all the stories euer yet recited,
Neuer could any make the mind more sorie,
Than that which he so dolefully indighted :
　Which sets in sight how for abhomination
　That goodly Citty came to desolation.

In all the world the like might not be seene,
To this faire Citty famous to behold :

A thoufand Towers ftood there the ftreetes between,
Whofe carued ftones great cunning did vnfold :
   The buildings all, fo ftately fine and rare,
   That with Ierufalem no place might compare.

In midft whereof the glorious Temple ftood,
Which Nehemia had fo faire erected,
Whofe Timber worke was all of precious wood,
By Gods appointment wounderoufly effected :
   Where all the People came with one accord,
   And offered facrifice, vnto the Lord.

Three / ftately walles begirt this Citty round,
Strongly raild vp of gallant fquared ftone,
Vnpoffible in fight foes fhould them confound,
By warlike Engines seized therevpon.
   The fpacious gates moft glorious to behold,
   Were all gilt ouer, with rich burnifht gould.

And round about *Ierufalem* likewife
Were pleafant walkes prepard for recreation,
Sweet daintie gardens feeding gazers eyes,
With workes of wonder and high admiration,
   Where in the midft of fweeteft fmelling flowers,
   They built for pleafure, many pleafant bowers.

In treafures ftore this Citty did excell,
For pompe and pride it was the onely place,

In her alone did richeſt Marchants dwell,
And famous Princes ſprung of Royall race :
   And fairer Dames did nature neuer frame,
   Then in that Citty dwelt and thither came.

Chriſts Propheſie of the deſtruction

of this Cittie and how it came to paſſe accordingly
within Forty yeares after, ſhewing the cauſe that
mooued the Emperour to come againſt it.

Vr / Sauiour Chriſt tracing the bordring hilles
   When he on this faire Cittie caſt his eye
The teares along his roſiall cheekes diſtilles :
Mourning for their deſtruction drawing nie.
   O *Ieruſalem*, *Ieruſalem* quoth hee,
   My heart bewailes thy great calamitie.

The time ſhall come and neere it is at hand,
When furious foes ſhall trench thee round about,
And batter downe thy Towers that ſtately ſtand,
All thy ſtrong holds within thee and without :
   Thy golden buildings ſhall they quite confound,
   And make thee equal with the lowly ground.

O woe to them that then giues ſucke he ſayes,
And lulles their Infants on their tender knees,

More woe to them that be with child thofe dayes,
Wherein fhalbe fuch extreame miferyes:
　　Thou mightft haue fhund thefe plagues hadft
　　　　thou bin wife
　　Which now for finne is hidden from thy eyes.

This dreadfull Prophefie fpoken by our Lord,
The ftubborne people naught at all regarded,
Whofe Adamantine heartes did ftill accord,
To follow finne, which was with fhame rewarded :
　　They flouted him for telling of this ftorie,
　　And crucifide in fpite the Lord of glorie.

Re / prochfully they fleeted in his face,
That wept for them in tender true compaffion,
They wrought his death and did him all difgrace,
That fought their life, and waild their defolation :
　　Their hardened heartes beleeu'd not what was
　　Vntill they faw the fiege about them layd. [faid,

Full fortie yeares after Chrifts paffion,
Did thefe proud people liue in peace and reft,
Whofe wanton eyes feeing no alteration,
Chrifts words of truth, they turned to a ieft :
　　But when they thought themfelues the fureft of
　　Lo then began their neuer raifed fall.　　　[all,

Their mounting minds that towred paſt their
Scorning ſubiection to the *Romaine* ſtate [ſtrength,
In boyling hatred loath'd their Lords at length,
Diſpiſ'd the Emperour with a deadly hate :
    Reiecting his authoritie each howre,
    Sought to expell the pride of forraine power.

Which foule contēpt the Emperours wrath inflam'd,
Mightie *Veſpatian* hot reueng did threat,
But all in vaine they would not be reclaim'd,
Relying on their ſtrength and courage great :
    And herevpon began the deadly iarre,
    And after followed bloody wofull warre.

The / ſignes and tokens ſhewed before

the deſtruction, alluring the Iewes to repentance,
and their little regard thereof, interpreting
all things to be for the beſt, flattering
themſelues in their ſinnes.

Et marke the mercy of our gracious God,
    Before the grieuous ſcourge to them was ſent,
That they might ſhun his heauie ſmarting rod
And hartely their filthy faultes repent :
    Strange ſignes and wonders did he ſhew them
    Fore-runners of their ruine, woe, and ill.   [ſtill

For one whole yeare as well by day as night,
A blazing ftarre appeared in the fkie,
Whofe bufhie tayle was fo excelling bright,
It dim'd the glory of the funns faire eye,
    And euery one that on this obiect gazed,
    At fight thereof ftood wonderous fore amazed.

In right proportion it refembled well,
A fharp two edged fword of mighty ftrength,
The percing poynt a needle did excell,
And fure it feem'd a miracle for length :
    So ftrange a ftarre before was neuer feene,
    And fince that time the like hath neuer been.

And / ouer right that goodly famous Cittie,
Hung ftill this dreadfull apparition,
Which might haue mou'd had they bin gracious
        witty,
For outward follies, inward hearts contrition :
    And neuer did that wonder change his place,
    But ftill *Ierufalem* with woe menace.

The wondring people neuer lookt thereon,
But their miftrufting heart fufpected much,
Saying great plagues would follow therevpon,
Such priuie motions did their confcience touch :
    But other-fome would fay it was not fo,
    But figne that they their foes would ouerthrow.

Thinke not quoth they that Iacobs God will leaue,
The bleffed feed of *Abraham* in diftreffe :
Firft fhall his Sword the heathens liues bereaue,
As by this token he doth plaine expreffe,
 His fierie fword fhall fhield this holy towne,
 And heaw in heapes the proudeft *Romains*
  downe.

Thus flattered they themfelues in finfull fort,
Their harts were hard, their deepeft iudgmc̄ts
What godly teachers did to them report, [blinded
They foone forgot, fuch things they neuer minded :
 Their chiefeft ftudy was delight and pleafure,
 And how they might by all meanes gather
  treafure.

Men / would haue thought this warning had bin
  faire,
When God his ftandard gainft them did aduance,
His flag of Iuftice waued in the ayre,
And yet they count it, but a thing of chance :
 This bad them yeild, and from their finnes
  conuart,
 But they would not till forrow made them
  fmart.

Then in the ayre God fhewed another wonder,
When azurd fkies were brighteft faire and cleere,

An hoaſt of armed men, like dreadfull thunder,
With hidious clamours, fighting did appeare :
　　And at each other eagerly they ran,
　　With burniſht Falchions murdering many a man.

And marching fiercely in their proud aray,
Their wrathfull eyes did ſparkle like the fier,
Or like inraged Lyons for their pray,
So did they ſtriue, in nature and deſire :
　　That all the plaine wherein they fighting ſtood,
　　Seem'd to mens ſight all ſtaind with purple
　　　　blood.

This dreadfull token many men amazed :
When they beheld the vncouth ſight ſo ſtrange,
On one another doubtfully they gazed,
With fearefull lookes their coulour quite did change :
　　Yet all, they did interpret to the beſt,
　　Thinking themſelues aboue all others bleſt.

The / conquering ſort that did with warlike hand,
Suppreſſe the other in the bloudy field,
Declares quoth they that *Iudaes* ſacred band
Shall make vnhallowed *Romaines* die or yeeld :
　　And ouer them we ſhall haue honour great,
　　That proudly now vſurpes King Dauids ſeat.

See how the Diuell doth ſinfull ſoules beguile,
Filling the ſame with vaine imagination,

Thinking themfelues cock-fure, when al the while,
They ftand vpon the brink of defolation :
    All faithfull Chriftians warning take by this,
    Interpret not Gods fearefull fignes amiffe.

Yet loe the Lord would not giue ouer fo,
But to conuert them, if that it might bee,
Hee doth proceed more wonders yet to fhow,
All to reclayme them from iniquitie :
    That fo he might remoue his plagues away,
    Which threatned their deftruction euery day.

The Temple gates all made of fhining braffe,
Whofe maffie fubftance was exceeding great,
Which they with yron barres each night did croffe,
And lockt with brazen bolts, which made them fweat,
    Did of themfelues ftart open and vndoe,
    Which twenty men of might could fcant put to.

Vpon / a day moft high and feftiuall,
The high Prieft went after a facred manner,
Into the glorious Temple moft maiefticall,
To offer facrifice their God to honour :
    What time the Lord a wonder did declare,
    To all mens fight, prodigious, ftrange, and rare.

A goodly *Calfe* prepar'd for facrifice
And layd vpon the holy Alter there,

Brought forth a *Lambe* moſt plaine before their eyes,
Which filled ſome mens hearts with ſodaine feare :
   And ſore perplext the paſſions of their mind,
   To ſee a thing ſo farre againſt all kind.

Soone after this they heard a wailefull voice,
Which in the Temple ſhreeking thus did ſay,
Let vs go hence, and no man heere reioyce :
Thus figuring foorth their ruine and decay,
   All men did heare theſe ſpeeches very plaine,
   But ſaw nothing, nor knew from whence it came.

And foure yeares ſpace before the bloody fight,
One *Ananias* had a youthfull ſonne,
Which like a Prophet cried day and night
About the ſtreetes as he did go and runne :
   Shewing the people without dread at all,
   Moſt wofull plagues ſhould on the Cittie fall.

And / in this ſort began his dolefull cry :
A fearefull voyce proceedeth from the Eaſt,
And from the Weſt, as great a voyce did fly,
A voyce likewiſe from bluſtering winds addreſt :
   A voyce vpon *Ieruſalem* ſhall goe,
   A voyce vpon the Temple full of woe.

A mournefull voyce on wretched man and wife,
A voyce of ſorrow on the people all,

Woe and deftruction, mortall war and ftrife,
Bitter pinching famine, mifery and thrall :
    In euery place thefe threatnings ftill he had,
    Running about like one diftraught and mad.

With lofty voyce thus ran he through the towne,
Nor day and night did he his clamours ceafe,
No man could make him lay thefe threatnings
By no intreaty would he hould his peace :   [downe
    Although he was in Dungeon deeply layd,
    Yet there his cryes did make them more afraid.

The Maieftrates that moft forbad his crie :
And faw his bouldneffe more and more arife,
With grieuous fcourges whipt him bitterly,
Yet came no teares out of his pleafant eyes :
    The more his ftripes, the higher went his voyce,
    In foreft torment did he moft reioyce.

But / when the *Iewes* perceau'd how he was bent,
And that their eares were cloyed with his cries,
They counted it but fportfull merriment.
A nine dayes wonder that in fhort time dyes :
    So that afrefh their follies they begin,
    And for his fpeech they paffed not a pin.

But as the holy Scriptures doe bewray,
To dainty cheere they iocundly fat downe,

And well refreſht, they roſe againe to play,
In ſmiling ſort when God did fircely frowne :
    And neuer more to mirth were they diſpoſed,
    Then when the Lord his wrath to them diſcloſed.

    ¶ *The tydings brought of the enimies approach,
and the feare of the citizens: their proviſiõ of
victuals for twenty yeares burnt in one night, by one
of their owne captaines, of meere malice, which
cauſed a ſodaine dearth to follow: their ſeditiõ
and diuiſiõ betweene thẽſelues while the cittie was
beſieged.*

B Vt whilſt that they their ſugred Iunkets taſted,
    Vnto the Citty came a tyred poſt,
Full weake and wearie, and with trauell waſted,
Who brought thẽ word their foes were on their
    coaſt :
    Which when they knew, their merriments were
    daſhed,
    Theſe dolefull newes made them full ſore
    abaſhed.

Three / Cipres Tables then to ground they throw,
Their ſiluer diſhes, and their cups of gould,

For hafte to meet the proud inuading foe,
Feare makes them mad, but courage makes thē
    bould :
    And to defend the brunt of future harmes,
    They leaue their Ladies and imbrace their
      Armes.

Inftead of Lutes and fweete refounding Vials,
They found the Trumpet and the ratling drum,
Their barbed Steeds they put to diuers tryals,
How they can manage, ftop, carrie, and run :
    Their cunning harpers now muft harneffe beare,
    Their nimble dauncers war-like weapons weare.

But ere their wrathfull foes approached neere,
The ftore-houfes the Gouernors did fill,
With wholfome victuals which for twenty yeare
Would ferue two hundred thoufand caft by bill,
    But all the fame by one feditious Squire
    Was in one night confum'd with flaming fire.

For why the Cittizens to difcord fell,
So giddy headed were they alwaies found,
And in their rage like furious fiends of hell,
In murdering fort they did each other wound :
    And when they entred in this diuellifh ftrife,
    They fpared neither Infant, man, nor wife.

Into / three parts the people were deuided,
And one againſt an other hatred bore,
The chiefeſt ſort ſedicioufly were guided,
Whereby vnciuell mutines vext them ſore :
    So that the ſorrow of the forreine warre
    Was nothing to their bloody ciuill iarre.

And ſo malicious did their rancor riſe,
That they the holy Temple did defile,
All ſuch as came to offer ſacrifice,
They murdered ſtraight, remorce they did exile :
    The Sacrificer with the ſacrifice,
    Both bath'd in blood, men ſaw before their eyes.

Thus did they make the ſacred Temple there
The ſlaughter houſe of many a humane ſoule,
So that the marble pauement euery where,
Was blacke with blood like to a butchers bowle :
    And with the fat of men ſo ſlippery made,
    That there for falling, none could goe vnſtayd.

And by this wicked meanes it came to paſſe,
The ſtreets and temple full of dead-men lay,
With wounds putrified, where buriall was,
Which raiſ'd a grieuous peſtilence that day :
    So hot, and fell, that thereof dyed a number,
    Whoſe foule infection all the towne did
        cumber.

And / that which was more heauie to behold,
As men and woemen paſt along the ſtreet :
Their weeping eyes did to their hearts vnfold,
A mappe of Murder at their trembling feete :
   Some ſaw their Fathers fetching deadly groanes,
   Some their Huſbands braines ſcattered on the
     ſtões.

Here lay a woman ſtabbed to the heart,
There a tender Infant one a ſouldiers ſpeare,
Strugling with death, and ſprawling with each part :
The channels ran with purple blood each wheare,
   A thouſand perſons might you daily ſee,
   Some gaſping, groaning, bleeding freſh to bee.

Lo all this miſchiefe was within the towne
Wrought twixt theſelues in wonderous hatefull ſort,
While noble *Tytus* beat their bulwarkes downe,
And at their walles did ſhew them warlike ſport :
   But by diſtreſſe to bring them vnto thrall,
   He brake their pipes, and ſtopt their cundits all.

¶ A defcrip / tion of the horrible Famine within
the Cittie of Ierufalem.

FOr true report rung in his royall eares,
That bitter Famine did afflict them fore,
Which was the caufe of many bitter teares,
And he to make their miferie the more,
Depriu'd them quit of all their water cleere,
Which in their want they did efteeme fo deere.

Alack, what pen is able to expreffe ?
The extreame miferie of this people then ?
Which were with Famine brought to great diftreffe,
For cruell hunger vext the wealthieft men :
When night approacht, well might they lye &
winke,
But cold not fleepe for want of meat and drinke.

For by this time full Fourteene monthes and more,
Had warlike *Titus* fieg'd that famous towne,
What time the *Iewes* had quite confum'd their ftore,
And being ftaru'd, like Ghofts went vp and downe :
For in the markets were no victuals found,
Though for a *Lambe*, they might haue twenty
pound.

When / bread was gone, then was he counted bleft,
That in his hand had either cat or dogge,

To fill his emptic maw : and thus diftreft,
A dozen men would fight for one poore frogge :
 The faireft Lady lighting one a mouce,
  Would keepe it from her beft friend in the
   houfe.

A weazell was accounted daynty meate,
A hiffing fnake efteem'd a Princes difh,
A Queene vpon a moule might feeme to eate,
A veanom neawt was thought a wholefome fifh :
 Wormes from the earth, were dig'd vp great
  & fmall,
 And poyfoned fpiders eaten from the wall.

A hundred men vnder this grieuous croffe,
With hunger-ftarued bodies wanting food,
Haue for a morfell of a ftinking horfe,
In deadly ftrife, fhed one anothers blood :
 Like famifht Rauens, that in a fhole doe pitch,
 To feaze a caryon in a noyfome ditch.

But when thefe things, were all confumed quite,
(For Famines greedy mawe deftroyeth all)
Then did they bend, their ftudy day and night,
To fee what next vnto their fhare might fall :
 Neceffitie doth feele an hundred wayes,
 Famines fell torment from the heart to rayfe.

D. I.   4

Then / did they take their horſes leather raignes,
And broyling them ſuppoſ'd thē wonderous ſweete:
A hungry ſtomack naught at all refraines:
Nor did they ſpare their ſhooes vpon their feete:
  But ſhooes, and bootes, and buſkins, all they eate,
  And would not ſpare one morſell of their
    meate.

But out alas my heart doth ſhake to ſhow, [made,
When theſe things fail'd, what ſhift theſe wretches
Without ſalt teares how ſhould I write their woe,
Sith ſorrowes ground-worke in the ſame is layd:
  All Engliſh hearts which Chriſt in armes doe hem
  Marke well the woes of fayre *Ieruſalem*.

When all was ſpent, and nothing left to eate,
Whereby they might maintaine their feeble life,
Then doth the wife her huſband deere intreat,
To end her miſery by his wounding knife:
  Maides weepe for foode & children make their
    mone,
  Their parents ſigh when they can giue them
    none.

Some men with hunger falleth raging mad,
Gnawing the ſtones and timber where they walke,

Some other ſtaggering, weake and wonderous ſad,
Dyes in the ſtreetes, as with their friends they
  And other ſome licks vp the vomit faſt, [talke?
  Which their ſick neighbours in their houſes caſt.

Nay / more then this, though this be all to much,
Ioſephus writes, that men and maidens young
The which of late did ſcorne brown-bread to touch,
Suſtain'd themſelues with one an others doong.
  Remember this you that ſo dainty bee,
  And praiſe Gods name for all things ſent to thee.

All things were brought by famine out of frame,
For modeſt Chaſtitie to it gaue place,
High honoured Virgins that for very ſhame,
Would hardly looke on men with open face,
  One bit of bread neuer ſo courſe and browne,
  Would winne them to the fouleſt knaue in towne.

¶ The feditious Captaines *Schimion* & *Iehocanā*
fearch *all the houfes in the Citty for Victuals, they
take from a noble* Lady *all her prouifion, leauing
her and her* Sonne *comfortleffe, fhewing the great
moane fhe made.*

THe curft feditious Captaines and their crue,
   When they perceiu'd the famine grow fo
     great,
In all mens houfes would they fearch, and view,
In euery corner both for bread and meat:
   If any did their bould requeft denie,
    On murdering fwords they were right fure to
     dye.

Among / the reft where they a fearching went,
Vnto a gallant Ladyes houfe they came,
And there before her victuals quite was fpent,
With hardened hearts, and faces void of fhame :
   They tooke her ftore with many a bitter threat,
   And left her not one bit of bread to eate.

The noble Lady on her tender knees,
With floods of teares diftilling from her eyes,
Their crueltie when fhe fo plainely fees,
In mournefull fort vnto them thus fhe cries :
   Vpon a wofull Lady take fome pittie,
   And let not famine flay me in this Cittie.

Of all the ſtore which you haue tooke away,
Leaue on browne loafe, for my poore child and me :
That we may eat but one bit in a day,
To ſaue our liues from extreame miſery.
 Thus holding vp her lillie hands ſhe cried,
 The more ſhe crau'd the more ſhe was denied.

If you quoth ſhe cannot afford me bread,
One dried ſtock-fiſh doe one me beſtow,
For my poore Infants life I greatly dread,
If thus diſtreſt you leaue me when you goe :
 Braue men of might, ſhew pittie for his ſake,
 And I thereof a thouſand meales will make.

O call / to minde my childe is nobly borne,
Of honorable blood and high degree :
Then leaue vs not braue Captaines thus forlorne,
Your countries friend one day this child may bee :
 O let me not this gentle fauour miſſe,
 I may one day requite far more then this.

Then anſwered they in harſh and churliſh ſort,
Tut tell not vs of honourable ſtate,
And if thou wilt we'l cut thy Infants throat,
So ſhall he neede no meate : then ceaſe to prate :
 Men muſt haue meate, let children dye and
  ſtarue,
 Yf we want foode, in warres how can we ſerue.

With bended browes they ſtroue to get away,
But ſhe vpon her knees did follow faſt,
And taking hould on their confuſ'd aray,
This ſad complaint from her hearts pallace paſt :
   Renouned Lords, our Citties ſure defence,
   O let me ſpeake once more, ere you go hence.

Yf you lack money, ſee I haue good ſtore,
Wherein great *Ceſars* Image is portrayde,
Therefore of gift, I will demaund no more,
To buy me ſome foode, let me not be denayd.
   For fiue red herrings, ten Crownes ſhall you haue,
   Ile pay it downe, with vantage if you craue.

That / damned coyne quoth they wee doe deteſt,
And therewithall thy ſelfe, which all this while,
Haſt kept our foes foule picture in thy cheſt,
Which ſeekes this holy Citty to defile :
   Thou getſt no foode, and therefore hold thy
      tounge,
   Hang, ſtarue, & dye, thou canſt not dye more
      young.

O pardon yet (quoth ſhe) my earneſt ſpeech,
Doe not my words to poyſon ſo conuert,

Take heere my chaine, I humbly doe befeech,
Of pearle and Diamonds for one filly fprat :
 One fprat (fweete men) caft vpon the ground,
 For this faire chayne, which coft a thoufand
  pound.

Talke not to vs, quoth they of Iems and chaines,
Of Diamonds, Pearls, or precious rings of Gould,
One fprat to vs is fweeter gotten gaines,
Then fo much filuer, as this houfe can hold :
 Gould is but droffe, where hunger is fo great,
 Hard hap hath hee, that hath but gould to eate.

With that the teftie Souldiers get them out,
Proud of the purchaft pray which they had got,
The woefull Ladye did they mocke and flout,
Her plaints and teares regarding not a iott :
 Shee fighes, they fmile, fhe mournes, and they
  reioyce,
 And of their pray they make an equall choyce.

But / Megar famine couetous of all
Enuying thofe that fhould thereof haue part,
In fharing out their purchaffe bread a brawle,
Wherein one ftabd the other to the heart :
 This fellow faid the other did deceiue him,
 He fwore againe enough they did not leaue him.

Lo thus about the victuals they did fight,
Looke who was ftrongeft bore away the prize,
And for a cruft of bread, in dead of night,
They cut their Fathers throats in wofull wife :
 The mother would her childrens victuals fnatch,
 And from his wife, the hufband he did catch.

¶ How the noble *Lady* and her young *Sonne* went to
 [*feeke*] *out the dung of beafts to eate, being ready*
 to dye with hunger, and could finde none : fhewing
 what moane they made comming home without.

BVt now of *Miriams* forrow will I fpeake,
 Whom the feditious Souldiers fo diftreft,
Her noble heart with grife was like to breake,
No kind of foode had fhe, then to reliue her.
 With gnawing hunger was fhe, fore oppreft
 Nor for her child, which moft of all did grieue her.

Alas, quoth fhee that euer I was borne,
To fee thefe gloomie daies of griefe and care,
Whome this falfe world hath made an open fcorne,
Fraught full of miferie paffing all compare
 Bleft had I been if in the painefull birth,
 I had receiu'd fweete fentence of my death.

Why hath the partiall heauens prolong'd my life,
Aboue a number of my deereft friends,
Whofe bleffed foules did neuer fee the ftrife?
How happy were they in their happy ends :
    Great God of *Abraham* heare my mournefull crie,
    Soone rid my life, or end this miferie.

With that her little fonne with eager looke,
Vnto his wofull mother crying came,
His pretty hands faft holde vpon her tooke,
Whofe prefence brought her praying out of frame :
    And to his Mother thus the child did fay,
    Giue mee fome meate, that eat nothing to day.

I am (deere Mother) hungry at the heart,
And fcalding thirft, makes me I cannot fpeake,
I feele my ftrength decay in euery part,
One bit of bread, for me good Mother breake :
    My leffon I haue learnd, where you did lay it,
    Then giue me fome-what : you fhall heere me
        fay it.

The / fighing Ladie looking quite a-fide,
With many fobs fent from her wofull foule,
Wroung both her hands, but not one word replide :
Sighes ftopt her toung, teares did her tongue
        cōtroul,
    Sweete Lady mother, mother fpeake (quoth he?)
    O let me not with hunger murdered bee.

D. I.   5

Deere child fhe faid, what wouldft thou haue of me?
Art thou a thirft, then come and drinke my teares,
For other fuccour haue I none for thee:
The time hath been, I could haue giuen thee peares:
   Rofe coulered apples, cherries for my child,
   But now alas, of all wee are beguild.

But come quoth fhe, giue me thy little finger,
And thou and I will to the back-yard goe,
And there feeke out a Cow-cake for thy dinner:
How faift thou fonne art thou contented fo?
   The ioyfull child did hereat giue a fmile,
   When both his eyes with water ran the while.

Then vp and downe with warie fearching eye,
In euery place for beafts dung doth fhe feeke,
As if a long loft Iewell there did lye,
Clofe hidden in fome narrow chink or creeke:
   When fhe lookt and nought at all had found,
   Then downe fhe coucheth on the fluttifh ground.

And / with her faire white fingers fine and fmall,
She fcrapes away the duft and draffe togeather,
And fo does fearch through out the Oxes ftall,
For dung or hoofes, or fome old peece of leather:
   But when in vaine her paines fhe did beftow,
   She paid her heart the intereft of her woe.

And lifting vp with forow her bright eyes,
She cald her little Sonne to come away,
Who fought as faft for fpiders, wormes and flies,
As fhe for Ordure mongft the mouldy hay.
 O ftay a while good mother did he cry,
 For heere euen now I did a maggot fpie.

At which fweete fight my teeth did water yet :
Euen as you cald, fhe fell her in the duft,
An hower were well fpent, this prize to get,
To let her flip, I thinke I was accurft :
 My hungry ftomacke, well it would haue ftayd,
 And I haue loft her I am fore affraid.

I, I, my Sonne, it may be fo (quoth fhee,)
Then come away : let vs togeather dye,
Our luckleffe ftarres alots it fo to be :
Peace my fweete boy, alack why doft thou cry ?
 Had I found any thing, thou fhouldft haue feen,
 That therewithall we would haue merry been.

Then / be thou ftill (my fonne) and weepe no more
For with my teares, thou kilft my wounded heart,
Thy neede is great, my hunger is as fore,
Which grieues my foule, and pinches euery part :
 Yet hope of helpe alack I know not any,
 Without, within, our foes they are fo many.

Deare mother heare me one word and no moe,
See heere my foote fo flender in your fight,
Giue me but leaue to eate my little toe,
No better fupper will I afke to night :
    Or elfe my thumbe : a morfell fmall you fee,
    And thefe two ioynts, me thinks may fpared be.

My fonne quoth fhe great are thy cares God wot,
To haue thy hungry ftomack fil'd with food,
Yet all be it we haue fo hard a lot
Difmember not thy felfe for any good :
    No brutifh beaft, will doe fo foule a deede,
    Then doe not thou gainft nature fo proceed,

But O my fonne, what fhall I doe quoth fhe ?
My griefe of hunger is as great as thine,
And fure no hope of comfort doe I fee,
But we muft yeild ourfelues to ftarue and pine :
    The wrath of God doth fiege the Citty round,
    And we within fell famine doth confound.

The / fword without, intends our defolation,
Confuming peftilence deftroyeth heere within,
Ciuell diffention breedes our hearts vexation,
The angry heauens, the fame hath fent for finne,
    Murders, and ruine through our ftreetes, doe run :
    Then how can I feede thee, my louing fonne ?

Yf pale fac't famine take away my life,
Why then, with whome fhould I truft thee my fonne
For heer's no loue, but hate and deadly ftrife :
Woe is that child, whofe parents dayes are done :
   One thee fweete boy no perfon would take pitty,
   For milde compaffion, hath forfooke the citty.

Once I retaynd, this ioyfull hope of thee,
When ripened yeares, brought thee to mans eftate,
That thou fhouldft be a comfort vnto me,
Feeding my age, when youthfull ftrength did bate:
   And haue my meate, my drinke and cloth of thee,
   Fit for a *Lady* of fo high degree.

And when the fpan length, of my life was done,
That God, and nature, claim'd of me their due,
My hope was then, that thou my louing Sonne,
In Marble ftone, my memorie fhould renew :
   And bring my corpes, with honour to the graue :
   The lateft dutie, men of children craue.

But / now I fee (my fweete and bonny boy)
This hope is fruitleffe, and thefe thoughts are vaine,
I fee grim death, hath feaz'd my earthly ioy,
For famines dart hath thee already flaine :
   Thy hollow eyes and wrinckled cheekes declare,
   Thou art not markt, to be thy Fathers heire.

Looke on thy legges, fee all thy flefh is gone,
Thy iollie thighes, are fallen quite away,
Thy armes and handes, nothing but fkin, and bone,
How weake thy heart is, thou thy felfe canft fay :
    I haue no foode, to ftrengthen thee (my child,)
    And heere thy buriall would be too too vilde.

Wherefore my Sonne leaft vgly Rauens and Crowes,
Should eate thy carcaffe in the ftincking ftreetes,
Thereby to be a fcorne vnto our foes,
And gaule to me, that gaue thee many fweets :
    I haue prepaird, this my vnfpotted wombe,
    To be for thee an honourable Tombe.

Then fith thou canft not liue to be a man,
What time thou mightft haue fed thy aged mother,
Therefore my child it lyes thee now vpon,
To be my foode, becaufe I haue no other :
    With my o[w]ne blood, long time I nourifht thee,
    Then with thy flefh, thou oughtft to cherifh mee./

Within this wombe thou firft receiuedft breath,
Then giue thy mother, that which fhee gaue thee,
Here hadft thou life, then lye here after death,
Sith thou hadft beene, fo welbeloude of me :
    In fpite of foes, be thou my dayly food,
    And faue my life, that can doe thee no good.

In bleſſed *Eden* ſhall thy ſoule remaine,
While that my belly is thy bodyes graue,
There, is no taſte of famine woe or paine
But ioyes eternall, more then heart can craue :
   Then who would wiſh, in ſorrow to perſeuer,
   That by his death might liue in heauen for euer.

The *Lady* with hunger is conſtrayned to kill her
   beſt beloued and onely Sonne, *and eate him :*
      whoſe body ſhe roaſted.

WHen this was ſaid, her feeble child ſhe tooke,
   And with a ſword which ſhe had lying by,
She thruſt him through, turning away her looke,
That her wet eyes might not behold him die :
   And when ſweete life was from his body fled,
   A thouſand times ſhe kiſt him being dead.

His / milke white body ſtaind with purple blood,
She clenſd and waſht with ſiluer dropping teares,
Which being done, ſhe wipte it as ſhe ſtood,
With nothing elſe, but her faire golden haires :
   And when ſhe ſaw, his litle lims were cold,
   She cut him vp, for hunger made her bold.

In many pecces did fhe then deuide him,
Some part fhe fod, fome other part fhe rofted,
Frō neighbours fight fhe made great fhift to hide him,
And of her cheere, in heart fhe greatly bofted :
　　Ere it was ready, fhe began to eate,
　　And from the fpit, pluckt many bits of meate.

The fmell of the meate is felt round about : the
feditious Captaine[s] therevpon came to the Lady,
　and threatens to kill her for meate.
　　Where vpon the Lady *fets part*
　　　before them.

THe fent thereof was ftraight fmelt round about,
　The neighbour[s] then out of their houfes ran,
Saying, we fmell roaft-meat out of all doubt,
Which was great wonder vnto euery man :
　　And euery one like to a longing wife,
　　In that good cheer did wifh his fharpeft knife.

This / newes fo fwift, in each mans mouth did flie :
The proud feditious, heard thereof at laft,
Who with all fpeed, vnto the houfe did hye,
And at the doores and windowes knocked faft :
　　And with vilde words & fpeeches rough and great,
　　They afkt the Lady where fhe had that meat.

Thou wicked woman how comes this quoth they ?
That thou alone haſt roaſt-meat in the towne?
While we with griping famine dye each day,
Which are your Lords, and leaders of renowne :
   For this contempt, we thinke it right and reaſon,
   Thou ſhouldſt be puniſht as in caſe of treaſon.

The louely Lady trembling at their ſpeech,
Fearing their bloody hands and cruell actions,
With many gentle words did them beſeech,
They would not enter into further factions :
   But liſten to her words and ſhe would tell,
   The certaine truth how euery thing befell.

Be not ſhe ſaid, at your poore hand-maid grieued,
I haue not eaten all in this hard caſe,
But that your ſelues might ſomething be relieued,
I haue kept part to giue you in this place :
   Then ſit you downe, right-welcome ſhall you be,
   And what I haue, your ſelues ſhall taſt and ſee.

With / diligence the Table then ſhe layde,
And ſiluer trenchers, on the boord ſhe ſet,
A golden ſalt, that many ounces wayde,
And Damaſk napkins, dainty, fine, and neate :
   Her gueſts were glad to ſe this preparation,
   And at the boord they ſat with contentation.

D. I.   6

In maſſie ſiluer platters brought ſhe forth
Her owne Sonnes fleſh whom ſhe did loue ſo deere,
Saying my maiſters take this well in worth,
I pray be merry : looke for no other cheere :
    See here my childs white hand, moſt finely dreſt,
    And here his foote, eate where it likes you beſt.

And doe not ſay this child was any others,
But my owne Sonne : whom you ſo well did know,
Which may ſeeme ſtrange, vnto all tender Mothers,
My owne childes fleſh, I ſhould deuoure ſo :
    Him did I beare, and carefully did feed,
    And now his fleſh ſuſtaines me in my need.

Yet allbeit this ſweet relieuing feaſt,
Hath deareſt beene to me that ere I made,
Yet niggardize I doe ſo much deteſt,
I thought it ſhame, but there ſhould ſome be layde,
    In ſtore for you : although the ſtore be ſmall,
    For they are gluttons which conſumeth all.

Herewith / ſhe burſt into a flood of teares,
Which downe her thin pale cheekes diſtilled faſt :
Her bleeding heart, no ſobs nor ſighes forbeares,
Till her weake voyce breath'd out theſe words at laſt :
    O my deere Sonne, my pretty boy (quoth ſhe)
    While thou didſt liue, how ſweet waſt thou to me?

Yet fweeter farre, a thoufand times thou art,
To thy poore mother, at this inftant howre,
My hungry ftomake haft thou eaf'd of fmart,
And kept me from the bloody Tyrants power,
 And they like friends doe at my table eat,
 That would haue kild me for a bit of meate.

When this was faid, wiping her watery eyes,
Vnto her felf, frefh courage then fhe tooke,
And all her guefts, fhe welcom'd in this wife,
Cafting on them a courteous pleafant looke :
 Be mery friends, I pray you doe not fpare.
 In all this towne, is not fuch noble fare.

The / Captaines and their company were fo amazed
at fight of the childs limbes being by his mother fet vpon
the table in platters, that wondring thereat, they
would not eat a bite, for the which the Lady
reproues them.

THe men amazed at this vncouth fight,
 One to another caft a fteadfaft eye, [fpight
Their hard remorceleffe hearts full fraught with
Were herewithall appalled fodenly.   [great,
 And though their extreame hunger was full
 Like fenceleffe men they fat and would not eate.

Oh why quoth fhe doe you refraine this food,
I brought it forth vnto you for good will,
Then fcorne it not (deere friends) for it is good :
And I euen now did thereof eate my fill :
   Taft it therefore and I dare fweare you'l fay,
   You eat no meate, more fweete this many a day.

Hard hearted woman, cruell and vnkind
Canft thou (quoth they) fo frankly feed of this?
A thing more hatefull did wee neuer finde,
Then keepe it for thy tooth, loe there it is.
   Moft wild and odious is it in our eye,
   Then feed on mans flefh, rather would wee dye.

Alack / quoth fhe, doth foolifh pity mooue ye,
Weaker then a womans, is your hearts become?
I pray fall too, and if that you doe loue me,
Eate where you will, and ile with you eat fome.
   What greater fhame to Captaines can befall,
   Then I in courage fhould furpaffe you all.

Why, waft not you, that did with many a threate,
Charge me with eager lookes to lay the cloth :
And as I lou'd my life to bring you meate,
And now to eate it doe you feeme fo loath ?
   More fit I fhould, then you, heerewith be moued,
   Since twas his flefh whom I fo deerly loued.

It was my fonne and not yours that is flaine,
Whofe roafted limbes lies here within the platter :
Then more then you I ought his flefh refraine,
And ten times more be greeued at this matter :
    How chance you are more mercifull then I,
    To fpare his flefh, while you for hunger dye?

Yet blame not me for this outragious deed,
For waft not you that firft did fpoyle my houfe?
And rob me of my food in my great need,
Leauing not behind a ratt or filly moufe :
    Then you alone are authors of this feaft,
    What need you then this action fo deteft ?

The / ftarued *Iewes* hearing this dolefull tale,
Were at the matter fmitten in fuch fadneffe,
That man by man with vifage wan and pale,
Dropt out of dores, accufing her of madneffe,
    And noting well, their famine, warre and ftrife,
    Wifht rather death, than length of mortall life.

And hereupon, much people of the Citty,
Fled to the *Romaines* fecret in the night,
Vpon their knees defiring them for pitty
To faue their liues that were in wofull plight :
    And finding mercie, tolde when that was done,
    How famine forc't a *Lady* eate her *Sonne*.

Tytus the Romaine Generall wept at the report of
the famine in Ierufalem, *efpecially when he heard
of the* Mother *that did eate her* Childe.

THe Romaine Generall hearing of the fame
  Tytus I meane, *Vefpafians* famous Sonne,
So grieu'd thereat, that griefe did teares conftraine,
Which downe his manly cheekes did ftreaming runne
  And holding vp to heauen his hands and eyes
  To this effect, vnto the Lord he cries.

          [round,
Thou / mighty God, which guides this mortall
That all hearts fecrets fees, and knowes my heart,
Witneffe thou canft, I came not to confound,
This goodly Cittie : or to worke their fmart :
  I was not author of their bloudie iarrs,
  But offred peace, when they imbraced wars.

Thefe eighteene moneths, that I with warlike force,
Befieged their Citty : (Lord thou knoweft it well,)
My heart was full of mercy and remorce,
And they alwayes did ftubbornely rebell :
  Therfore good Lord, with their moft hatefull rage,
  And wondrous deeds do not my confcience
   charge.

My eyes doe fee, my heart doth likewife pity,
The great calamitie that they are in,
Yet Lord, except thou wilt yeeld me the Cittie,
I'le raife my power, and not behold more finne :
   For they with famine are become fo wilde,
   That hunger made a woman eate her childe.

When noble *Titus* thus had made his moane,
All thofe that from *Ierufalem* did fly,
He did receaue to mercy euery one,
And nourifht famifht men at poynt to dye :
   But cruell *Schimion* that feditious *Iewe*,
   And Proud Iehocanan, more mifchiefe ftill did
     brew.

For / albeit braue *Tytus* by his power
And warlike Engines, brought vnto that place,
Had layde their ftrong walles, flat vpon the flower,
And done their Citty wonderfull difgrace.
   Yet ftubbornly they did refift him ftill,
   Such place they gaue, to their feditious will.

Tytus overthrowing the walls of Ierusalem enters the
Cyty and Temple with his power burning downe
the filuer gate thereof, which led the way to the
Sanctum Sanctorū : *and setteth Souldiers to keepe*
it from further hurt.

ABout that time, with wonderous dilligence,
They rais'd a wall, in secret of the night,
Which then was found their Citties best defence,
For to withstand the conquering *Romaines* might :
    Which once rac't the Citty needs must yeeld,
    And *Iewes* giue place to *Romaines* sword and
      shield,

Renowned *Tytus* well perceiuing this,
To his best proued Captaines, gaue a charge,
That new rais'd wall, the *Iewes* supposed blis,
Should scattered be, with breaches wide and large :
    And hervpon, the troopes togither met,
    And to the walles, their battering Engines set.

The / feare of this, made many a *Iewish* Lord,
That ioynde themselues with the seditious traine,
To steale away, and all with one accord,
At *Tytus* feete, sought mercie to obtaine :
    Whose milde submission, he accepted then,
    And gaue them honour, mong'st his noble men.

By this the mellow wall was broke and fcaled,
With fierce allarms, the holy towne was entred,
Romaines tooke courage, but the *Iewes* harts failed,
Thoufands loft their liues, which for honour ven-
    Schimion, *Iehocanan*, all did flie for feare,   [tred :
    Iewes mournd and *Romaines* triumpht euery
      where.

The faire Temple, Gods holy habitation,
The world *non pareli*, the heathens wonder,
Their Citties glory, their ioyes preferuation,
To the Romaine power, muft now come vnder :
    There many *Ifralites* for liues defence,
    Had lockt themfelues, & would not come from
      thence.

The famous Citty being thus fubdued,   [crowned
The *Romaines* heads, with glad-foe baies wer
For blesfull victory on their fide eufued,
While on the *Iewes* the worlds Creator frowned :
    The Captaines of the foule feditious rout,
    To hide their heades did feeke odd corners
      out.

The / *Romaines* refting in triumphant ftate
Vnto the holy Temple turned their courfe,

And finding fhutt the filuer fhining gate,
They fir'd it, retayning no remorce :
   And when the fiers flamde did fore abound,
   The melting filuer ftreamd along the ground.

Their timber worke into pale afhes turning,
Downe dropt the goodly gate vpon the flower,
What time the wrathfull *Romaines* went in running,
Shouting and crying with a mighty power :
   The glory of which place, their bright fight drew,
   To take thereof a wondring greedy view.

Yet did that place but onely lead the way,
Vnto the holyeft place, where once a yeare,
The high Prieft went, vnto the Lord to pray,
The figure of whofe glory, did there appeare :
   Sanctum Sanctorum fo that place was called,
   Which *Tytus* wondring mind the moft appalled.

Which holy holyeft place when *Tytus* fawe,
Hauing a view but of the outward part,
So glorious was it that the fight did draw,
A wounderous reuerence in his foule and heart :
   And with all meeknefle on his Princely knees,
   He honors there the Maieftie he fees.

This / place was clofed in with goulden gates,
So beautifull and fuper excellent,

That Princely *Tytus* and the *Romaine* ſtates
Said ſure this is Gods houſe omnipotent :
    And therefore *Tytus* who did loue and feare it,
    Cōmanded ſtraightly, no man ſhould come
        nere it.

And through his Camp, he made a proclamation,
That whoſoeuer did come neere the ſame,
He ſhould be hanged vp, without compaſſion,
Without reſpect of birth, deſert, or fame :
    And more, a band of men he there ordained,
    To keepe the Temple not to be prophaned.

The ſeditious ſet vpon the *Romaine* guard that kept
the Temple, and ſodenly ſlew them : whereupon the
Romaine *ſouldiers ſet fire on the golden gate of*
Sanctum Sanctorum, *and ſpoyled the holy place with*
fire. Titus *ſought to quench it but could not, for*
which he made great lamentation.

VVHile quiet thus the *Romaine* prince did ly,
    Without miſtruſt of any bloudy broyle,
Proclaiming pardon, life and liberty,
To euery yeelding ſoule, in that faire ſoyle :
    A crew of trayterous *Iewes* of baſe condition,
    Aſſayled the *Romaine* guard, without ſuſpition.

All / *Tytus* gallant Souldiers which he fet,
So carefully, the Temple gates to keepe,
Vpon a fodaine, they againft them get,
In dead of night, when moft were falne a fleepe :
  And there without all ftay, or further wordes,
  Each man they murdered on their drawn
    fwordes.

Not one efcap'd their bloody butchering hands :
Which noble *Tytus* hearing, grieued fore,
And thereon raif'd, his beft prepared bandes,
Slaying thofe *Iewes*, and many hundreds more.
  And with fuch fury, he purfu'd them ftill,
  That who efcapt, fled vp to *Syon* hill.

But yet the *Romaines* full of hot reuenge,
For this vilde deede, by wicked *Iewes* committed,
Troopt to the Temple, with a mighty fwinge,
And hauing all things for their purpofe fitted :
  Did in their rage, fet on fiers flame,
  Thofe goodly goulden gates, of greateft fame.

And as the flaming fier gather'd ftrength,
Great fpoyle was practif'd by the Romaine rout,
The melting gould that ftreamed downe at length,
Did guild the marble pauement round about :
  The gates thus burned with a hidious din,
  Sanctum Sanctorum Romaines entred in.

Who / hauing hereby won their hearts defier,
With mighty fhoutes they fhewed fignes of ioy,
While the holy place burnt with flaming fier,
Which did, earthes heauenly paradice deftroy:
    This woefull fight when *Tytus* once did fee
    He fought to quench it: but it would not be.

For many wicked hands, had bufie beene,
To worke that holy houfe all foule difgraces,
Which *Tytus* would haue fau'd as well was feene,
But it was fier'd in fo many places:
    That by no meanes, the fpoyle he could preuent,
    Which thing he did moft grieuoufly lament.

He ran about and cri'd with might and maine,
O ftay your hands, and faue this houfe I charge
Fetch water vp, and quench this fire againe, [yee,
Or you fhall fmart, before I doe enlarge yee:
    Thus fome he threatned, many he intreated,
    Till he was hoarfe, with that he had repeated.

But when his voyce was gone with crying out,
He drew his fword, and flew the difobedient,
Till faint and weary, running round about,
He fat him downe, as it was expedient:
    And there twixt wrath and forrow he bewayled,
    With froward Souldiers, he no more preuayled.

The / Priefts & *Iewes* that earft themfelues had
Within the compaffe of that holy ground, [hidden,
Againft the Romaines fought : and had abidden,
For to defend it many a bleeding wound :
    But when they faw, there was no way to fly,
    They lept into the fier, and there did die.

So long they fought, vntill the parching fier,
Did burne the clothes, from their fweating backes :
The more they fought, the more was their defier,
For to reuenge the Temples wofull wrackes :
    They layd about, as long as they could ftand ;
    Or moue a legge, or lift a feeble hand.

And all this while did noble *Tytus* mourne,
To fee *Sanctorum* fpoyled in fuch fort :
Layde on the ground, there did he toffe and turne,
And fmote at fuch as did to him report,
    The woefull ruine of that holy place,
    And from his fight, with frownes he did them
      chace.

Titus / with great reuerence, entred into the *Sanctum*
Sanctorum, and greatly wondred at the beautie
thereof, affirming it to be the houfe
of the God of heauen.

THe cruell fier hauing wrought her worft,
   When that at length the fury thereof ceaft,
Titus arofe, all open and vntruft,
Of many teares vnburdned and releaft :
   With head vncouered, mild and reuerently,
   Into *Sanctorum* humbly entred he.

And feeing the glorie and magnificence,
The wondrous beautie of that facred place,
Which there appeared, for all the vehemence,
The flaming fier made, fo long a fpace :
   Tytus did ftand amazed at the fight,
   When he confidered euery thing a right.
‘

And thereupon into this fpeech he broke,
How came I in this Paradice of pleafure?
This Place Celeftiall, may all foules Prouoke,
To fcorne the world, and feeke no other treafure :
   Doe I from earth afcend by eleuation ?
   Or fee I heauen by diuine reuelation ?

Vndoubtedly / the mightie God dwelt here,
This was no mortall creatures habitation,

For earthly Monarkes, it was all to deere,
Fit for none, but him who is our foules faluation :
   O earthly heauen, or heauenly Saintes receauer,
   Thy fweete remembrance fhall I keepe for euer.

Now well I wot, no maruell t'was indeed,
The *Iewes* fo ftoutly ftood in fence of this :
O who could blame them, when they did proceed
By all deuices to preferue their blis :
   Since firft I faw the Sunne, I neuer knew
   What heauens ioy ment, till I this place did view.

Nor did the Gentiles, without fpeciall caufe,
From fardeft partes both of the Eaft and Weft,
Send heapes of gold by ftraight commaund of lawes,
This facred place with glory to inueft :
   For rich and wounderous is this holy feat,
   And in mans eye the Maiefty is great.

Farre doth it paffe the *Romaine* Temples all,
Yea all the Temples of the world likewife,
They feeme to this like to an Affes ftall,
Or like a ftie where fwine ftill grunting lies.
   Great God of heauen, God of this glorious place,
   Plague thou their foules that did thy houfe
      deface.

Tytus, / thus wearied, gazing vp and downe,
Yet not fatisfied, with the Temples fight,

Departed thence, to lodge within the towne,
Things out of frame, to fet in order right :
 Where while he ftayd the ftubborne harted *Iewes*,
 Did there moft wicked actions dayly vfe.

For when they faw that fier had fo fpoyled,
Sanctum Sanctorum in fuch pitious fort,
Their diuillifh harts that ftill with mifchiefe broyled,
The treafure houfes all, they burnt in fport,
 And precious Iewells wherefoeuer they ftood,
 With all things elfe that fhould doe *Romaines*
  good.

The reft of the Temple, likewife did they burne,
In defperàt manner, without all regard :
Which being wrought, away they did returne,
But many fcapt not, without iuft reward ;
 The *Romaine* Souldiers, quickly quencht the fier,
 And in the Temple wrought their heartes defire.

Where they fet vp, their heathen Idolls all,
Their fence-leffe Images, of wood and ftone,
And at their feete, all proftrate did they fall,
There offering facrifice to them alone :
 In plaine derifion of the conquered fort,
 Of whom the Romaines made a mocking fport.

A / falſe Prophet aroſe among the *Iewes*, telling them *that the Temple ſhould againe be builded by it ſelfe, without the help of mans hand: willing therefore to deſtroy the* Romaines : *which they going about to doe, brought further ſorrow vpon themſelues.*

A Falſe and lying Prophet then aroſe,
     Among the *Iewes*, at faire *Ieruſalem*,
Which then an abſurd fancie did diſcloſe,
Among them all, who thus incourag'd them :
    Moſt valiant *Iewes* play you the men and fight,
    And God will ſhew a wonder in your ſight.

Againſt the curſed Romaines turne againe,
And beate the boaſting heathen to the ground,
For God will ſhew vnto your ſights moſt plaine,
His mightie power : if you doe them confound,
    The Temple by it ſelfe ſhall builded be,
    Without mans hand or helpe, moſt glorious ly.

That *Iacobs* God, thereby may ſhew his power,
To thoſe proud *Romaines* : which doe glory ſo,
In their owne ſtrength : tryumphing euery hower,
In this our ſpoyle, and wofull ouerthrow :
    Then fight O *Iewes*, the temple ſanz delay,
    Shall by it ſelfe be builded vp this day.

The / wilde ſeditious beleeuing this lye,
Did ſet a freſh vpon the *Romaine* band,

In fuch fierce fort, that many men did dye,
But yet the *Romaines* got the vpper hand :
   Who in new wakened wrath, that late did fleepe
   Slew downe the *Iewes* like to a fort of fheepe.

Schimion and *Iehocanan* come to feeke peace with
  Tytus, but refufe to be in fubieEtion to the Romaines:
  wherevpon Tytus *will fhew them no fauour, but*
  prefently affayled them with his power, wherevpon
  Schimion *and* Iehocanans *followers by fome, and*
  fome forfake them, leauing them in diftreffe : who
  there-vpon hid them-felues in Caues.

THen came falfe *Schimion* and *Iehocanan,*
    Chiefe Captaines, to the feditious trayne,
With many followers, weapned euery man,
Requiring peace, if peace they could obtaine :
   To whome Prince *Tytus* with his chiefeft ftate,
   Did thus reply, you feeke this thing to late.

How / comes it now that yee intreate for life,
After fo many mifcheiefes by you wrought,
When you haue flaine and murthered man and wife,
And thoufand thoufands to deftruction brought :
   [O wretched man, vpon thy head fhall come
   Sudden and fwift and fure a rafcal doom.]

How oft haue I intreated you to peace,
And offered mercie, without all defert,
When you refufing it, did ftill increafe,
Your trayterous dealings, your chiefeft fmart :
    It pittied me to fee your woefull cafe,
    With your innumerable men dead in each place.

How can I pardon thefe outragious acts,
Your many murders and falfe fedition,
With diuers other abhominable facts,
For which I fee in you, no hearts contrition :
    You feeke for peace, yet armed do you ftand,
    You craue for pardon, with your fwords in hand.

Firft lay a fide your fwords and weapons all,
And in fubmiffiue manner afk for grace,
So fhall you fee what fauour may befall,
Perhaps I may take pitty on your cafe :
    And gracioufly withall your faults fufpence,
    And giue you pardon, ere you goe from hence.

With / bended browes proud *Schimion* then did
On gentle *Tytus*: *Iehocanan* likewife,   [looke
In fcornfull manner all his fpeeches tooke,
And both of them difdainefully replies :
    By heauens great God, we both haue fworne
        quoth they
    To make no feruile peace with thee this day.

For neuer fhall earths mifery prouoke,
Our vndaunted heartes to ftoope vnto thy will,
Or bend our neckes vnto the *Romaine* yoake,
While vitall breath our inward parts doth fill :
    Then vnto vs this fauour doe expreffe,
      To let vs part and liue in wilderneffe.

At this contempt was *Tytus* greatly moued :
And doth your pride continue yet quoth he ?
Will not your impudency be yet reproued ?
Nor yet your ftubborne heartes yet humbeld be ?
    And dare you fay that you will fweare and vow,
      That to the *Romaine* yoke you will not bow ?

At this his wrath was wounderous fore inflamed,
Who herevpon gaue ftraight commandement,
By ftrength of fword to haue thofe rebels tamed ;
On whom the *Romaines* fet incontinent :
    Who chac'd the *Iewes* and fcattered them fo fore,
      That they were found to gather head no more.

For / fecretly the *Iewes* from *Schimion* fled,
By fome and fome they all forfooke him quite,
With falfe *Iehocanan* which fo mifled,
And forĉt thē gainft them felues to murderous
    Who leauing them, to noble *Tytus* came, [fight :
      Defiring grace, who graunted them the fame.

Iehocanan and *Schimion* feeing this,
They were forfaken, and left poft alone,
In their diftreffe lamented their amiffe :
Cloffe hid in caues, they lay and made their mone :
    Where they remained perplext with famine great,
    Till they were ready, their owne flefh to eate.

✠✠✠✠✠✠✠✠✠✠✠✠✠✠✠✠✠

Iehocanan inforced by hunger comes out of his caue,
  & fubmits him-felfe to Tytus, *who caufed
    him to be hanged.*

AT length out of a deepe darke hollow caue,
    With bitter hunger *Iehocanan* was driuen,
Like to a Ghoft new rifen from his graue,
Or like Anotamy of all flefh beryuen :
    Who then as faint as euer he could ftand,
    Came to fubmit himfelfe, to *Tytus* hand.

Into / this Princely prefence when he came,
With all fubmiffion fell he at his feete,
Saying O King of moft renouned fame,
Here am I come as it is right and meete :
    To yeeld my felfe into thy Princely hand,
    Whofe life doth reft, vpon thy great command.

My difobedience, doe I fore repent,
That euer I, refuf'd thy offered grace,
Bewayling my lewd life, fo badly bent,
And my foule actions, gainft this holy place :
　　Yet with thy mercy fhadow my amiffe,
　　And let me taft what thy compaffion is.

Not from my felfe, did all my finne proceede,
Though I confeffe, my faults were too too many,
But was prouokte to many a bloody deede,
By him that yet was neuer good to any :
　　Blood-thirfty *Schimeon*, led me to all euill,
　　Who doth in malice, far exceed the Diuell.

Too long alaffe, he ouer-ruld my will,
And made me actor, of a thoufand woes :
What I refuf'd his outrage did fulfill,
And his deuife, did make my friends my foes :
　　Then worthy Victor, mittigate my blame,
　　And let thy glory, ouer-fpread my fhame.

No / more quoth *Tytus*, ftay thy traiterous tounge
Infect vs not with thy impoyfoned breath,
Ile doe thee right that haft done many a wrong,
Thy end of forrow, fhall begin thy death :
　　And by thy death, fhall life arife to fuch,
　　To whom thou thoughtft a minutes life too much.

With that he wild his Captaines take him thence,
When he with yron chaines was fettered faſt,
And afterward (meete meed for his offence)
Through all the Campe they led him at the laſt,
    That he of them, might mockt and ſcorned be,
    And then in chaines they hangd him one a tree.

This was the end of proud *Iehocanan*,
That in *Ieruſalem* did ſuch harme,
And this likewiſe was that accurſed man,
That in his malice with a fierce alarme
    Burnd all the Victuals laid in by the Peeres,
    That was inough to ſerue them twenty yeeres.

Which was the cauſe, that in ſo ſhort a ſpace,
So great a famine fell within the towne:
Yea this was he burnt King *Agrippaes* place,
And in the temple ſlew ſo many downe:
    But not long after he was gone and dead,
    Out of his den did *Schimion* ſhew his head.

✹✹✹✹✹✹✹✹✹✹✹✹✹✹✹✹✹✹✹✹✹✹ ✹✹✹✹✹

SCHIMION / *in like fort being driuen with hunger out of his den, apparelling himfelfe in princely attire, defired to be brought before* Titus, *fuppofing he would haue faued his life : but he commanded his head to be ftricken off, and his body to be cut in peces and caft to the dogges.*

WHo ftaring vp and downe with feareful
   lookes,
Leaft any one were nigh to apprehend him,
Like to a Panther doubting hidden hookes,
That any way might lye for to offend him :
 Driuen out with famine, hungry at the hart,
 He fought for fuccour of his earned fmart.

And hauing dreft himfelfe in Kingly tire,
In richeft manner that he could deuife,
That men at him might wonder : and defire,
To know what Monarke did from earth arife,
 Farre off he walked as it were in boaft,
 And fhewd himfelfe vnto the Romaine hoaft.

For his great heart could not abid to yeeld,
Though gnawing hunger vext his very foule :
Thus faintly walkt he vp and downe the field
With lofty thoughts, which famine did controule :
 Suppofing firmely, though he liu'd in hate,
 He fhould finde fauour, for his high eftate :

D. I.   9

For though (quoth he) I did the *Romaines* wrong,
Yet in my deeds I fhewed a Princely courage,
Bearing a heart, that did to honour throng,
And therevpon their Campe fo oft did forage :
    To haughty acts all Princes honour owes,
     For they muft thinke that war hath made vs foes.

Confidering this, Prince *Tytus* may be proude,
To fuch an enemie he may fauour fhew,
And herein may his action be allowd,
That magnanimitie he will nourifh fo :
    And by his mercie make a friend of him,
     That in his warres fo great a foe hath beene.

Which in this honour, hee himfelfe did flatter,
Of him the *Romaines* had a perfect fight,
And round about him, they themfelues did fcatter,
Yet were afraid, to come within his might :
    And that they fear'd ; this was the onely reafon,
     They knew his craft, and doubted hidden treafon.

But *Schimion* feeing, that they fhund him fo,
He cald vnto them in couragious wife,
Maiestically walking to and fro
And in this fort, his fpeech to them applies :
    If any gallant Captaine with you be,
     Let him approch, and talke one word with me.

With / that ftept out a braue couragious Knight,
With weapons well prouided euery way:
A noble *Romaine* of great ftrength and might,
Who with his weapon drawne thefe words did fay :
 Tell me, who art thou that in fuch attire,
 Walkes in this place, and what is thy defire?

I am (quoth he) vndaunted *Schimeon*,
The wrathfull Captaine of feditious *Iewes*,
That flew the *Romaines*, in their greateft throng,
The deed whereof I come not to excufe :
 Nor doe I paffe what you can fay thereto,
 I am the man made you fo much adoe.

Yet let me thus much fauour craue of thee,
As to conduct me to great *Tytus* fight,
Thy noble friend, but enemie to me :
Yet doubt I not, but he will doe me right:
 Bring me to him, what chaunce fo ere I finde,
 That he may heare, and I may fhew my minde.

The *Romaine* Captaine his requeft fulfild,
To *Tytus* royall prefence was he brought :
Whofe hatefull perfon, when the Prince beheld,
He did refufe to heare him fpeake in ought :
 Away with him he fayd, let him be bound,
 For of all woe this villaine was the ground.

And / like a Captiue firſt let him be led,
About the Campe to ſuffer ſcoffes and ſcornes,
And after that ſtrike of his hatefull head,
The manſion houſe of miſchiefes pricking thornes :
   And let his carcaſe be in peeces torne,
   And euery gobbet vnto dogges be throwne.

What *Titus* charg'd was put in execution,
And in this ſort was *Schimions* hatefull end,
Who went to death with wonderous reſolution,
Not like a man, but like an helliſh fiend :
   Thus *Titus* conquer'd that moſt pretious Iem,
   The beautious Cittie faire *Ieruſalem*.

The number of thoſe that had bin ſlaine at the ſiege
of Ieruſalem, and the number of the Priſoners that
Titus carried with him to Rome.

THe perfect number of the people there,
   The which with hunger & with ſword was
Eleauen hundred thouſand did appeare,   [ſlaine :
As bookes of records did declare it plaine :
   Beſide all ſuch as did vnburied lye,
   And diuers moe that did in fier dye.

And when to *Rome* the Conquerer went his way,
The number of his Priſoners were full great,

Full fixteene thoufand men that inftant day,
Were carried captiue to the *Romaine* Seat:
   Among the reft the man that wrote this ftory,
   Who by his wifedome purchaft endless glory.

Thus Chrifts prophefie truely came to paffe,
Which Forty yeares before he had expreffed:
But with the *Iewes* of fmall account it was,
Till they did finde themfelues fo fore diftreffed:
   He foght their life, his death they wrought with
      fpite
   Wifhing his blood on them and theirs to light.

The which according to their owne requeft,
The Lord in wrath did perfectly fulfil:
There channels ran with blood and did not reft,
Their blood was fpilt, that *Iefus* blood did fpill:
   God grant we may our hatefull fins forfake,
   And by the *Iewes* a Chriftian warning take.

FINIS.

II.

THE WONDERFULL YEARE.

1603.

NOTE.

For the ' Wonderfull Yeare (1603) ' I am again indebted to the British Museum.   See Memorial-Introduction on it.—G.

THE
VVonderfull yeare.
1603.

Wherein is ſhewed the picture of *London*, lying ſicke of the Plague.

At the ende of all (like a mery Epilogue to a dull Play) cer-
taine Tales are cut out in ſundry faſhions, of purpoſe
to ſhorten the liues of long winters nights,
that lye watching in the darke for vs.

Et me rigidi legant Catones.

LONDON

Printed by Thomas Creede, and are to be ſolde
in Saint Donſtones Church-yarde
in Fleet-ſtreete.

TO HIS VVEL-

RESPECTED GOOD

friend, M. *Cuthbert Thure∫by*, *VVa-*
ter-Bayli∫∫e of London.

Ookes are but poore gifts, yet *Kings*
receiue them: vpō which I pre∫ume,
you will not turne *This* out of deores.
You cannot for ∫hame but bid it welcome, becau∫e
it bringes to you a great quantitie of my loue:
which, if it be worth litle (and no maruell if *Loue*
be ∫olde vnder-foote, when the God of *Loue*
him∫elfe goes naked) yet I hope you will not ∫ay
you haue a hard bargaine, Sithēce you may take
as much of it as you plea∫e for nothing. I
haue clapt the *Cognizance* of your name, on the∫e
∫cribled papers, it is their liuery. So that now
they are yours: being free frō any vile imputation,
∫aue only, that they thru∫t them∫elues into your
acquaintance. But generall errors, haue generall
pardons: for the title of / other mens names, is
the common *Heraldry* which all tho∫e laie claime

too, whofe creft is a Pen-and-Inckhorne. If you read, you may happilie laugh ; tis my defire you fhould, becaufe mirth is both *Phiſicall*, and whole-fome againſt the *Plague* : with which ficknes (to tell truth) this booke is (though not forely) yet fomewhat infected. I pray, driue it not out of your companie for all that ; for (affure your foule) I am fo iealous of your health, that if you did but once imagine, there were gall in mine Incke, I would caſt away the Standiſh, and for-fweare medling with anie more *Muſes*.

To the Reader.

ND why to the *Reader?* Oh good Sir! theres as found law to make you giue good words to the *Reader*, as to a *Conſtable* when hee carries his watch about him to tell how the night goes, tho (perhaps) the one (oftentimes) may be ſerued in for a *Gooſe*, and the other very fitly furniſh the ſame meſſe. Yet to maintaine the ſcuruy faſhion, and to keepe *Cuſtome* in reparations, he muſt be honyed, and come ouer with *Gentle Reader*, *Courteous Reader*, and *Learned Reader*, though he haue no more *Gentilitie* in him than *Adam* had (that was but a gardner) no more *Ciuilitie* than a *Tartar*, and no more *Learning* than the moſt errand *Stinkard*, that (except his owne name) could neuer finde any thing in the Horne-book.

How notoriouſly therfore do good wits diſhonor, not only their *Calling*, but euen their *Creation*, that worſhip *Glow-wormes* (in ſtead of the Sun) becauſe of a litle falſe gliſtering? In the name of

Phœbus what madneſſe leades them vnto it ? For
he that dares hazard a preſſing to death (thats to
ſay, *To be a man in Print*) muſt make account
that he ſhall ſtand (like the olde Weathercock
ouer Powles ſteeple) to be beaten with all ſtormes.
Neither the ſtinking Tabacco-breath of a *Sattin-
gull*, the *Aconited* ſting of a narrow-eyde *Critick*,
the faces of a phantaſtick Stage-monkey, nor the
Indeede-la of a Puritanicall Citizen muſt once ſhake
him. No, but deſperately reſolue (like a French
Poſt) to ride through thick & thin : indure to
ſee his lines torne pittifully on the rack : ſuffer
his Muſe to take the *Baſtoone*, yea the very ſtab,
& himſelfe like a new ſtake to be a marke for
euery *Hagler*, and therefore (ſetting vp all theſe
reſts) why ſhuld he regard what tooles bolt is
ſhot at him ? Beſides, / if that which he preſents
vpon the Stage of the world be *Good*, why ſhould
he baſely cry out (with that old poeticall mad-cap
in his *Amphitruo*) *Iouis ſummi cauſa clarè plaudite.*
I beg a *Plaudite* for God ſake ! If *Bad*, who (but
an Aſſe) would intreate (as Players do in a
cogging *Epilogue* at the end of a filthie Comedy)
that, be it neuer ſuch wicked ſtuffe, they would
forbeare to hiſſe, or to dam it perpetually to lye
on a Stationers ſtall. For he that can ſo coſen
himſelfe, as to pocket vp praiſe in that ſilly ſort,
makes his braines fat with his owne folly.

But *Hinc Pudor*! or rather *Hinc Dolor*, heeres the Diuell! It is not the ratling of all this former haile-fhot, that can terrifie our *Band* of *Caftalian Pen-men* from entring into the field: no, no, the murdring Artillery indeede lyes in the roaring mouthes of a company that looke big as if they were the fole and fingular *Commanders* ouer the maine Army of *Poefie*, yet (if *Hermes* mufter-booke were fearcht ouer) theile be found to be moft pitifull pure frefh-water fouldiers: they giue out, that they are heires-apparent to *Helicon*, but an eafy *Herald* may make them meere yonger brothers, or (to fay troth) not fo much. Beare witnes all you whofe wits make you able to be witneffes in this caufe, that here I meddle not with your good Poets, *Nam tales, nufquàm funt hic amplius*, If you fhould rake hell, or (as *Ariftophanes* in his Frog fayes) in any Celler deeper than hell, it is harde to finde Spirits of that *Fafhion*. But thofe Goblins whom I now am cōiuring vp, haue bladder-cheekes puft out like a *Swizzers* breeches (yet being prickt, there comes out nothing but wind) thin-headed fellowes that liue vpon the fcraps of inuention, and trauell with fuch vagrant foules, and fo like Ghofts in white fheetes of paper, that the Statute of Rogues may worthily be fued vpon them becaufe their wits haue no abiding place, and

yet wander without a paffe-port. Alas, poore
wenches (the nine Mufes!) how much are you
wrongd, to haue fuch a number of Baftards lying
vpō your hands? But turne them out a begging;
or if you cannot be rid of their Riming company
(as I thinke it will be very hard) then lay your
heauie and immortal curfe vpon them, that /
whatfoeuer they weaue (in the motley-loome of
their ruftie pates) may like a beggers cloake, be
full of ftolne patches, and yet neuer a patch like
one another, that it may be fuch true lamentable
ftuff, that any honeft Chriftian may be fory to
fee it. Banifh thefe *Word-pirates*, (you facred
miftreffes of learning) into the gulfe of *Bar-
barifme* : doome them euerlaftingly to liue among
dunces : let them not once lick their lips at the
Thefpian bowle, but onely be glad (and thanke
Apollo for it too) if hereafter (as hitherto they
haue alwayes) they may quench their poeticall
thirft with fmall beere. Or if they will needes
be ftealing your *Heliconian Nectar*, let them (like
the dogs of *Nylus*,) onely lap and away. For
this *Goatifh* fwarme are thofe (that where for
thefe many thoufand yeares you went for pure
maides) haue taken away your good names, thefe
are they that deflowre your beauties. Thefe are
thofe ranck-riders of Art, that haue fo fpur-gald
your luftie wingd *Pegafus*, that now he begins

to be out of flefh, and (euen only for prouander
fake) is glad to fhew tricks like *Bancks* his Curtall.
O you Bookes-fellers (that are Factors to the
Liberall Sciences) ouer whofe Stalles thefe Drones
do dayly flye humming ; let *Homer, Hefiod, Euri-
pides,* and fome other mad Greekes with a band
of the Latines, lye like mufket-fhot in their way,
when thefe Gothes and Getes fet vpon you in
your paper fortifications ; it is the only Canon,
vpon whofe mouth they dare not venture: none
but the Englifh will take their parts, therefore
feare them not, for fuch a ftrong breath haue
thefe chefe-eaters, that if they do but blow vpon
a booke they imagine ftraight tis blafted: *Quod
fupra nos ; Nihil ad nos,* (they fay) that which
is aboue our capacitie, fhall not paffe vnder our
commendation. Yet would I haue thefe *Zoilifts*
(of all other) to reade me, if euer I fhould write
any thing worthily: for the blame that knowne-
fooles heape vpon a deferuing labour, does not
difcredit the fame, but makes wife men more
perfectly in loue with it. Into fuch a ones hands
therefore if I fortune to fall, I will not fhrink
an inch, but euen when his teeth are fharpeft,
and moft ready to bite, I will ftop his mouth
only with this, *Hæc mala funt, fed tu, non meliora
facta. /*

Reader.

*W*Hereas there ſtands in the Rere-ward of this Booke a certaine mingled Troope of ſtraunge Diſcourſes, faſhioned into Tales, Know, that the intelligence which firſt brought them to light, was onely flying Report : whoſe tongue (as it often does) if in ſpreading them it haue tript in any materiall point, and either ſlipt too farre, or falne too ſhort, beare with the error : and the rather, becauſe it is not wilfully committed. Neither let any one (whome thoſe Reports ſhall ſeeme to touch) cauill or complaine of iniury, ſithence nothing is ſet downe by a malitious hand. Farewell. |

THE VVONDER-
full yeare.

*Ertumnus* being attired in his accuftomed habit of changeable filke, had newly paffed through the firft and principall Court-gate of heauen : to whom for a farewell, and to fhewe how dutifull he was in his office, *Ianus* (that beares two faces vnder one hood) made a very mannerly lowe legge, and (becaufe he was the onely Porter at that gate) prefented vnto this king of the Moneths, all the New-yeares gifts, which were more in number, and more worth than thofe that are giuen to the great Turke, or the Emperour of *Perfia* : on went *Vertumnus* in his luftie progreffe, *Priapus, Flora*, the *Dryades*,

Vertumnus God of the yeare.

Description of the Spring.

and *Hamadryades*, with all the woodden rabble of
thofe that dreft Orchards & Gardens, perfuming
all the wayes that he went, with the fwéete
Odours that breathed from flowers, hearbes and
trées, which now began to péepe out of prifon :
by vertue of which excellent aires, the fkie got
a moft cleare complexion, lookte fmug and
fmoothe, and had not fo much as a wart fticking
on her face : the Sunne likewife was frefhly and
very richly apparelled in cloth of gold like a
Bridegroome, and inftead of gilded Rofemary,
the hornes of the Ramme, (being the figne of
that celeftiall bride-houfe where he lay, to be
marryed to the Spring) were not like

Vpon the 23,
of March the
Spring begins,
by reason of
the Sunnes en-
trance into
Aries.

your common hornes parcell-gilt, but
double double-gilt, with the liquid gold
that melted from his beames, for ioy
w[h]ereof the Larke fung at his windowe
euery morning, the Nightingale euery night : the
Cuckooe (like a fingle fole / Fidler, that réeles
from Tauerne to Tauerne) plide it all the day
long : Lambes frifkte vp and downe in the
vallies, kids and Goates leapt too and fro on
the Mountaines : Shepheards fat piping, country
wenches finging : Louers made fonnets for their
Laffes, whileft they made Garlands for their
Louers : And as the Country was frolike, fo
was the Citie mery : Oliue Trées (which grow

no where but in the Garden of peace) ftood (as
common as Béech does at Midfomer) at euery
mans doore, braunches of Palme were in euery
mans hand : Stréetes were full of people, people
full of ioy : euery houfe féemde to haue a Lorde
of mifrule in it, in euery houfe there was fo much
iollity : no Scritch-Owle frighted the filly Country-
man at midnight, nor any Drum the Citizen
at noone-day ; but all was more calme than a
ftill water, all hufht, as if the Spheres had bene
playing in Confort : In conclufion, heauen lookt
like a Pallace, and the great hall of the earth, like
a Paradice. But O the fhort-liude Felicitie of
man ! O world of what flight and thin ftuffe
is thy happineffe ! Iuft in the midft of this
iocund Holi-day, a ftorme rifes in the Weft :
Weftward (from the toppe of a *Ritch-* The Queenes
mount) defcended a hidious tempeft, that ficknes.
fhooke Cedars, terrified the talleft Pines, and
cleft in funder euen the hardeft hearts of Oake :
And if fuch great trées were fhaken, what thinke
you became of the tender Eglantine, and humble
Hawthorne ; they could not (doubtleffe) but
droope, they could not choofe but die with the
terror. The Element (taking the Deftinies part,
who indeed fet abroach this mifchiefe) fcowled
on the earth, and filling her hie forehead full of
blacke wrinckles, tumbling long vp and downe

(like a great bellyed wife) her fighes being whirle-
windes, and her grones thunder, at length fhe fell
in labour, and was deliuered of a pale, meagre,
weake child, named *Sickneffe*, whom Death (with
a peftilence) would néedes take vpon him to
nurfe, and did fo.   This ftarueling being come
to his full growth, had an office giuen him for
nothing (and thats a wonder in this age) Death
made him his Herauld : attirde him like a
Courtier, and (in his name) chargde him to goe
into the Priuie Chamber of the Englifh Quéene,
to fommon her to appeare in the Star-chamber
of heauen.

The fommons made her ftart, but (hauing an
inuincible fpirit) / did not amaze her : yet whom
would not the certaine newes of parting from a
Kingdome amaze ! But fhe knewe where to finde
Her death. a richer, and therefore lightlie regarded
the loffe of this, and thereupon made readie for
that heauenlie Coronation, being (which was moft
ftrange) moft dutifull to obay, that had fo many
yeares fo powrefully commaunded.   She obayed
Deaths meffenger, and yéelded her body to the
hands of death himfelfe.   She dyed, refigning her
Scepter to pofteritie, and her Soule to immortalitie.

The report of her death (like a thunder clap)
was able to kill thoufands, it tooke away hearts
from millions: for hauing brought vp (euen

vnder her wing) a nation that was almoſt begotten
and borne vnder her; that neuer ſhouted any
other *Aue* than for her name, neuer ſawe the
face of any Prince but her ſelfe, neuer vnder-
ſtoode what that ſtrange out-landiſh word *Change*
ſignified: how was it poſſible, but that her ſicknes
ſhould throw abroad an vniuerſall feare, and her
death an aſtoniſhment? She was the
Courtiers treaſure, therefore he had
caufe to mourne: the Lawyers ſword

The generall
terror that her
death bred.

of iuſtice, he might well faint: the Merchants
patroneſſe, he had reaſon to looke pale: the
Citizens mother, he might beſt lament: the
Shepheards Goddeſſe, and ſhould not he droope?
Onely the Souldier, who had walkt a long time
vpon wodden legs, and was not able to giue
Armes, though he were a Gentleman, had briſſeld
vp the quills of his ſtiffe Porcupine muſtachio,
and ſwore by no beggers that now was the houre
come for him to beſtirre his ſtumps: Vſurers
and Brokers (that are the Diuels Ingles, and
dwell in the long lane of hell) quakt like aſpen
leaues at his oathes: thoſe that before were the
onely cut-throates in *London*, now ſtoode in feare
of no other death: but my *Signior Soldado* was
deceiued, the Tragedie went not forward.

Neuer did the Engliſh Nation behold ſo much
black worne as there was at her Funerall: It was

then but put on, to try if it were fit, for the great
day of mourning was fet downe (in the booke of
heauen) to be held afterwards : that was but the
dumb fhew, the Tragicall Aɛ̃t hath bene playing
euer fince.   Her Herfe (as it was borne) feémed
to be an Iland fwimming in water, for round /
about it there rayned fhowers of teares, about her
death-bed none : for her departure was fo fudden
and fo ftrange, that men knew not how to wéepe,
becaufe they had neuer bin taught to fhed teares
of that making.   They that durft not fpeake their
forrowes, whifperd them : they that durft not
whifper, fent them foorth in fighes.   O what an
Earth-quake is the alteration of a State!   Looke
from the Chamber of Prefence, to the Farmers
cottage, and you fhall finde nothing but diftraction:
the whole Kingdome feemes a wildernes, and the
people in it are tranfformed to wild men. ˙ The
Map of a Countrey fo pitifullie diftracted by the
horror of a change, if you defire perfectlie to
behold, caft your eyes then on this that followes,
which being heretofore in priuate prefented to the
King, I thinke may very worthily fhew it felfe
before you : And becaufe you fhall fee them
attirde in the fame fafhion that they were before
his Maiefty, let thefe fewe lines (which ftood then
as Prologue to the reft) enter firft into your
eares.

*N*Ot for applau∫es, ∫hallow fooles aduenture,
     I plunge my ver∫e into a ∫ea of cen∫ure,
But with a liuer dre∫t in gall, to ∫ee
So many Rookes, catch-polls of poe∫y,
That feed vpon the fallings of hye wit ;
And put on ca∫t inuentions, mo∫t vnfit ;
For ∫uch am I pre∫t forth in ∫hops and ∫talls,
Pa∫ted in Powles, and on the Lawyers walls,
For euery ba∫ili∫k-eyde Criticks bait,
To kill my ver∫e, or poi∫on my conceit :
Or ∫ome ∫moakt gallant who at wit repines,
To dry Tabacco with my hole∫ome lines,
And in one paper ∫acrifice more braine,
Than all his ignorant ∫cull could ere containe :
But merit dreads no martyrdome, nor ∫troke,
My lines ∫hall liue when he ∫hall be all ∫moke.

Thus farre the Prologue, who leauing the Stage
cléere, the feares that are bred in the wombe of
this altring kingdome do / next ∫tep vp, acting
thus.

*T*He great impo∫tume of the realme was drawne
     Euen to a head : the multitudinous ∫pawne
Was the corruption, which did make it ∫well
With hop'd ∫edition (the burnt ∫eed of hell,)
Who did expeᴕ but ruine, blood, and death,
To ∫hare our kingdome, and diuide our breath.

D. I.   I 2

Religions without religion,
To let each other bload, confusion
To be next Queene of England, *and this yeere*
The ciuill warres of France *to be plaid heere*
By Englifh-men, ruffians, and pandering flaues,
That faine would dig vp gowtie vfurers graues :
At fuch a time, villaines their hopes do honey,
And rich men looke as pale as their white money :
Now they remoue, and make their filuer fweat,
Cafting themfelues into a couetous heate,
And then (vnfeene) in the confederate darke,
Bury their gold, without or Prieft, or Clarke.
And fay no prayers ouer that dead pelfe :
True, Gold's no Chriftian, but an Indian elfe.
Did not the very kingdome feeme to fhake
Her precious maffie limbes ? did fhe not make
All Englifh cities (like her pulfes) beate
With people in their veines ? the feare fo great,
That had it not bene phifickt with rare peace
Our populous power had leffend her increafe.
The Spring-time that was dry, had fprung in blood,
A greater dearth of men, than e're of foode :
In fuch a panting time and ga'ping yeare,
Victuals are cheapeft, only men are deare.
Now each wife-acred Landlord did difpaire,
Fearing fome villaine fhould become his heire,
Or that his fonne and heire before his time,
Should now turne villaine, and with violence clime

Vp to his life, saying father you haue seene
King / Henry, Edward, Mary, and the Queene,
I wonder you'le liue longer ! then he tells him
Hees loth to see him kild, therfore he kills him,
And each vast Landlord dyes lyke a poore slaue :
Their thousand acres makes them but a graue.
At such a time great men conuey their treasure
Into the trusty Citie : wayts the leisure
Of bloud and insurrection, which warre clips,
When euery gate shutts vp her Iron lips :
Imagine now a mighty man of dust,
Standeth in doubt, what seruant he may trust, [more:
With Plate worth thousands : Iewels worth farre
If he proue false, then his rich Lord proues poore :
He calls forth one by one, to note their graces,
Whilst they make legs he copies out their faces,
Examines their eye-browe, consters their beard,
Singles their Nose out, still he rests afeard :
The first that comes by no meanes heele alow,
Has spyed three Hares starting betweene his brow,
Quite turnes the word, names it Celeritie,
For Hares do run away, and so may he :
A second shewne : him he will scarce behold,
His beard's too red, the colour of his gold :
A third may please him, but tis hard to say,
A rich man's pleasde, when his goods part away.
And now do cherrup by, fine golden nests
Of well hatcht bowles : such as do breed in feasts.

For warre and death cupboords of plate downe pulls,
Then Bacchus *drinkes not in gilt-bowles, but fculls.*
Let me defcend and ftoope my verfe a while,
To make the Comicke cheeke of Poefie fmile ;
Ranck peny-fathers fcud (with their halfe hammes,
Shadowing their calues) to faue their filuer dammes ;
At euery gun they ftart, tilt from the ground,
One drum can make a thoufand Vfurers found,
In vnfought Allies and vnholefome places,
Back-wayes and by-lanes, where appeare fewe faces.
In / fhamble-fmelling roomes, loathfome profpects,
And penny-lattice-windowes, which reiects
All popularitie : there the rich Cubs lurke,
When in great houfes ruffians are at worke,
Not dreaming that fuch glorious booties lye
Vnder thofe nafty roofes : fuch they paffe by
Without a fearch, crying there's nought for vs,
And wealthie men deceiue poore villaines thus :
Tongue-trauelling Lawyers faint at fuch a day,
Lye fpeechleffe, for they haue no words to fay.
Phifitions turne to patients, their Arts dry,
For then our fat men without Phifick die.
And to conclude, againft all Art and good,
Warre taints the Doctor, lets the Surgion blood.

Such was the fashion of this Land, when the
great Land-Lady thereof left it: Shée came in
with the fall of the leafe, and went away in the

Spring: her life (which was dedicated to Virginitie,)
both beginning & clofing vp a miraculous Mayden
circle : for fhe was borne vpon a Lady Eue, and
died vpon a Lady Eue : her Natiuitie & death
being memorable by this wonder : the firft and
laft yeares of her Raigne by this, that a *Lee* was
Lorde Maior when fhe came to the Crowne, and
a *Lee* Lorde Maior when fhe departed from it.
Thrée places are made famous by her for thrée
things, *Greenewich* for her birth, *Richmount* for
her death, *White-Hall* for her Funerall : vpon her
remouing from whence, (to lend our tiring profe
a breathing time) ftay, and looke vpon thefe
Epigrams, being compofed.

1. Vpon the Queenes last Remoue
being dead.

*T*He *Queene's remou'de in folemne fort,*
  Yet this was ftrange, and feldome feene,
The Queene vfde to remoue the Court,
But now the Court remou'de the Queene.

2. Vpon her bringing by water
to White Hall.

*T*He *Queene was brought by water to White Hall,*
  At euery ftroake, the Oares teares let fall.
More clung about the Barge : Fifh vnder water
Wept out their eyes of pearle, and fwom blind after.

I thinke the Barge-men might with eafier thyes
Haue rowde her thither in her peoples eyes:
For howfoe're, thus much my thoughts haue fkand,
S'had come by water, had fhe come by land.

3. Vpon her lying dead at
White Hall.

*T*He Queene lyes now at *White Hall* dead,
  And now at *White Hall* liuing,
To make this rough obiection euen,
  Dead at White Hall at Weftminfter,
But liuing at White Hall in Heauen.

Thus you fée that both in her life and her
death fhée was appointed to bee the mirror of her
time : And furely, if fince the firft ftone that
was layd for the foundation of this great houfe
of the world, there was euer a yeare ordained to
be wondred at, it is only this : the *Sibils, Octo-*
gefimus, Octauus Annas, That same terrible 88.
which came fayling hither in the Spanifh Armado,
1603. A more and made mens hearts colder then the
wonderfull
yeare than 88. frozen Zone, when they heard but an
inckling of it : That 88 by whofe horrible pre-
dictions, Almanack-makers ftood in bodily feare
their trade would bée vtterly ouerthrowne, and
poore *Erra Pater* was threatned (becaufe he was
a Iew) to be put to bafer offices than the ftopping

of muſtard-pots : That ſame 88. which had more
prophecies waiting at his héeles, thã euer *Merlin*
the Magitian had in his head, was a yeare of
Iubile to this. *Platoes Mirabilis Annus,* (whether
it be paſt alreadie, or to come within theſe foure
yeares) may throwe *Platoes* cap at *Mirabilis,* for
that title of wonderfull is beſtowed vpon 1603.
If that ſacred Aromatically perfumed fire of wit
(out of whoſe flames *Phœnix* poeſie doth ariſe)
were burning in any breſt, I would féede it with
no other ſtuffe for a twelue-moneth and a day, than
with kindling papers full of lines, that ſhould tell
only of the chances, changes, and ſtrange ſhapes
that this Protean Climaðtericall yeare hath meta-
morphoſed himſelfe into. It is able to finde ten
Chroniclers a competent liuing, and to ſet twentie
Printers at worke. You ſhall perceiue I lye not, if
(with *Peter Bales*) you will take the paines to drawe
the whole volume of it into the compaſſe of a
pennie. As firſt, to begin with the Quéene's death,
then the Kingdomes falling into an Ague vpon
that. Next, followes the curing of that feauer
by the holeſome receipt of a proclaymed King.
That wonder begat more, for in an houre, two
mightie Nations were made one : wilde *Ireland*
became tame on the ſudden, and ſome Engliſh
great ones that before ſéemed tame, on the
ſudden turned wilde : The ſame Parke which

great *Iulius Cæsar* inclofed, to hold in that Déere whome they before hunted, being now circled (by a fecond *Cæfar*) with ftronger pales to kéepe them from leaping ouer. And laft of all (if that wonder be the laft and fhut vp the yeare) a moft dreadfull plague. This is the abftract, and yet (like *Stowes* Chronicle of *Decimo Sexto* to huge *Hollinfhead*) thefe fmall pricks in this Set-card of ours, reprefent mightie Countreys ; whilft I haue the quill in my hand, let me blow them bigger.

The Quéene being honoured with a Diademe of Starres, *France*, *Spaine*, and *Belgia*, lift vp their heads, preparing to do as much for *England* by giuing ayme, whilft fhe fhot arrowes at her owne breft (as they imagined) as fhe had done (many a yeare together) for them : and her owne Nation betted on their fides, looking with diftracted countenance for no better guefts than Ciuill Sedition, Vprores, Rapes, Murders, and Maffacres. But the whéele of Fate turned, a better Lottery was drawne, *Pro Troia ftabat Apollo*, God ftuck valiantlie to vs. For behold, vp rifes a comfortable Sun out of the North, whofe glorious beames / (like a fan) difperfed all thick and contagious clowdes. The loffe of a Queene, was paid with the double intereft of a King and Quéene. The Cedar of her gouern-ment which ftood alone and bare no fruit, is

changed now to an Oliue, vpon whofe fpreading
branches grow both Kings and Quéenes. Oh it
were able to fill a hundred paire of writing
tables with notes, but to fée the parts plaid in
the compaffe of one houre on the ftage of this
new-found world! Vpon Thurfday it was treafon to cry God faue king *Iames* king King Iames
of *England*, and vppon Friday hye proclaimed.
treafon not to cry fo. In the morning no voice
hearde but murmures and lamentation, at noone
nothing but fhoutes of gladnes & triumphe.
S. George and *S. Andrew* that many hundred
yeares had defied one another, were now fworne
brothers: *England* and *Scotland* (being parted
only with a narrow Riuer, and the people of
both Empires fpeaking a language leffe differing
than englifh within it felfe, as tho prouidence had
enacted, that one day thofe two Nations fhould
marry one another) are now made fure together, and
king *Iames* his Coronation, is the folemne wedding
day. Happieft of all thy Anceftors (thou mirror of
all Princes that euer were or are) that at feauen of
the clock wert a king but ouer a péece of a little
Iland, and before eleuen the greateft Monarch in
Chriftendome. Now

Siluer Crowds
Of blisful Angels and tryed Martyrs tread
On the Star-feeling ouer England's *head :*

Now heauen broke into a wonder, and brought forth
Our omne bonum *from the holesome North*
(Our fruitfull Souereigne) Iamus, *at whose dread*
   name
Rebellion swounded, and (erc since) became
Groueling and nerue-lesse, wanting bloud to nourish ;
For Ruine gnawes her selfe when kingdomes flourish.
Nor are our hopes planted in regall springs,
Neuer to wither, for our aire breedes kings :
And in all ages (from this Soueraigne time)
England shall still be calde the royall clime.
Most blisfull Monarch of all earthen powers,
Seru'd with a messe of kingdomes, foure such bowers
(For | prosperous   hiues,   and   rare   industrious
   swarmes)
The world containes not in her solid armes.
O thou that art the Mecter of our dayes,
Poets Apollo ! deale thy Daphnaan bayes
To those whose wits are bay-trees, euer greene,
Vpon whose hye tops Poesie chirps vnseene :
Such are most fit, t'apparell Kings in rimes,
Whose siluer numbers are the Muses chimes ;
Whose spritely caraéters (being once wrought on)
Out-liue the marble th'are insculpt vpon :
Let such men chaunt thy vertue, then they flye
On Learnings wings vp to Eternitie.
As for the rest, that limp (in cold desert)
Hauing small wit, lesse iudgement, and least Art :

Their verſe! tis almoſt hereſie to heare;
Baniſh their lines ſome furlong, from thine eare:
For tis held dang'rous (by Apolloes ſigne)
To be infeĉted with a leaprous line.
O make ſome Adamant Aĉt (n'ere to be worne)
That none may write but thoſe that are true-
   borne:
So when the worlds old cheekes ſhall race and
   peele,
Thy Aĉts ſhall breath in Epitaphs of Steele.

By theſe Comments it appeares that by this time
King *Iames* is proclaimed: now does freſh blood
leape into the cheekes of the Courtier: The ioyes that
the Souldier now hangs vp his armor, followed vpon
and is glad that he ſhall féede vpon his pro-clayming.
the bleſſed fruites of peace: the Scholler ſings
Hymnes in honor of the Muſes, aſſuring himſelfe
now that *Helicon* will bée kept pure, becauſe
Apollo himſelfe drinkes of it. Now the thriftie
Citizen caſts beyond the Moone, and ſéeing the
golden age returned into the world againe, re-
ſolues to worſhip no Saint but money. Trades
that lay dead & rotten, and were in all mens
opinion vtterly dambd, ſtarted out of their trance,
as though they had drunke of *Aqua Cæleſtis*, or
Vnicorns horne, and ſwore to fall to their olde
occupatioꞙs. Taylors meant no more to be called

Merchant-taylors, but Merchants, for their fhops were all lead foorth in leafes to be turned into fhips, and with their fheares (in ftead of a Rudder) would they haue / cut the Seas (like Leuant Taffaty) and fayld to the Weft Indies for no worfe ftuffe to make hofe and doublets of, than beaten gold : Or if the neceflitie of the time (which was likely to ftand altogether vpon brauery) fhould preffe them to ferue with their iron and Spanifh weapons vpon their ftalls, then was there a fharpe law made amongft them, that no workman fhould handle any néedle but that which had a pearle in his eye, nor any copper thimble, vnleffe it were linde quite through, or bumbafted with Siluer. What Mechanicall hard handed Vulcanift (feeing the dice of Fortune run fo fwéetly, and refoluing to ftrike whilft the iron was hote) but perfwaded himfelfe to bée Maifter or head Warden of the company ere halfe a yeare went about? The worft players Boy ftood vpon his good parts, fwearing tragicall and bufking oathes, that how vilainoufly foeuer he randed, or what bad and vnlawfull action foeuer he entred into, he would in defpite of his honeft audience be halfe a fharer (at leaft) at home, or elfe ftrowle (thats to fay trauell) with fome notorious wicked floundring company abroad. And good reafon had thefe time-catchers to be led into this fooles

paradice, for they fawe mirth in euery mans face,
the ftréetes were plumd with gallants, Tabac-
conifts fild vp whole Tauernes : Vintners hung
out fpicke and fpan new Iuy bufhes (becaufe
they wanted good wine) and their old raine-
beaten lattices marcht vnder other cullors, hauing
loft both company and cullors before. *London*
was neuer in the high way to preferment till
now ; now fhe refolued to ftand upon her pan-
toffles : now (and neuer till now) did fhe laugh
to fcorne that worme-eaten prouerbe of *Lincolne*
was, *London* is, & *Yorke* fhall bée, for fhe faw
her felfe in better ftate then *Ierufalem*, fhe went
more gallant then euer did *Antwerp*, was more
courted by amorous and luftie fuiters then *Venice*
(the minion of *Italy*) more loftie towers ftood
(like a Coronet, or a fpangled head-tire) about
her Temples, then euer did about the beautifull
forehead of *Rome* : *Tyrus* and *Sydon* to her were
like two thatcht houfes, to *Theobals* : ỹ grand
Cayr but a hogfty. *Hinc illæ lachrymæ.* She
wept her belly full for all this. Whilft *Troy* was
fwilling fack and fugar, and mowfing fat venifon,
the mad Gréekes made bonefires of their houfes :
Old Priam was drinking a health to the / wooden
horfe, and before it could be pledgd had his
throat cut. Corne is no fooner ripe, but for all
the pricking vp of his eares hée is pard off by

the fhins, and made to goe vpon ftumps.   Flowers
no fooner budded, but they are pluckt vp and
dye.   Night walks at the héeles of the day, and
forrowe enters (like a tauerne-bill) at the taile
of our pleafures: for in the Appenine heigth of
this immoderate ioy and fecuritie (that like
Powles Stéeple ouer-lookt the whole Citie) Behold, that miracle-worker, who in one minute
turnd our generall mourning to a generall mirth,
does now againe in a moment alter that gladnes
to fhrikes & lamentation.   Here would I faine
make a full point, becaufe pofteritie fhould not
be frighted with thofe miferable Tragedies, which
The Plague. now my Mufe (as *Chorus*) ftands ready
to prefent.   Time, would thou hadft neuer bene
made wretched by bringing them forth: Obli-
uion, would in all the graues and fepulchres, whofe
ranke iawes thou haft already clofd vp, or fhalt
yet hereafter burft open, thou couldft likewife
bury them for euer.

A ftiffe and fréezing horror fucks vp the riuers
of my blood : my haire ftands an ende with the
panting of my braines : mine eye balls are ready
to ftart out, being beaten with the billowes of my
teares : out of my wéeping pen does the inck
mournefully and more bitterly than gall drop on
the pale fac'd paper, euen when I do but thinke
how the bowels of my ficke Country haue bene

torne : *Apollo* therefore and you bewitching filuer-
tongd Mufes, get you gone, I inuocate none of your
names : Sorrow & Truth, fit you on each fide of
me, whilft I am deliuered of this deadly burden :
prompt me that I may vtter ruthfull and paffionate
condolement : arme my trembling hand, that it
may boldly rip vp and Anetimize the vlcerous
body of this *Anthropophagized* plague : Anthropo-
lend me Art (without any counterfeit Scithians. that
phagi are
feed on mens
fhadowing) to paint and delineate to the flesh.
life the whole ftory of this mortall and peftiferous
battaile, & you the ghofts of thofe more (by many)
then 40000. that with the virulent poifon of infection haue bene driuen out of your earthly
dwellings : you defolate hand-wringing widowes
that beate your bofomes ouer your departing
hufbands : you wofully diftracted mothers that
with difheueld haire falne into fwounds, whilft you
lye kiffing the infenfible cold lips / of your breathleffe Infants : you out-caft and downe-troden
Orphanes, that fhall many a yeare hence remember
more frefhly to mourne, when your mourning
garments fhall looke olde and be forgotten ; and
you the *Genij* of all thofe emptyed families, whofe
habitations are now among the *Antipodes* : Ioyne,
all your hands together, and with your bodies caft
a ring about me : let me behold your ghaftly
vizages, that my paper may receiue their true

pictures: *Eccho* forth your grones through the hollow truncke of my pen, and raine downe your gummy teares into mine Incke, that euen marble bofomes may be fhaken with terrour, and hearts of Adamant melt into compaffion.

What an vnmatchable torment were it for a man to be bard vp euery night in a vaft filent Charnell-houfe? hung (to make it more hideous) with lamps dimly & flowly burning, in hollow and glimmering corners : where all the pauement fhould in ftead of gréene rufhes, be ftrewde with blafted Rofemary : withered Hyacinthes, fatall Ciprefle and Ewe, thickly mingled with heapes of dead mens bones : the bare ribbes of a father that begat him, lying there : here the Chaplefle hollow fcull of a mother that bore him : round about him a thoufand Coarfes, fome ftanding bolt vpright in their knotted winding fhéetes : others halfe mouldred in rotten coffins, that fhould fuddenly yawne wide open, filling his nofthrils with noyfome ftench, and his eyes with the fight of nothing but crawling wormes. And to kéepe fuch a poore wretch waking, he fhould heare no noife but of Toads croaking, Scréech-Owles howling, Mandrakes fhriking : were not this an infernall prifon? would not the ftrongeft-harted man (befet with fuch a ghaftly horror) looke wilde? and run madde? and die?   And euen fuch a

formidable fhape did the difeafed Citie appeare in:
For he that durft (in the dead houre of gloomy
midnight) haue bene fo valiant, as to haue walkt
through the ftill and melancholy ftréets, what
thinke you fhould haue bene his muficke? Surely
the loud grones of rauing ficke men ; the ftrugling
panges of foules departing: In euery houfe griefe
ftriking vp an Allarum : Seruants crying out for
maifters: wiues for hufbands, parents for children,
children for their mothers : here he fhould haue
met fome frantickly running to knock vp Sextons ;
there, others fearfully / fweating with Coffins, to
fteale forth dead bodies, leaft the fatall hand-writing
of death fhould feale vp their doores.   And to
make this difmall confort more full, round about
him Bells heauily tolling in one place, and ringing
out in another.   The dreadfulneffe, of fuch an
houre, is invtterable: let vs goe further.   If fome
poore man, fuddeinly ftarting out of a fwéete and
golden flumber, fhould behold his houfe flaming
about his eares, all his family deftroied in their
fléepes by the mercileffe fire ; himfelfe in the very
midft of it, wofully and like a madde man calling
for helpe : would not the mifery of fuch a dis-
treffed foule, appeare the greater, if the rich Vfurer
dwelling next doore to him, fhould not ftirre,
(though he felt part of the danger) but fuffer him
to perifh, when the thrufting out of an arme might

haue faued him?   O how many thoufands of
wretched people haue acted this poore mans part?
how often hath the amazed hufband waking, found
the comfort of his bedde lying breathleffe by his
fide! his children at the fame inftant gafping for
life! and his feruants mortally wounded at the
hart by ficknes! the diftracted creature, beats at
death doores, exclaimes at windowes, his cries
are fharp inough to pierce heauen, but on earth
no eare is opend, to receiue them.   And in this
manner do the tedious minutes of the night ftretch
out the forrowes of ten thoufand : It is now day,
let vs looke forth and try what Confolation rizes
with the Sun : not any, not any : for before the
Iewell of the morning be fully fet in filuer, hundred hungry graues ftand gaping, and euery one
of them (as at a breakfaft) hath fwallowed downe
ten or eleuen liueleffe carcafes : before dinner, in
the fame gulfe are twice fo many more deuoured :
and before the Sun takes his reft, thofe numbers
are doubled : Thrée fcore that not many houres
before had euery one feuerall lodgings very
delicately furnifht, are now thruft altogether into
one clofe roome : a litle noifome roome : not
fully ten foote fquare.   Doth not this ftrike coldly
to ỹ hart of a worldly mifer?   To fome, the very
found of deaths name is in ftead of a paffing-bell :
what fhall become of fuch a coward, being told

that the felfe-fame bodie of his, which is now fo
pampered with fuperfluous fare, fo perfumed and
bathed in odoriferous waters, and fo gaily apparelled
in varietie of fafhiōs, muft one day be throwne
(like ftinking carion) into a rank & rotten graue ;
where his goodly eies ỹ did on c fhoote foorth /
fuch amorous glances, muft be beaten out of his
head : his lockes that hang wantonly dangling,
troden in durt vnder-foote : this doubtleffe (like
thunder) muft néeds ftrike him into the earth.
But (wretched man !) when thou fhalt fée, and be
affured (by tokens fent thée from heauen) that
to-morrow thou muft be tumbled into a Mucke-
pit, and fuffer thy body to be bruifde and preft
with thrée fcore dead men, lying flouenly vpon
thée, and thou to be vndermoft of all ! yea and
perhaps halfe of that number were thine enemies !
(and fée howe they may be reuenged, for the
wormes that bréed out of their putrifying car-
kaffes, fhall crawle in huge fwarmes from them,
and quite deuoure thée) what agonies will this
ftrange newes driue thée into?   If thou art in
loue with thy felfe, this cannot choofe but poffeffe
thée with frenzie.   But thou art gotten fafe (out
of the ciuill citie Calamitie) to thy Parkes and
Pallaces in the Country, lading thy affes and thy
Mules with thy gold (thy god), thy plate, and thy
Iewels : and the fruites of thy wombe thriftily

growing vp but in one onely fonne (the young
Landlord of all thy carefull labours) him alfo haft
thou refcued from the arrowes of infection : Now
is thy foule iocund, and thy fences merry.   But
open   thine   eyes,   thou   Foole   and   behold   that
darling of thine eye (thy fonne) turnd fuddeinly
into a lumpe of clay : the hand of peftilence hath
fmote him euen vnder thy wing : Now doeft thou
rent thine haire, blafpheme thy Creator, curfeft
thy creation, and bafely defcendeft into bruitifh
& vnmanly paffions, threatning in defpite of death
& his Plague, to maintaine the memory of thy
childe, in the euerlafting breft of Marble : a tombe
muft now defend him from tempefts : and for that
purpofe, the fwetty hinde (that digs the rent he
paies thee out of the entrailes of the earth) he is
fent for, to conuey forth that burden of thy
forrow : But note how thy pride is difdained :
that weather-beaten fun-burnt drudge, that not a
month fince fawnd vpon thy Worfhip like a
Spaniell, and like a bond-flaue, would haue ftoopt
lower than thy feete, does now ftoppe his nofe at
thy prefence, and is ready to fet his Maftiue as
hye as thy throate, to driue thee from his doore :
all thy gold and filuer cannot hire one of thofe
(whom before thou didft fcorne) to carry the dead
body to his laft home : the Country round about
thee fhun thee, as a Bafilifke, / and therefore to

London (from whofe armes thou cowardly fledft away) poaft vpon poaft muft be galloping, to fetch from thence thofe that may performe that Funerall Office: But there are they fo full of graue-matters of their owne, that they haue no leifure to attend thine : doth not this cut thy very heart-ftrings in funder? If that doe not, the fhutting vp of the Tragicall Act, I am fure will : for thou muft be inforced with thine owne handes, to winde vp (that blafted flower of youth) in the laft linnen, that euer he fhall weare : vpon thine owne fhoulders muft thou beare part of him, thy amazed feruant the other: with thine owne hands muft thou dig his graue, (not in the Church, or common place of buriall,) thou haft not fauour (for all thy riches) to be fo happie, but in thine Orcharde, or in the proude walkes of thy Garden, wringing thy palfie-fhaking hands in ftead of belles, (moft miferable father) muft thou fearch him out a fepulcher.

My fpirit growes faint with rowing in this Stygian Ferry, it can no longer endure the transportation of foules in this dolefull manner : let vs therefore fhift a point of our Compaffe, and (fince there is no remedie, but that we muft ftill bee toft vp and downe in this *Mare mortuum*) hoift vp all all our failes, and on the merry winges of a luftier winde feeke to arriue on fome profperous fhore.

Imagine then that all this while, Death (like a

Spanifh Leagar, or rather like ftalking *Tamberlaine*) hath pitcht his tents, (being nothing but a heape of winding fhéetes tackt together) in the finfully-polluted Suburbes : the Plague is Mufter-maifter and Marfhall of the field : Burning Feauers, Boyles, Blaines, and Carbuncles, the Leaders, Lieutenants, Serieants, and Corporalls : the maine Army confifting (like *Dunkirke*) of a mingle-mangle, *viz.*, dumpifh Mourners, merry Sextons, hungry Coffin-fellers, fcrubbing Bearers, and naftie Graue-makers : but indéed they are the Pioners of the Campe, that are imployed onely (like Moles) in cafting vp of earth and digging of trenches ; Feare and Trembling (the two Catch-polles of Death) arreft euery one : No parley will be graunted, no compofition ftood vpon, But the Allarum is ftrucke vp, the *Toxin* ringes out for life, and no voyce heard but *Tue*, *Tue*, Kill, Kill ; the little Belles / onely (like fmall fhot) doe not yet goe off, and make no great worke for wormes, a hundred or two loft in euery fkirmifh, or fo : But alas thats nothing : yet by thofe defperat fallies, what by open fetting vpon them by day, and fecret Ambufcadoes by night, the fkirts of *London* were pittifully pared off, by litle and litle : which they within the gates perceiuing, it was no boot to bid them take their héeles, for away they trudge thick and thrée fold ; fome riding,

fome on foote: fome without bootes, fome in
their flippers, by water, by land : In fhoales fwom
they Weft-ward, mary to *Grauefend* none went
vnleffe they be driuen, for whofoeuer landed
there neuer came back again : Hacknies, water-
men & Wagons, were not fo terribly imployed
many a yeare ; fo that within a fhort time, there
was not a good horfe in Smith-field, nor a Coach
to be fet eye on.   For after the world had once
run vpon the wheeles of the Peft-cart, neithe[r]
coach nor caroach durft appeare in his likeneffe.

   Let vs purfue thefe runawayes no longer, but
leaue them in the vnmercifull hands of the
Country-hard-hearted *Hobbinolls*, (who are ordaind
to be their Tormentors) and returne backe to
the fiege of the Citie, for the enemie taking
aduantage by their flight, planted his ordinance
againft the walls ; here the Canons (like their
great Bells) roard : the Plague took fore paines
for a breach ; he laid about him cruelly, ere he
could get it, but at length he and his tiranous
band entred : his purple colours were prefently
(with the found of Bow-bell inftead of a trumpet)
aduanced, and ioynd to the Standard of the Citie ;
he marcht euen thorow Cheapfide, and the capitall
ftréets of *Troynouant* : the only blot of difhonor
that ftruck vpon this Inuader, being this, that
hée plaide the tyrant, not the conqueror, making

hauocke of all, when he had all lying at the foote
of his mercy. Men, women & children dropt
downe before him : houfes were rifled, ftréetes
ranfackt, beautifull maidens throwne on their
beds, and rauiſht by ficknes: rich mens Cofers
broken open, and ſhared amongſt prodigall heires
and vnthriftie feruants : poore men vſde poorely,
but not pittifully ; he did very much hurt, yet
fome fay he did very much good. Howfoeuer
he behaued himfelfe, this intelligence runs currant,
that euery houfe lookt like S. *Bartholmewes*
Hofpitall, and / euery ftréete like Bucklerſbury for
poore *Methridatum* and *Dragon-water* (being both
of them in all the world, fcarce worth thrée-pence)
were bort in euery corner, and yet were both
drunke euery houre at other mens coſt. *Lazarus*
lay groning at euery mans doore : mary no *Diues*
was within to fend him a crum, (for all your
Gold-finches were fled to the woods) not a dogge
left to licke vp his fores, for they (like Curres)
were knockt downe like Oxen, and fell thicker
then Acornes.

I am amazed to remember what dead Marches
were made of thrée thoufand trooping together ;
hufbands, wiues & children being led as ordinarily
to one graue, as if they had gone to one bed.
And thofe that could fhift for a time, and fhrink
their heads out of the collar (as many did) yet

went they (moſt bitterly) miching and muffled
vp & downe, with Rue and Wormewood ſtuft
into their eares and noſthrils, looking like ſo many
Bores heads ſtuck with branches of Roſemary, to
be ſerued in for Brawne at Chriſtmas.

This was a rare worlde for the Church, who
had wont to complaine for want of liuing, and
now had more liuing thruſt vpon her, than ſhe
knew how to beſtow : to haue bene Clarke now
to a pariſh Clarke, was better then to ſerue ſome
fooliſh Iuſtice of Peace, or than the yeare before
to haue had a Benefice. Sextons gaue out, if
they might (as they hoped) continue theſe doings
but a tweluemonth longer, they and their poſteritie
would all ryde vppon footecloathes to the ende
of the world. Amongſt which worme-eaten
generation, the thrée bald Sextons of limping
Saint *Gyles*, Saint *Sepulchres*, and Saint *Olaues*,
rulde the roaſte more hotly, than euer did the
Triumuiri of *Rome*. *Iehochanan*, *Symeon*, and
Eleazar, neuer kept ſuch a plaguy coyle in
Ieruſalem among the hunger-ſtarued Iewes, as
theſe thrée Sharkers did in their Pariſhes among
naked Chriſtians. Curſed they were I am ſure
by ſome to the pitte of hell, for tearing money
out of their throates, that had not a croſſe in
their purſes. But alas ! they muſt haue it, it
is their Fee, and therefore giue the Diuell his

due : Onely Hearbe-wiues and Gardeners (that
neuer prayed before vnleffe it were for Raine or
faire weather,) were now day and night vppon
their marybones, that God would bleffe the
labors of thofe mole-catchers, / becaufe they fucke
fwéetneffe by this ; for the price of flowers,
Hearbes and garlands, rofe wonderfully, in fo
much that Rofemary which had wont to be fold
for 12. pence an armefull, went now for fix
fhillings a handfull.

A fourth fharer likewife (thefe winding-fhéete-
weauers) deferues to haue my penne giue his
lippes a Iewes Letter, but becaufe he worfhips
the Bakers good Lord & Maifter, charitable S.
Clement (whereas none of the other thrée euer had
to do with any Saint) he fhall fcape the better :
only let him take heede, that hauing all this
yeare buried his praiers in the bellies of Fat ones,
and plump Capon eaters, (for no worfe meat
would downe this *Bly*-foxes ftomach) let him
I fay take héede leaft (his flefh now falling
away) his carcas be not plagude with leane ones,
of whom (whilft the bill of *Lord haue mercy
vpon vs,* was to be denied in no place) it was
death for him to heare.

In this pittifull (or rather pittileffe) perplexitie
ftood *London,* forfaken like a Louer, forlorne like
a widow, and difarmde of all comfort: difarmde

I may well fay, for fiue Rapiers were not ftirring all this time, and thofe that were worne, had neuer bin féene, if any money could haue bene lent vpon them: fo hungry is the Eftridge difeafe, that it will deuoure euen Iron: let vs therefore with bag & baggage march away from this dangerous fore Citie, and vifit thofe that are fled into the Country. But alas! *Decidis in Scyllam*, you are pepperd if you vifit them, for they are vifited alreadie: the broad Arrow of Death, flies there vp & downe, as fwiftly as it doth here: they that rode on the luftieft geldings could not out-gallop the Plague. It ouer-tooke them, and ouer-turnd them too, horfe and foote.

You whom the arrowes of peftilence haue reacht at eightéen and twenty fcore (tho you ftood far enough as you thought frō the marke) you that fickning in the hie way, would haue bene glad of a bed in an Hofpitall, and dying in the open fieldes, haue bene buried like dogs, how much better had it bin for you, to haue lyen fuller of byles and plague-fores than euer did *Iob*, fo you might in that extremity haue receiued both bodily & fpiritual comfort, which there was denied you? For thofe mifbeléeuing Pagans, the plough-driuers, thofe worfe then Infidels, that (like their Swine) neuer / looke vp

fo high as Heauen : when Citizens boorded them
they wrung their hands, and wifht rather they
had falne into the hands of Spaniards: for the
fight of a flat-cap was more dreadfull to a Lob,
then the difcharging of a Caliuer : a treble-ruffe
(being but once named the Merchants fet) had
power to caft a whole houfhold into a cold fweat.
If one newe fuite of Sackcloth had béene but
knowne to haue come out of Burchin-lane (being
the common Wardrope for all their Clowne-
fhips) it had béene enough to make a Market
towne giue vp the ghoft. A Crow that had
béene féene in a Sunne-fhine day, ftanding on
the top of Powles, would haue béene better than
a Beacon on fire, to haue raizd all the townes
within ten miles of *London*, for the kéeping her
out.

Neuer let any man afke me what became of
our Phifitions in this Maffacre : they hid their
Synodicall heads afwell as the prowdeft : and
I cannot blame them, for their Phlebotomies,
Lofinges, and Electuaries, with their Diacatholi-
cons, Diacodiens, Amulets, and Antidotes had
not fo much ftrength to hold life and foule
together, as a pot of *Pinders* Ale and a Nutmeg :
their Drugs turned to Durt, their fimples were
fimple things, *Galen* could do no more good, than
Sir Giles Goofecap: Hipocrates, Auicen, Parafelfus,

Rasis, *Fernelius*, with all their succéeding rabble
of Doctors and Water-casters, were at their wits
end, or I thinke rather at the worlds end, for
not one of them durst péepe abroad; or if any
one did take vpon him to play the ventrous
Knight, the Plague put him to his *Nonplus*; in
such strange, and such changeable shapes did this
Cameleon-like sicknes appeare, that they could
not (with all the cunning in their budgets) make
pursenets to take him napping.

Onely a band of Desper-vewes, some few
Empiricall madcaps (for they could neuer be
worth veluet caps) turned themselues into Bées
(or more properly into Drones) and went humming vp and downe, with hony-brags in their
mouthes, sucking the swéetnes of Siluer (and
now and then of *Aurum Potabile*) out of the
poison of Blaines and Carbuncles: and these
iolly Mountibanks clapt vp their bils vpon euery
post (like a Fencers Challenge) threatning to
canuas the Plague, and to fight / with him at
all his owne feuerall weapons: I know not how
they sped, but some they sped I am sure, for I
haue heard them band for the Heauens, becaufe
they sent thofe thither, that were wisht to tarry
longer vpon earth.

I could in this place make your chéekes looke
pale, and your hearts shake, with telling how

fome haue had 18. fores at one time running vpon them, others 10. and 12., many 4. and 5. and how thofe that haue bin foure times wounded by this yeares infection, haue dyed of the laft wound, whilft others (that were hurt as often) goe vp and downe now with founder limmes, then many that come out of *France*, and the *Netherlands.* And defcending from thefe, I could draw forth a Catalogue of many poore wretches, that in fieldes, in ditches, in common Cages, and vnder ftalls (being either thruft by cruell maifters out of doores, or wanting all worldly fuccour but the common benefit of earth and aire) haue moft miferably perifhed. But to chronicle thefe would weary a fecond *Fabian.*

We will therefore play the Souldiers, who at the end of any notable battaile, with a kind of fad delight rehearfe the memorable acts of their friends that lye mangled before them : fome fhewing how brauely they gaue the onfet : fome, how politickly they retirde : others, how manfully they gaue and receiued wounds: a fourth fteps forth, and glories how valiantly hee loft an arme : all of them making (by this meanes) the remembrance euen of tragicall and mifchieuous euents very delectable. Let vs ftriue to do fo, difcourfing (as it were at the end of this mortall fiege of the Plague) of the feuerall moft worthy accidents

and ſtrange birthes which this peſtiferous yeare
hath brought foorth : ſome of them yeelding
Comicall and ridiculous ſtuffe, others lamentable :
a third kind, vpholding rather admiration, then
laughter or pittie.

As firſt, to reliſh the pallat of lickeriſh ex-
pectation, and withall to giue an *Item* how ſudden
a ſtabber this ruffianly ſwaggerer (Death) is, You
muſt beléeue, that amongſt all the weary number
of thoſe that (on their bare féete) haue trauaild
(in this long and heauie vocation) to the Holy-
land, one (whoſe name I could for néede beſtow
vpon you, but that I know you haue no néed /
of it, tho many want a good name) lying in that
cõmon Inne of ſick-men, his bed, & ſeeing the
black & blew ſtripes of the plague ſticking on
his fleſh, which he receiued as tokens (from
heauen) that he was preſently to goe dwell in
the vpper world, moſt earneſtly requeſted, and
in a manner coniured his friend (who came to
enterchange a laſt farewell) that hée would ſée
him goe handſomely attirde into the wild Iriſh
countrey of wormes, and for that purpoſe to
beſtow a Coffin vpon him : his friend louing him
(not becauſe he was poore yet he was poore) but
becauſe hée was a Scholler : Alack that the Weſt
Indies ſtand ſo farre from Vniuerſities ! and that
a minde richly apparelled ſhould haue a thréed-

bare body!) made faithfull promife to him, that
he fhould be naild vp, he would boord him: and
for that purpofe went inftantly to one of the new-
found trade of Coffin-cutters, befpake one, and
(like the Surueyour of deaths buildings) gaue
direction how this little Tenement fhould be
framed, paying all the rent for it before hand.
But note vpon what flippery ground life goes!
little did he thinke to dwell in that roome himfelfe
which he had taken for his friend: yet it féemed
the common law of mortalitie had fo decréede,
for hée was cald into the cold companie of his
graue neighbours an houre before his infected
friend, and had a long leafe (euen till doomes
day) in the fame lodging, which in the ftrength
of health he went to prepare for another. What
credit therefore is to be giuen to breath, which
like an harlot will runne away with euery minute?
How nimble is fickneffe, and what fkill hath
he in all the weapons he playes withall? The
greateft cutter that takes vp the Mediterranean
Ile in Powles for his Gallery to walke in, cannot
ward off his blowes. Hées the beft Fencer in
the world: *Vincentio Sauiolo* is no body to him:
He has his Mandrittaes, Imbrocataes, Stramazones,
and Stoccataes at his fingers ends: hécle make
you giue him ground, though ye were neuer
worth foote of land, and beat you out of breath,

though *Aeolus* himfelfe plaid vp̄o your wind-pipe.

To witnes which, I will call forth a Dutch-man (yet now hées paft calling for, has loft his hearing, for his eares by this time are eaten off with wormes) who (though hée dwelt in *Bedlem*) was not mad, yet the very lookes of the Plague (which indéed / are terrible) put him almoft out of his wits, for when the fnares of this cunning hunter (the Peftilence) were but newly layd, and yet layd (as my Dutch-man fmelt it out well enough) to intrap poore mens liues that meant him no hurt, away fneakes my clipper of the kings englifh, and (becaufe Mufket-fhot fhould not reach him) to the Low-countries (that are built vpon butter-firkins, and Holland chéefe) failes this plaguie fugitiue, but death, (who hath more authoritie there then all the feauen Electors, and to fhew him that there were other Low-countrey befides his owne) takes a little Frekin (one of my Dutch runnawayes children) and fends her packing, into thofe Netherlands fhée departed : O how pitifully lookt my Burgomaifter, when he vnderftood that the ficknes could fwim ! It was an eafie matter to fcape the Dunkirks, but Deaths Gallyes made out after him fwifter then the great Turkes. Which he perceiuing, made no more adoo, but drunke to the States fiue or fixe healths (becaufe he would be fure to liue well) and backe againe comes he, to try the ftrength of Englifh Béere: his old *Randeuous* of mad men was the place of méeting, where he was no fooner arriued, but the Plague had him by the backe, and arrefted him vpon an *Exeat Regnum*, for running to the enemie, fo that for the mad tricks he plaid to cozen our Englifh wormes of his Dutch carkas (which had béene fatted héere) ficknefſe and death clapt him vp in *Bedlem* the fecond time, and there he lyes, and there he fhall lye till he rot before ile meddle any more with him.

But being gotten out of *Bedlem*, let vs make a iourney to *Briſtow*, taking an honeſt knowne Citizen along with vs, who with other company trauailing thither (onely for feare the aire of *London* fhould confpire to poifon him) and fetting vp his reft not to heare the found of Bow-bell till next Chriſtmas, was notwithſtanding in the hye way fingled out from his company, and fet vpon by the Plague, who bad him ſtand, and deliuer his life. The reft at that word fhifted for themfelues, and went on, hée (amazed to fée his friends flye, and being not able to defend himfelfe, for who can defend himfelfe méeting fuch an enemye?) yéelded, and being but about fortie miles from *London*, vfed all the flights he could to get loofe out of the handes of death, and fo to

hide / himfelfe in his owne houfe, whereupon he
call'd for help at the fame Inne, where not long
before he and his fellowe pilgrimes obtained for
their money (mary yet with more prayers then
a beggar makes in thrée Termes) to ftand and
drinke fome thirtie foote from the doore. To
this houfe of tipling iniquitie hée repaires againe,
coniuring the *Lares* or walking Sprites in it, if it
were Chriftmas (that if was well put in) and in the
name of God, to fuccor and refcue him to their
power out of the handes of infection, which now
affaulted his body : the Diuell would haue bene
afraid of this coniuration, but they were not, yet
afraid they were it féemed, for prefently the doores
had their woodden ribs crufht in pieces, by being
beaten together : the cafements were fhut more
clofe than an Vfurers greafie veluet powch : the
drawing windowes were hangd, drawne, and
quartred : not a creuis but was ftopt, not a
moufe-hole left open, for all the holes in the
houfe were moft wickedly dambd vp : mine
Hofte and Hofteffe ran ouer one another into
the backe-fide, the maydes into the Orchard,
quiuering and quaking, and ready to hang themfelues on the innocent Plumb-trées (for hanging to
them would not be fo fore a death, as the Plague,
and to die maides too ! O horrible !) As for the
Tapfter, he fled into the Cellar, rapping out fiue

or fixe plaine Country oathes, that hée would
drowne himfelfe in a moft villanous Stand of Ale,
if the ficke Londoner ftoode at the doore any
longer. But ftand there he muft, for to go away
(well) he cannot, but continues knocking and
calling in a faint voyce, which in their eares
founded, as if fome ftaring ghoft in a Tragedie
had exclaimd vpon *Rhadamanth* : he might
knocke till his hands akte, and call till his heart
akte for they were in a worfe pickle within, then
hée was without : hée being in a good way to
go to Heauen, they being fo frighted, that they
fcarce knew whereabout Heauen ftoode, onely
they all cryed out, Lord haue mercie vpon vs :
yet Lord haue mercy vpon vs was the only thing
they feared. The dolefull cataftrophe of all is,
a bed could not be had for all *Babilon* : not a
cup of drinke, no, nor cold water be gotten,
though it had bin for *Alexander* the great : [if] a
draught of *Aqua vitæ* might haue faued his foule,
the towne denyed to do God that good feruice.

What / miferie continues euer ? the poore man
ftanding thus at deaths doore, and looking euery
minute when hée fhould be let in, behold, another
Londoner that had likewife bene in the *Frigida
zona* of the Countrey, and was returning (like
Æneas out of hell) to the heauen of his owne
home, makes a ftand at this fight, to play the

Phyfition, and feeing by the complexion of his patient that he was ficke at heart, applies to his foule the beft medicines that his comforting fpéech could make, for there dwelt no Poticary néere enough to helpe his body. Being therefore driuen out of all other fhiftes, he leads him into a field (a bundle of Strawe, which with much adoe he bought for money, feruing inftead of a Pillow.) But the Deftinies hearing the difeafed partie complaine and take on, becaufe hée lay in a field-bedde, when before hée would haue béene glad of a mattraffe, for very fpight cut the threade of his life, the crueltie of which deede made the other that playd Charities part at his wittes end, becaufe hée knew not where to purchafe tenne foote of ground for his graue : the Church nor Churchyard would let none of their lands. Maifter Vicar was ftrucke dumbe, and could not giue the dead a good word, neither Clarke nor Sexton could be hired to execute their Office ; no, they themfelues would firft be executed : fo that he that neuer handled fhouell before, got his implements about him, ripped vp the belly of the earth, and made it like a graue, ftript the cold carcaffe, bound his fhirt about his féete, pulled a linnen night cappe ouer his eyes, and fo layde him in the rotten bedde of the earth, couering him with cloathes cut out of the fame piece : and learning by his laſt words his name and habitation, this ſad Trauailer arriues at *London*, deliuering to the amazed widdow and children, inſtead of a father and a huſband, onely the out-ſide of him, his apparell. But by the way note one thing, the bringer of theſe heauy tydings (as if he had liued long enough when ſo excellent a worke of pietie and pittie was by him finiſhed) the very next day after his comming home, departed out of this world, to receiue his reward in the Spirituall Court of heauen.

It is plaine therefore by the euidence of theſe two witneſſes, that death, like a thiefe, ſets vpon men in the hie way, dogs them into / their owne houſes, breakes into their bed chambers by night, aſſaults them by day, and yet no law can take hold of him : he deuoures man and wife : offers violence to their faire daughters : kils their youthfull ſonnes, and deceiues them of their ſeruants : yea, ſo full of trecherie is he growne (ſince this Plague tooke his part) that no Louers dare truſt him, nor by their good wils would come neare him, for he workes their downfall, euen when their delights are at the higheſt.

Too ripe a proof haue we of this, in a paire of Louers ; the maide was in the pride of freſh bloud and beautie: ſhe was that which to be now is a wonder, yong and yet chaſte: the gifts

of her mind were great, yet thofe which fortune
beſtowed vpon her (as being well deſcended)
were not much inferiour: On this louely creature
did a yong man ſo ſtedfaſtly fixe his eye, that
her lookes kindled in his boſome a deſire, whoſe
flames burnt the more brightly, becauſe they were
fed with ſwéet and modeſt thoughts : *Hymen* was
the God to whome he prayed day and night that
he might marry her : his praiers were receiued :
at length (after many tempeſts of her deniall,
and frownes of kinsfolk) the element grew cléere,
& he ſaw ſ̃ happy landing place, where he had
long ſought to ariue : the prize of her youth
was made his own, and the ſolemne day appointed
when it ſhould be deliuered to him. Glad of
which bleſſednes (for to a louer it is a bleſſednes)
he wrought by all the poſſible art he could vſe
to ſhorten the expećted houre, and bring it néerer,
for, whether he feared the interception of parents,
or that his owne ſoule, with exceſſe of ioy, was
drowned in ſtrange paſſions, he would often, with
ſighs mingled with kiſſes, and kiſſes halfe ſinking
in teares, prophetically tell her, that ſure he ſhould
neuer liue to enioy her. To diſcredit which
opinion of his, behold, the ſunne had made haſt
and wakened the bridale morning. Now does
he call his heart traitour, that did ſo falſly con-
ſpire againſt him : liuely bloud leapeth into his

chéekes: hées got vp, and gaily attirde to play
the bridegroome, fhée likewife does as cunningly
turne her felfe into a bride : kindred and friends
are mette together, foppes and mufcadine run
fweating vp and downe till they drop againe, to
comfort their hearts, and becaufe fo many coffins
peftred London Churches, that / there was no room
left for weddings, Coaches are prouided, and away
rides all the traine into the Countrey.   On a
monday morning are thefe luftie Louers on their
iourney, and before noone are they alighted, entring
(inftead of an Inne) for more ftate into a Church,
where they no fooner appeared, but the Prieft fell
to his bufines : the holy knot was a tying, but he
that fhould faften it, comming to this, *In fickneffe and in health,* there he ftopt, for fodainely
the bride tooke holde of, *in ficknes,* for *in health*
all that ftoode by were in feare fhée fhould neuer
be kept.   The maiden-blufh into which her
chéekes were lately died, now beganne to loofe
colour : her voyce (like a coward) would haue
fhrunke away, but that her Louer reaching her a
hand, which he brought thither to giue her, (for
hée was not yet made a full hufband) did with
that touch fomewhat reuiue her; on went they
againe fo farre, till they mette with *For better, for
worfe*: there was fhe worfe than before, and had not
the holy Officer made hafte, the ground on which

fhée ftood to be marryed might eafily haue béene broken vp for her buryall. All ceremonies being finifhed, fhe was ledde betwéene two, not like a Bride, but rather like a Coarfe, to her bed: *That,* muft now be the table, on which the wedding dinner is to be ferued vppe (being at this time, nothing but teares, and fighes, and lamentations) and Death is chief waiter: yet at length her weake heart wraftling with the pangs, gaue them a fall, fo that vp fhée ftoode againe, and in the fatall funeral Coach that carried her forth, was fhe brought back (as vpon a béere) to the Citie: but fée the malice of her enemy that had her in chafe, vpon the wenfday follow-ing being ouertaken, was her life ouercome. Death rudely lay with her, and fpoild her of a maiden-head in fpite of her hufband. Oh the forrow that did round befet him! now was his diuination true, fhe was a wife, yet continued a maide: he was a hufband and a widdower, yet neuer knew his wife: fhe was his owne, yet he had her not: fhe had him, yet neuer enioyed him: hére is a ftrange alteration, for the rofemary that was wafht in fwéete water to fet out the Bridall, is now wet in teares to furnifh her buri-all: the mufike that was heard to found forth dances, can not now be heard for the ringing of belles: all the comfort that / happened to

either fide being this, that he loft her, before fhe
had time to be an ill wife, and fhe left him, ere
he was able to be a bad hufband.

Better fortune had this Bride, to fall into the
handes of the Plague, then one other of that
fraile female fex (whofe picture is next to be
drawne) had to fcape out of them.   An honeft
cobler (if at leaft coblers can be honeft that liue
altogether amongeft wicked foales) had a wife,
who in the time of health treading her fhooe
often awry, determined in the agony of a fickneffe (which this yeare had a faying to her) to
fall to mending afwell as her hufband did.   The
bed that fhe lay vpon (being as fhe thought or
rather feared) the laft bed that euer fhould beare
her, (for many other beds had borne her you
muft remember) and the worme of finne tickling
her confcience, vp fhe calls her very innocent
and fimple hufband out of his vertuous fhoppe,
where like Iuftice he fat diftributing amongft
the poore, to fome, halfe-penny péeces, penny
péeces to fome, and two-penny péeces to others,
fo long as they would laft, his prouident care
being alway, that euery man and woman fhould
goe vpright.   To the beds fide of his plaguy
wife approacheth Monfieur Cobler, to vnderftand
what deadly newes fhe had to tell him, and the
reft of his kinde neighbours that there were affem-

bled: fuch thicke teares ftanding in both the
gutters of his eies, to fée his beloued lie in fuch
a pickle, that in their falt water, all his vtterance
was drownd: which fhe perceiuing, wept as faft
as he: But by the warme counfell that fat about
the bed, the fhower ceaft, fhe wiping her chéekes
with the corner of one of the fhéetes: and he,
his fullied face, with his leatherne apron. At laft,
two or three fighes (like a *Chorus* to the tragedy
enfuing) ftepping out firft, wringing her handes
(which gaue the better action) fhée told the pittifull *Aŭæon* her hufband, that fhe had often done
him wrong: hée onely fhooke his head at this,
and cried humb! which humb, fhe taking as the
watch-word of his true patience, vnraueld the
bottome of her frailetie at length, and concluded,
that with fuch a man (and named him; but I hope
you would not haue me follow her fteppes and
name him too) fhe practifed the vniuerfall &
common Art of grafting, and that vpon her good
mans head, they two / had planted a monftrous
paire of inuifible hornes: At the found of the
hornes, my cobler ftarted vppe like a march Hare,
and began to looke wilde: his awle neuer ranne
through the fides of a boote, as that word did
through his heart: but being a polliticke cobler,
and remembring what péece of worke he was
to vnder-lay, ftroking his beard, like fome graue

headborough of the Parifh, and giuing a nodde,
as who fhould fay, goe on, bade her goe on indéed, clapping to her fore foule, this generall
falue, that *All are Sinners, and we muft forgiue,*
&c. For hée hoped by fuch wholefome Phificke
(as Shooemakers waxe being laide to a byle) to
draw out all the corruption of her fecret villanies.
She good heart being tickled vnder gilles, with
the finger of thefe kind fpéeches, turnes vp the
white of her eye, and fetches out an other. An
other, (O thou that art trained vp in nothing but
to handle péeces :) Another hath difcharged his
Artillery againft thy caftle of fortification : here
was paffion predominant: *Vulcan* ftrooke the
coblers ghoft (for he was now no cobler) fo
hardy vpon his breaft, that he cryed Oh! his
neighbours taking pitte to fée what terrible ftitches
pulld him, rubde his fwelling temples with the
iuice of patience, which (by vertue of the blackifh
fweate that ftoode reaking on his browes, and
had made them fupple) entred very eafily into
his now-parlous-vnderftanding fcull: fo that he
left winching, and fate quiet as a Lamb, falling
to his old vomite of councell, which he had
caft vp before, and fwearing (becaufe he was in
ftrong hope, this fhoo fhould wring him no more)
to fcale her a generall acquittance : prickt forward
with this gentle fpur, her tongue mends his pace,

fo that in her confeffion fhée ouertooke others, whofe bootes had béene fet all night on the Coblers laaft, beftowing vppon him the poefie of their names, the time, and place, to thintent it might be put into his next wifes wedding ring. And although fhée had made all thefe blots in his tables, yet the bearing of one man falfe (whom fhe had not yet difcouered) ftucke more in her ftomacke than all the reft. O valiant Cobler, cries out one of the Auditors, how art thou fet vpon? how art thou tempted? happy arte thou, that thou art not in thy fhop, for in ftead of cutting out péeces of leather, thou wouldft doubtleffe now pare away thy hart: for I fée and / fo do all thy neighbours here (thy wifes ghoftly fathers) fée that a fmall matter would now caufe thée turne turk, & to meddle with no more patches: but to liue within the compaffe of thy wit: lift not vp thy collar: be not horne mad: thanke heauen that the murther is reueald: ftudy thou *Baltazars* Part in *Ieronimo*, for thou haft more caufe (though leffe reafon) than he, to be glad and fad.

Well, I fée thou art worthy to haue patient *Grifeld* to thy wife, for thou beareft more than fhe: thou fhewft thy felfe to be a right cobler, and no fowter, that canft thus cleanely clowt vp the feam-rent fides of thy affection. With this learned Oration the Cobler was tutord : layd his finger on his mouth, and cried *paucos palabros* : he had fealed her pardon, and therefore bid her not feare : héer vpon [f]he named the malefactor : I could name him too, but that he fhall liue to giue more Coblers heads the Baftinado. And told, that on fuch a night when he fupt there (for a Lord may fup with a cobler that hath a pretty wench to his wife) when the cloth, O treacherous linnen ! was taken vp, and *Menelaus* had for a parting blow, giuen the other his fift : downe fhe lights (this half-fharer) opening the wicket, but not fhutting him out of the wicket, but conueis him into a by-room (being the ward-rob of old fhooes and leather) from whence the vnicorne cobler (that dreamt of no fuch fpirits) being ouer head and eares in fléepe, his fnorting giuing the figne that he was cock-fure, foftly out-fteales fir *Paris*, and to *Helenaes* téeth prooued himfelfe a true Troian.   This was the creame of her confeffion, which being fkimd off from the ftomach of her confcience, we looked euery minute to goe thither, where we fhould be farre enough out of the Coblers reach.   But the Fates laying their heades together, fent a repriue, the plague that before meant to pepper her, by little and little left her company : which newes being blowne abroad, Oh lamentable ! neuer did the

old buſkind tragedy beginne till now : for the
wiues of thoſe huſbands, with whom ſhe had
playd at faſt and looſe, came with nayles ſharpened
for the nonce, like cattes, and tongues forkedly
cut like the ſtings of adders, firſt to ſcratch out
falſe *Creſſidaes* eyes, and then (which was worſe)
to worry her to death with ſcolding.

But / the matter was tooke vp in a Tauerne ;
the caſe was altered, and brought to a new
reckoning (mary the blood of the *Burdeaux* grape
was firſt ſhead about it) but in the end, all anger
on euery ſide was powred into a pottle pot, &
there burnt to death. Now whether this Recanta-
tion was true, or whether the ſtéeme of infection,
fuming vp (like wine) into her braines, made her
talke thus idlely, I leaue it to the Iury.

And whilſt they are canuaſing her caſe, let
vs ſee what doings the Sexton of *Stepney* hath :
whoſe ware-houſes being all full of dead commodities, ſauing one : that one hée left open a
whole night (yet was it halfe full too) knowing
ẙ théeues this yeare were too honeſt to break
into ſuch cellers. Beſides thoſe that were left
there, had ſuch plaguy pates, that none durſt
meddle with them for their liues. About twelue
of the clock at midnight, when ſpirites walke,
and not a mowſe dare ſtirre, becauſe cattes goe
a catter-walling : Sinne, that all day durſt not

fhew his head, came réeling out of an ale-houfe, in the fhape of a drunkard, who no fooner fmelt the winde, but he thought the ground vnder him danced the Canaries : houfes féemed to turne on the toe, and all things went round : infomuch, that his legges drew a paire of Indentures, be-twéene his body and the earth, the principal couenant being, that he for his part would ftand to nothing what euer he faw : euery trée that came in his way, did he iuftle, and yet chalenge it the next day to fight with him. If he had clipt but a quarter fo much of the Kings filuer, as he did of the Kings englifh, his carkas had long ere this bene carrion for Crowes. But he liued by gaming, and had excellent cafting, yet feldome won, for he drew reafonable good hands, but had very bad féete, that were not able to carry it away. This fetter-vp of Malt-men, being troubled with the ftaggers, fell into the felfe-fame graue, that ftood gaping wide open for a breakfaft next morning, and imagining (when he was in) that he had ftumbled into his owne houfe, and that all his bedfellowes (as they were indéede) were in their dead fléepe, he, (neuer complaining of colde, nor calling for more fhéete) foundly takes a nap til he fnores again : In the morning the Sexton comes plodding along, and cafting vpon his fingers ends what he hopes ꝑ dead pay of that

day will come too, by that which / he receiued
the day before, (for Sextons now had better doings
than either Tauernes or bawdy-houfes). In that
filuer contemplation, fhrugging his fhoulders together, he fteppes ere he be aware on the brimmes
of that pit, into which this worfhipper of *Bacchus*
was falne, where finding fome dead mens bones,
and a fcull or two, that laie fcattered here and
there ; before he lookt into this Coffer of wormes
thefe he takes vp, and flinges them in : one of
the fculls battered the fconce of the fléeper, whilft
the bones plaide with his nofe ; whofe blowes
waking his muftie worfhip, the firft word that he
caft vp, was an oath, and thinking the Cannes
had flyen about, cryed zoundes, what do you
meane to cracke my mazer? the Sexton fmelling
a voice, (feare being ftronger than his heart)
beleeued verily fome of the coarfes fpake to him,
vpon which, féeling himfelfe in a cold fweat,
tooke to his héeles, whilft the Goblin fcrambled
vp and ranne after him : But it appeares the
Sexton had the lighter foote, for he ran fo fafte,
that hée ranne out of his wittes, which being left
behinde him, he had like to haue dyed prefently
after.

A meryer bargaine than the poore Sextons did
a Tincker méete withall in a Countrey Towne ;
through which a Citizen of *London* being driuen

(to kéepe himfelfe vnder the lée-fhore in this tempeftuous contagion) and cafting vp his eye for fome harbour, fpied a bufh at the end of a pole, (the auncient badge of a Countrey Ale-houfe :) Into which as good lucke was, (without any refiftance of the Barbarians, that all this yeare vfed to kéepe fuch landing places) veiling his Bonnet, he ftrucke in.   The Hoft had bene a mad Greeke, (mary he could now fpeake nothing but Englifh,) a goodly fat Burger he was, with a belly Arching out like a Béere-barrell, which made his legges (that were thicke & fhort, like two piles driuen vnder *London*-bridge) to ftradle halfe as wide as the toppe of Powles, which vpon my knowledge hath bene burnt twice or thrice. A leatherne pouch hung at his fide, that opened and fhut with a Snap-hance, and was indéede a flafke for gunpowder when King Henry went to *Bulloigne*.   An Antiquary might haue pickt rare matter out of his Nofe, but that it was worme-eaten (yet that proued it to be / an auncient Nofe :)   In fome corners of it there were blewifh holes that fhone like fhelles of mother of Pearle, and to fée his nofe right, Pearles had bene gathered out of them : other were richly garnifht with Rubies, Chrifolites and Carbunckles, which glis-tered fo oriently, that the Hamburgers offered I know not how many Dollars, for his companie in

an Eaft-Indian voyage, to haue ftoode a nightes
in the Poope of their Admirall, onely to faue
the charges of candles. In conclufion, he was
an Hoft to be ledde before an Emperour, and
though he were one of the greateft men in all
the fhire, his bignes made him not proude, but
he humbled himfelf to fpeake the bafe language
of a Tapfter, and vppon the Londoners firft
arriuall, cryed welcome, a cloth for this Gentleman : the Linnen was fpread, and furnifht
prefently with a new Cake and a Can, the roome
voided, and the Gueft left (like a French Lord)
attended by no bodie : who drinking halfe a
Can (in conceit) to the health of his beft friend
in the Citie, which laie extreame ficke, and had
neuer more neede of health, I knowe not what
qualmes came ouer his ftomach, but immediately
he fell downe without vttering any more wordes,
and neuer rofe againe.

Anon (as it was his fafhion) enters my puffing
Hoft, to relieue (with a frefh fupply out of his
Cellar,) the fhrinking Can, if hée perceiued it
ftoode in daunger to be ouerthrowne. But féeing
the chiefe Leader dropt at his féete, and imagining
at firft hée was but wounded a little in the head,
held vp his gowty golles and bleft himfelfe, that
a Londoner (who had wont to be the moft valiant
rob-pots) fhould now be ftrooke downe only with

two hoopes : and therevpon iugd him, fembling
out thefe comfortable words of a fouldier. If
thou be a man ftand a thy legges: he ftird not
for all this : wherevpon the Maydes being raifde
(as it had bene with a hue and cry) came hobling
into the room, like a flocke of Geefe, and hauing
vpon fearch of the bodie giuen vp this verdict,
that the man was dead, and murthered by the
Plague ; Oh daggers to all their hearts that heard
it ! Away trudge the wenches, and one of them
hauing had a freckled face all her life time, was
perfwaded prefently that now they were the /
tokens, and had like to haue turned vp her heeles
vpon it : My gorbelly Hoft that in many a yeare
could not without grunting, crawle ouer a threfh-
old but two foote broad, leapt halfe a yarde from
the coarfe (It was meafured by a Carpenters rule)
as nimbly as if his guts had béene taken out by
the hangman : out of the houfe he wallowed
prefently, being followed with two or thrée dozen
of napkins to drie vp the larde, that ranne fo faft
downe his héeles, that all the way he went, was
more greazie than a kitchin-ftuffe-wifes bafket :
you would haue fworne, it had béene a barrell of
Pitch on fire, if you had looked vpon him, for
fuch a fmoakie clowde (by reafon of his owne
fattie hotte ftéeme) compaffed him rounde, that
but for his voyce, hée had quite béene loft in

that ftincking myft: hanged himfelfe hée had
without all queftion (in this pittifull taking) but
that hée feared the weight of his intollerable
paunch, would haue burft the Roape, and fo hée
fhould bée put to a double death. At length
the Towne was raifed, the Countrey came downe
vpon him, and yet not vpon him neither, for
after they vnderftood the Tragedie, euery man
gaue ground, knowing my purfie Ale-cunner
could not follow them: what is to bée done in
this ftraunge Allarum? The whole Village is in
daunger to lye at the mercy of God, and fhall
bée bound to curfe none, but him for it: they
fhould doe well therefore to fet fire on his
houfe, before the Plague fcape out of it, leaft it
forrage higher into the Countrey, and knocke
them downe, man, woman, and childe, like
Oxen, whofe blood (they all fweare) fhall bée
required at his handes. At thefe fpéeches my
tender-hearted Hofte, fell downe on his maribones,
meaning indéede to entreat his audience to bée
good to him; but they fearing hée had béene
pepperd too, as well as the Londoner, tumbled
one vpon another, and were ready to breake
their neckes for hafte to be gone: yet fome of
them (being more valiant then the reft, becaufe
they heard him roare out for fome helpe) very
defperately ftept backe, and with rakes and

pitch-forkes lifted the gulch from the ground. Cōcluding (after they had laid their hogſheads togither, to draw out ſom holeſome counſel) that whoſoeuer would venter vpon the dead man & bury him, ſhould haue fortie ſhillings / (out of the common towne-purſe though it would bée a great cut to it) with the loue of the Church-wardens and Side-men, during the terme of life. This was proclaimed, but none durſt appeare to vndertake the dreadfull execution: they loued money well, [but] mary the plague hanging ouer any mans head that ſhould meddle with it in that ſort, they all vowde to dye beggers before it ſhould be Chronicled they kild themſelues for forty ſhillings: and in that braue reſolution, euery one with bagge & baggage marcht home, barricadoing their doores & windowes with fir buſhes, ferne, and bundels of ſtraw to kéepe out the peſtilence at the ſtaues end.

At laſt a Tinker came ſounding through the Towne, mine Hoſts houſe being the auncient watring place where he did vſe to caſt Anchor. You muſt vnderſtand hée was none of thoſe baſe raſcally Tinkers, that with a ban-dog and a drab at their tayles, and a pike-ſtaffe on their necks, will take a purſe ſooner then ſtop a kettle: No, this was a deuout Tinker, he did honor God *Pan*: a Muſicall Tinker, that vpon his kettle-drum

could play any Countrey dance you cald for, and
vpon Holly-dayes had earned money by it, when
no Fidler could be heard of. Hée was onely
feared when he ftalkt through fome townes where
Bées were, for he ftrucke fo fwéetely on the
bottome of his Copper inftrument, that he would
emptie whole Hiues, and leade the fwarmes after
him only by the found.

This excellent egregious Tinker calls for his
draught (being a double Iugge): it was fild for him,
but before it came to his nofe, the lamentable
tale of the Londoner was tolde, the Chamber doore
(where hée lay) being thruft open with a long pole,
(becaufe none durft touch it with their hands) and
the Tinker bidden (if he had the heart) to goe in
and fée if hée knew him. The Tinker being not
[vnwilling] to learne what vertue the medicine
had which hée held at his lippes, powred it downe
his throate merily, and crying trillill, he feares no
plagues. In hée ftept, tofling the dead body too
and fro, and was forrie hée knew him not : Mine
Hoft that with griefe began to fall away villanoufly,
looking very ruthfully on the Tinker, and thinking
him a fit inftrument to be playd vpon, offred a
crowne out of his owne / purfe, if he would bury
the partie. A crown was a fhrewd temptation to
a Tinker : many a hole might he ftop, before hée
could picke a crowne of it, yet being a fubtill

Tinker (& to make all Sextons pray for him,
becaufe hée would raife their fées) an Angell he
wanted to be his guide, and vnder ten fhillings
(by his ten bones) he would not put his finger into
the fire. The whole parifh had warning of this
prefently, thirtie fhillings was faued by the bargaine, and the Towne like to be faued too, therefore ten fhillings was leuyed out of hand, put into
a rag, which was tyed to the ende of a long pole
and deliuered (in fight of all the Parifh, who
ftood aloofe ftopping their nofes) by the Head-
boroughs owne felfe in proper perfon, to the
Tinker, who with one hand receiued the money,
and with the other ftruck the boord, crying hey,
a frefh double pot. Which armour of proofe
being fitted to his body, vp he hoifts the Londoner
on his backe (like a Schoole-boy) a Shouell and
Pick-axe are ftanding ready for him : And thus
furnifhed, into a field fome good diftance from
the Towne he beares his deadly loade, and there
throwes it downe, falling roundly to his tooles,
vpon which the ftrong béere hauing fet an edge,
they quickely cut out a lodging in the earth for
the Citizen. But the Tinker knowing that wormes
néeded no apparell, fauing onely fhéetes, ftript
him ftarke naked, but firft diude nimbly into his
pockets, to fée what linings they had, affuring himfelfe, that a Londoner would not wander fo farre

without filuer : his hopes were of the right ftampe, for from out of his pockets he drew a leatherne bagge with feuen poundes in it : this muficke made the Tinkers heart dance : he quickely tumbled his man into the graue, hid him ouer head and eares in duft, bound vp his cloathes in a bundle, & carying that at the end of his ftaffe on his fhoulder, with the purfe of feuen pounds in his hand, backe againe comes he through the towne, crying aloud, Haue yée any more Londoners to bury, hey downe a downe dery, haue ye any more Londoners to bury : the Hobbinolls running away from him, as if he had béene the dead Citizens ghoft, & he marching away from them in all the haft he could, with that fong ftill in his mouth.

You fée therefore how dreadfull a fellow Death is, making fooles / euen of wifemen, and cowards of the moft valiant; yea, in fuch a bafe flauerie hath it bound mens fences, that they haue no power to looke higher than their owne roofes, but féemes by their turkifh and barberous actions to belieue that there is no felicitie after this life, and that (like beafts) their foules fhall perifh with their bodyes. How many vpon fight onely of a Letter (fent from *London*) haue ftarted backe, and durft haue layd their faluation vpon it, that the plague might be folded in that empty paper, belieuing verily, that the arme of Omnipotence could neuer

reach them, vnleſſe it were with ſome weapon
drawne out of the infected Citie; in ſo much that
euen the Weſterne Pugs receiuing money there,
haue tyed it in a bag at the end of their barge,
and ſo trailed it through the Thames, leaſt plague-
ſores ſticking vpon ſhillings, they ſhould be naild
vp for counterfeits when they were brought home.

More ventrous than theſe block-heads was a
certaine Iuſtice of peace, to whoſe gate being ſhut
(for you muſt know that now there is no open
houſe kept) a company of wilde fellowes being
lead for robbing an Orchyard, the ſtout-hearted
Conſtable rapt moſt couragiouſly, and would haue
a bout with none but the Iuſtice himſelfe, who at
laſt appeard in his likeneſſe aboue at a window,
inquiring why they ſummond a parlie.   It was
aeliuered why : the caſe was opened to his examin-
ing wiſedome, and that the euill doers were onely
Londoners : at the name of Londoners the Iuſtice
clapping his hand on his breſt (as who ſhould ſay,
Lord haue mercie vpon vs) ſtarted backe, and
being wiſe enough to ſaue one, held his noſe hard
betwéene his fore-finger and his thumbe, and
ſpeaking in that wiſe (like the fellow that deſcribed
the villainous motion of *Iulius Cæſar* and the Duke
of *Guize*, who (as he gaue it out) fought a
combat together,) pulling the caſement cloſe to him
cryed out in that quaile-pipe voice, that if they

were Londoners away with them to *Limbo* : take
onely their names : they were fore fellowes, and he
would deale with them when time fhould ferue :
meaning, when the plague and they fhould not be
fo great together ; and fo they departed : The very
name of Londoners being worfe then ten whet-
ftones to fharpen the fword of Iuftice againft them.

I / could fill a large volume, and call it the fecond
part of the hundred mery tales, onely with fuch
ridiculous ftuffe as this of the Iuftice, but *Dij
meliora*, I haue better matters to fet my wits about :
neither fhall you wring out of my pen (though
you lay it on the rack) the villanies of that damnd
Kéeper, who kild all fhe kéept ; it had bene good
to haue made her kéeper of the common Iayle,
and the holes of both Counters, (for a number lye
there, that wifh to be rid out of this motley world,)
fhée would haue tickled them and turned them
ouer the thumbs. I will likewife let the Church-
warden in Thames ftréet fléepe (for hees now paft
waking) who being requefted by one of his neighbors to fuffer his wife or child (that was then dead)
to lye in the Churchyard, anfwered in a mocking
fort, he kéept that lodging for himfelfe and his
houfhold : and within thrée dayes after was driuen
to hide his head in a hole himfelfe. Neither will
I fpeake a word of a poore boy (feruant to a
Chandler) dwelling thereabouts, who being ftruck

to the heart by ſicknes, was firſt caryed away by water, to be left any where, but landing being denyed by an army of browne bill men that kept the ſhore, back againe was he brought, and left in an out-celler, where lying groueling and groning on his face (amongſt fagots, but not one of them ſet on fire to comfort him) there continued all night, and dyed miſerably for want of ſuccor. Nor of another poore wretch in the Pariſh of *Saint Mary Oueryes*, who being in the morning throwne, as the faſhion is, into a graue vpon a heape of carcaſes, that kayd for their complement, was found in the afternoone, gaſping and gaping for life : but by theſe tricks, imagining that many a thouſand haue bene turned wrongfully off the ladder of life, and praying that *Derick* or his executors may liue to do thoſe a good turne, that haue done ſo for others :
Hic finis Priami, héeres an end of an old Song.

Et iam tempus Equum fumantia ſoluere colla.

FINIS.

III.

THE BATCHELARS BANQUET.

1603.

NOTE.

For 'The Batchelar's Banquet' (1603) I again owe thanks to the British Museum. See Memorial-Introduction on it.—G.

THE BATCHELARS Banquet:

OR

A Banquet for Batchelars : Wherein is prepared ſundry daintie diſhes to furniſh their
Table, curiouſly dreſt, and ſeri-
ouſly ſerued in.

*Pleaſantly diſcourſing the variable humours of VVo-
men, their quickneſſe of wittes, and vnſearch-
able deceits.*

*View them well, but taſte not,
Regard them well, but waſte not.*

LONDON
Printed by T. C. and are to be ſolde
by T. P.   1603.

The Batchelars Banquet,

Or a Banquet for Batchelars: wherein is prepared fundry difhes to furnifh their
Table: curioufly dreft, and
ferioufly ferued in.

CHAP. I.

The humour of a young wife new married.

IT is the naturall inclination of a
young gallant, in the pleafant
prime, and flower of his florifh-
ing youth, being frefh, lufty,
iocond, to take no other care,
but to imploy his mony to buy
gay prefents for pretty Laffes, to frame his gréen
wits in penning loue ditties, his voice to fing
them fwéetly, his wandring eyes to gaze one the
faireft dames, and his wanton thoughts to plot
meanes for the fpéedy accomplifhment of his

wished defires, according to the compaffe of his eftate. And albeit his parents or fome other of his kindred, doe perhaps furnifh him with necesfary maintenance, fo that he wants nothing, but liues in all eafe and delight, yet cannot this content him, or fatisfie his vnexperienced mind : for although he dayly fée many married men, firft lapt in lobbes pound, wanting former libertie, and compaffed round in a cage of many cares, yet notwithftanding being ouer-ruled by felfe will, and blinded by folly : he fuppofes them therein to haue the fulnes of their delight, becaufe they haue fo neare them the Image of content. *Venus* ftarre glorioufly blazing / vpon them, I meane a daintie faire wife, brauely attired, whofe apparell perhaps is not yet paid for, (howfoeuer to draw their hufbands into a fooles paradice) they make him beléeue, that their father or mother haue of their coft and bounty affoorded it. This luftie youth (as I earft faid) feeing them already in this maze of bitter fwéetnes, he goes round about, turmoyling himfelfe in féeking an entrance, and taking fuch paines to finde his owne paine, that in the end, in he gets, when for the haft he makes, to haue a tafte of thefe fuppofed delicates, he hath no leifure to thinke, or no care to prouide thofe things that are hereunto requifite. The iolly yonker being thus gotten in, doth for a time ſwim in delight, and hath no deſire at all to wind him ſelfe out againe, till time and vſe, which makes all things more familiar and leſſe pleaſing, doe qualifie this humor: then glutted with ſacietie, or pinched with penury, he may perhaps begin to ſee his follie, and repent as well his fondnes, as his too much forwardnes, but all too late, he muſt haue patience perforce: his wife muſt be maintained according to her degrée, and withall (cōmonly it happes [if] ſhe carie the right ſtomacke of a woman) ſlender maintenance will not ſerue, for as their mindes mount aboue their eſtates, ſo commonly wil they haue their abillements. And if at a feaſt or ſome other goſſeps méeting whereunto ſhe is inuited, ſhe ſée any of the companie gaily attyred for coſt, or faſhion, or both, & chiefly the latter, (for generally women do affect nouelties,) ſhe forthwith moues a queſtion in her ſelfe, why ſhe alſo ſhould not be in like ſort attyred, to haue her garments cut after the new faſhion as well as the reſt, and anſwers it with a reſolution, that ſhe will, and muſt haue the like : Awaiting onely fit time and place, for the mouing and winning of her huſband there-vnto, of both which ſhe will make ſuch choice, that when ſhe ſpeakes ſhe will be ſure to ſpéede : obſeruing her opportunitie when ſhe might take her huſband at the moſt aduantage, which is

cōmonly in the bed, the gardaine of loue, the
ftate of marriage delights, & the life wherein the
weaker fexe hath euer the better : when therefore
this luftie gallant would profecute his / defired
pleafures, for which caufe he chiefly ran wil-
fully into the perill of Lobs pound, then
fqueamifhly fhe begins thus, faying ; I pray you
hufband let me alone, trouble me not, for I am
not well at eafe : which he hearing prefently
makes this reply. Why my fwéethart what ailes
you, are you not well ? I pray thée wife tell
me, where lies thy griefe? or what is the caufe
of your difcontent : wherevpon the vile woman
fetching a déepe figh, makes this anfwere. O
hufband God help me, I haue caufe enough to
gréeue, and if you knew all you would fay fo :
but alas it is in vaine to tell you any thing, féeing
that whatfoeuer I fay, you make but light reck-
ning of it : and therfore it is beft for me to bury
my forrowes in filence, being out of hope to haue
any help at your hands. Iefus wife (faith he)
why vfe you thefe words? is my vnkindnes fuch
that I may not knowe your griefes? tell me I
fay what is the matter ? In truth hufband it
were to no purpofe, for I knowe your cuftome
well inough, as for my words, they are but waft
wind in your eares ; for how great foeuer my
griefe is, I am affured you will but make light

of it, and thinke that I ſpeake it for ſome other purpoſe.

Goe too wife, ſaith her huſband, tell it me, for I wil know it. Well huſband, if you will needs, you ſhal : you know on Thurſday laſt, I was ſent for, and you willed me to goe to Miſtreſſe M. churching, and when I came thither I found great cheare, & no ſmal companie of wiues, but the meaneſt of them all was not ſo ill attired as I, and ſurely I was neuer ſo aſhamed of my ſelfe in my life, yet I ſpeake it not to praiſe my ſelfe : but it is well knowne, and I dare boldly ſay, that the beſt woman there came of no better ſtocke then I. But alas I ſpeake not this for my ſelfe, for God wot I paſſe not how meanely I am apparelled, but I ſpeake it for your credit & my friends. Why wife, ſaith he, of what calling & degrée were thoſe you ſpeak of ? Truly good huſband (ſaith ſhe) the meaneſt that was there, being but of my degrée, was in her gowne with trunck ſléeues, her vardingale, her turkie grograin kirtle, her taffety hat with a gold band, and theſe with ẙ reſt of her attire, made of ẙ neweſt faſhiõ, which is knowne / the beſt : whereas I poore wretch had on my threadbare gowne, which was made me ſo long agoe, againſt I was married, beſides that it was now too ſhort for me, for it is I remember ſince it was made aboue three yeares

agoe; fince which time I am growne very much,
and fo changed with cares and griefes, that I
looke farre older then I am: Truft me I was fo
afhamed, being amongft my neighbours, that I
had not the heart to looke vp; but that which
grceued me moft was, when miftreffe *Luce* B. &
miftreffe T. faid openly that it was a fhame both
for you and me, that I had no better apparell.
Tufh wife (quoth the good man) let them fay
what they lift, we are neuer a whit the worfe
for their words, we haue enough to doe with
our money though we fpend it not in apparell:
you knowe wife when we met together, we
had no great ftore of houfhold ftuffe, but were
fain to buy it afterward by fome and fome
as God fent mony, and yet you fee we want
many things that is neceffary to be had: befides,
the quarter day is néere, and my Landlord
you know wil not forbeare his rent: moreouer
you fee how much it cofts me in law about the
recouering of the Tenement which I fhould haue
by you. God fend me to get it quickly, or els
I fhal haue but a bad bargaine of it, for it hath
already almoft coft me as much as it is worth.
At thefe words his wiues coller begins to rife,
whereupon fhe makes him this anfwere. Iefus
God (faith fhe) when you haue nothing els to
hit in the téeth withall, yée twit me with the

Tenement: but it is my fortune. Why how now wife faith her hufband, are you now angry for nothing? Nay I am not angry, I muft be content with that which God hath ordained for me : but I wis the time was, when I might haue bene better aduifed : there are fome yet liuing that would haue bene glad to haue me in my fmock, whom you know well enough, to be propper young men, and therewithall wife and wealthy, but I verily fuppofe I was bewitcht to match with a man that loues me not; though I purchafed the ill-will of all my friends for his fake, this is all the good that I haue gotten there-by : I may truly fay I am the moft vnhappie woman in the / world : doe you thinke that *Law. Tom* & N. M. (who were both futers to me) doe kéepe their wiues fo? no by cocks body, for I know the worft cloathes that they caft off, is better then my very beft, which I weare on the cheifeft daies in the yeare : I know not what the caufe is that fo many good women die, but I would to God that I were dead too, that I might not troble you no more, féeing I am fuch an eie fore vnto you. Now by my faith wife faith he, you fay not well, there is nothing that I thinke too good for you, if my abillitie can compaffe it. But you knowe our eftate, we muft doe as we may, & not as we would; yet be of

good cheare, and turne to me, and I will ſtraine
my ſelf to pleaſe you in this or any other thing.
Nay for Gods ſake let me alone, I haue no mind
on ſuch matters, and if you had no more deſire
therto then I, I promiſe you, you would neuer
tuch me. No wife (ſaith he) hoping ſo with a
ieſt to make her mery, by my honeſtie I ſweare,
I verily thinke that if I were dead, you would
not be long without another huſband. No
maruaile ſure ſaith ſhe, I lead ſuch a good life
with you now. By my chriſtian ſoule I ſweare,
there ſhould neuer man kiſſe my lipps againe.
And if I thought I ſhould liue long with you, I
would vſe meanes to make my ſelfe away : herewithall ſhe puts finger in the eye making ſhew
as though ſhe wept. Thus plaies ſhe with the
ſillie ſot her huſband (meaning nothing leſſe then
to doe as ſhe ſaies) while he poore foole is in
mind both wel and ill apaid : he thinkes himſelfe
well, becauſe he imagines her of a cold conſtitu-
tion, and therefore exceeding chaſt : he thinkes
himſelfe ill, to ſee her fained teares, for that he
verily ſuppoſes ſhe loues him, which doth not a
little gréeue him, being ſo kind and tender harted.
Therefore he vſeth all meanes poſſible to make
her quiet, neither wil he giue her ouer, til he
hath effected it. But ſhe proſecuting her former
purpoſe, which ſhe hath alreadie ſet in ſo faire a

forwardnes, makes as though ſhe were nothing
moued with his gentle perſwaſions; therefore to
croſſe him, ſhe gets her vp betimes in the morning, ſooner a great deale then ſhe was wont,
pouting and lowring all the day, & not giuing
him one good word. But when night comes,
and / they againe both in bed, laying her ſelfe
ſullenly downe, and continuing ſtill ſilent, the
good man harkens whether ſhe ſleep or no, féeles
if ſhe be wel couered or not, he ſoftly plucks
vp the cloaths vpon her, lapping her warme,
being dubble diligent to pleaſe her. She lying
all this while winking, noting his kindnes and
carefulnes towards her, ſéemes on a ſuddaine to
awake from a ſound ſléepe, gruntling and nuſling
vnder the ſhéets, giuing him occaſion thereby
thus to begin. How now ſwéet hart, what are
you a ſléepe? A ſléepe (ſaith ſhe) I faith ſir no :
a troubled mind can neuer take good reſt. Why
womã are you not quiet yet? No doubt (ſaith
ſhe) you care much whether I be or no. By
lady wife, and ſo I doe: and ſince yeſternight
I haue bethought me (hauing well conſidered
your words) that it is very méete and requiſite,
that you ſhould be better furniſhed with apparell
then heretofore you haue bene, for indeed I
muſt confeſſe thy cloaths are too ſimple. And
therfore I mean againſt my couſin M. wedding

(which you know wil be fhortly) that you fhall haue a new gowne, made on the beſt faſhion, with all things ſutable thereunto, in ſuch ſort that the beſt woman in the pariſh ſhall not paſſe you. Nay (quoth ſhe) God willing I mean to go to no weddings this twelve moneths, for the goodly credit I got by the laſt. By my faith (ſaith he) but you ſhall : what? you muſt not be ſo head-ſtrong and ſelfe-wild. I tell you if I ſay the word, you ſhall goe, and you ſhal want nothing that you aſke or require. That I aſke? alas huſband (quoth ſhe) I aſke nothing, neither did I ſpeake this for any deſire that I haue to goe braue : truſt me for mine owne part I care not if I neuer ſtirre abroad, ſaue onely to church: but what I ſaid was vpon the ſpéeches which were there vſed, and ſuch other like words, which my goſſip N. told me that ſhe had alſo heard in company where ſhe was. With theſe words ẏ good kind foole her huſband is netled, for on the one ſide he conſiders his ſundry other occaſions to vſe money, and his ſmall ſtore thereof, which is perhaps ſo ſlender, that his ſingle purſe cannot extempory change a double piſtolet. And ſo ill beſted is he of houſhold ſtuffe, that perhaps the third part is not a ſufficiēt pawne / for ſo much money, as this new ſuite of his wiues will ſtand him in. But on the other ſide he waighes his difcontent, the report of neighbours fpeeches, and laftly how good a wife he hath of her : how chaft, how louing, how religious; whereof the kind Affe hath fuch an opinion, that he thanks God with al his heart, for blefling him with fuch a Iewell. In this thought he refolues that all other things fet afide he muft and will content her. And herewithall he fets his braines afrefh on worke, to confider how beft he may compaffe it : And in this humor he fpends the whole night without fléepe, in continuall thought. And it comes to paffe that the wife perceiuing to what a point fhe hath brought her purpofe, doth not a litle reioyce and fmile in her fléeue to fee it. The next morning by the break of day the poore man gets vp, who for care and thought could take no reft all night, and goes prefently to the Drapers ; of whom he takes vp cloth for thrée monthes time, paying for it after an exceffiue rate, by reafon of their forbearance, and in like fort makes prouifion for the reft ; or perhappes becaufe he would buy it at a better rate, he pawnes for ready mony the leafe of his houfe, or fome faire péece of plate (which his grandfather bought, and his father charily kéeping) left for him, which now he is inforced to part with, to furnifh therby his wiues pride : and hauing thus dis-patched his bufines, he returnes home with a merry heart, and fhewes his wife what he had done : who being now fure of all, begins to curfe the firft inuentors of pride, and exceffe in apparell : faying fye vpon it, what pride is this? but I pray you hufband, do not fay hereafter, that I made you lay out your mony in this needles fort, for I proteft that I haue no delight or defire to goe thus garifhly : If I haue to couer my body and keepe me warme it contents me. The good man hearing his wife fay fo, doth euen leape for joy, thinking all her words gofpel, & therefore prefently he fets the Taylor a worke, willing him to difpatch out of hand, that his wife may be braue fo foone as may be. She hauing thus obtained her purpofe doth inwardly triumph for very ioy, howfoeuer outwardly fhe doth diffemble. And whereas before fhe vaunted, that fhe could find in / her heart to keepe alwayes within doores, fhe will bee fure now euery good day to goe abroad, and at each feaft and Goffips meeting to bee a continuall gueft, that all may fee her brauery, and how well fhe doth become it ; to which caufe fhe alfo comes euery Sunday dayly to the Church, that there fhee may fee and be feene, which her hufband thinkes fhe doth of meere deuotion. But in the meane while the time runs on, and the day comes, wherein the poore man muft pay his creditors, which beeing

vnable to do, he is at length arrefted, and after
due proceeding in law, he hath an execution
ferued vpon him, or elfe his pawne is forfaited,
and by either of both hée is almoft vtterly vndone. Then muft his fine wife of force vaile her
peacocke-plumes, and fall againe to her old byas,
kéeping her houfe againft her will, becaufe fhe
could not be furnifht with gay attire according
to her mind. But God knoweth in what mifery
the fillie man doth liue, being dayly vexed with
her brawling and fcolding, exclaiming againft him,
that all the houfe doth ring thereof, and in this
fort fhe begins her fagaries. Now curfed be the
day that euer I fawe thy face, and a fhame take
them that brought me firft acquainted with thée:
I would to God I had either died in my cradle,
or gone to my graue when I went to   Alas poore
be married with thee. Was euer woman   soule.
of my degrée and birth brought to this beggery?
Or any of my bringing vp kept thus bafely, and
brought to this fhame? I which little knew what
labour meant, muft now toyle and tend the
houfe as a drudge, hauing neuer a coate to my
backe, or fcant hanfome hofe to my legs, and
yet all little enough, whereas I wis I might haue
had twentie good mariages, in the meaneft of
which I fhould haue liued at eafe and pleafure,
without being put to any paine, or fuffering

any penurie. Wretch that I am, why do I
liue? now would to God I were in my graue
already, for I am wearie of the worlde, weary of
my life, and weary of all. Thus doth fhe dayly
complaine, and lay all the fault of her fall on him
which leaft deferued it, nothing remembring her
owne pride, in coueting things aboue her eftate
or abilitie, her mifgouernment, & dayly gadding /
with her goffips to banquets and bridals, when
fhe fhould haue lookt to the houfe, and followed
her owne bufines at home. And his folly is alfo
fuch, that being blinded with dotage through too
much louing her, [he] cannot perceiue that fhe is
the caufe of all this euill, of all the cares, griefes,
& thoughts, which perplexe and torture him ; and
yet nothing cuts him fo much as this, to fee her
fo fumifh and vnquiet, when if he can at any
time fomewhat pacifie, then is his heart halfe at
reft. Thus doth the filly wretch toffe and tur-
moile himfelfe in lobs pound, wrapt in a kind of
pleafing woe, out of the which he hath neither
power nor will to wind himfelf, but therein doth
confume the remnant of his languifhing life, and
miferably endes his dayes.

CHAP. II.

*The humour of a woman, pranked vp in braue
apparell.*

THe nature of a woman inclined to another
kind of humor, which is this, when the
wife féeing her felfe brauely apparelled, and that
fhe is therewith faire & comely (or if fhe be not)
yet thinking her felfe fo (as women are naturally
giuen to footh themfelues,) fhe doth as I faid
before, hunt after feafts and follemne méetings,
wherwith her hufband perhaps is not very well
pleafed ; which fhe perceiuing, the more to bleare
his eyes, fhe takes with her fome kinfwoman or
goffip, or poffible fome lufty gallant, of whom
fhe claimes kinred, though in very déed there be
no fuch matter, but only a fmooth cullor to
deceiue her hufband : And perchance to induce
him the fooner to beléeue it, her mother which
is priuie to the match, will not ftick to fay and
fweare it is fo: yet fometime the hufband to
preuent his wiues gadding, will faine fome let,
as want of horfes, or other like hinderances :
then prefently the goffip or kinfwoman, of whom
before I fpeake, will thus follemnely affault him.
Beléeue / me goffip I haue as little pleafure, as
who hath leaft in going abroad, for I wis I had not

fo much bufineſſe to doe this twelue moneth as
I haue at this inſtant: yet ſhould I not goe to
this wedding, being ſo kindly bidden, I know
the young bride would take it in very ill part:
yea, and I may ſay to you, ſo would our neighbours, and other our friends, which will be there,
who would verily imagine, we kept away for
ſome other cauſe: and were it not for this, I
proteſt I would not ſtirre out of doores, neither
would my couſen your wife haue any defire to
goe thither : thus much I can truly witnes, that
I neuer knewe any woman take leſſe delight in
ſuch things then your wife, or which being abroad,
will make more haſt to be at home againe.   The
filly man her huſband being vanquiſhed by theſe
words, and no longer able to deny their requeſt,
demands onely what other women doe appoint
to goe, and who ſhall man them.   Marrie ſir
(faith ſhe) that ſhall my couſen H.   And befides
your wife and I, there goes my kinſwoman T.
and her mother, Miſtreſſe H. and her Aunt : my
Vncle T. and his brother be met, with both their
wiues : Miſtreſſe C. my next neighbour : and to
conclude, all the women of account in this ſtréete :
I dare boldly ſay, that honeſter company there
cannot be, though it were to conuey a Kings
daughter.

Now it oft chaunceth that this ſmooth tongued

Oratrix who pleades thus quaintly with womans art, muſt haue for her paines a gowne cloth, a Iewell, or ſome other recompence, if ſhe preuaile with the good man & cunningly play her part. He after ſome pauſe, perhaps will reply in this ſort : Goſſip, I confeſſe it is very good company, but my wife hath now great buſineſſe at home, and beſides ſhe vſeth to goe very much abroad, yet for this time I am content ſhe ſhall goe : But I pray you dame quoth he, be at home betimes. His wife ſeeing that her goſſip had gotten leaue, makes as if ſhe cares not for going forth, ſaying : By my faith man I haue ſomething els to do, then to goe to bridaile at this preſent : what, we haue a great houſhold, and rude ſeruants God wot : whoſe idlnes is ſuch, that they / will not doe any thing, if a bodies backe be turned : for it is an old prouerbe, When the cat is away, the mouſe will play. And therefore goſſip hold you content, we muſt not be altogether careles, nor ſet ſo much by our pleaſure, to neglect our profit : And therefore hold me excuſed, for I cannot now be ſpared, nor I will not goe, that is flat. Nay good goſſip (ſaith the other) ſeeing your huſband hath giuen you leaue, let vs haue your company this once, & if it be but for my ſake, ſuch a chaunce as this comes not euery day. With that the good man taking the Cib aſide, whiſpers her thus in her eare : were it not goffip for the confidence I repofe in you, I proteft fhe fhould not ftir out of doores at this time. Now as I am an honeft woman (quoth fhe) and of my credit goffip you fhall not néed to doubt any thing.

Thus to horfe they get, and away they fpurre with a merry gallop, laughing to themfelues, mocking and flouting the filly man for his fimplicitie : the one faying to the other, that he had a fhrewde Iealous braine, but it fhould auaile him nothing. Tufh faid the young woman, it is an olde faying, he had need of a long fpoone that will eate with the diuell : and fhe of a good wit, that would preuent the furie of a iealous foole : and with this and the like talke, they paffe the time till they come to the place appointed, where they meet with luftie gallants, who per-aduenture had at the former feaft made the match, and were come thither of purpofe to ftrike vp the bargaine. But howfoeuer it is, this luftie Laffe lackes no good cheare, nor any kindnes which they can fhew her. Imagin now how forward fhe will be to fhew her beft fkill in dauncing and finging, and how lightly fhe will afterward eftéeme her hufband : being thus courted and cōmended by a crew of luftie gallants, who féeing her fo brauely attired, and graced with fo fwéet & fmooth a tongue, fo fharpe a wit, fo amiable a countenance,

will each to ftriue to excéed other in feruing,
louing, and pleafing her: for the gallant carriage
and wanton demeanour of fo beautifull a péece,
cannot chufe but incorage a méere coward, and
heat (if not inflame) a frozen heart : One aſſaies
her with fugred tearmes, / and fome pleafing
difcourfe, painting forth his affection with louers
eloquence: another giues her a priuie token by
ftraining her foft hand, or treading on her prettie
foote : another eyes her with a piercing and
pittifull looke, making his countenance his fancies
herrold : and perhaps the third which is moſt
likely to fpéede, beſtowes vpon her a gold Ring, a
Diamond, a Ruby, or fome fuch like coſtly toy :
By all which aforefaid tokens fhe may well con-
ceiue their meanings (if fhe haue any conceit at
all) and fometimes it fo fals out, that they fall in
where they fhould not, and fhe ftepping fomewhat
afide, doth fo fhrewdly ftraine her honeſty, that
hardly or neuer the griefe can be cured. But to
procéed, this ouer gorgious wantoning of his wife,
brings the poore man behind hand, and doth
withall caufe a greater inconuenience, for in the
end by one meanes or other, either through her
too much boldnes, or her louers want of warineſſe,
the matter at length comes to light, whereof fome
friend or kinfman giues him notice.   He being
tickled by this bad report, therupon fearching

further, finds it true, or gathers more likelyhood
of fufpitiō, & that prefently infects his thoughts
with iealoufie, into which mad tormēting humor
no wife man will euer fall: for it is an euill both
extreame & endles, efpecially if it be iuftly con-
ceiued vpon the wiues knowne leaudnes, for then
there is no hope of curing.   She on the other fide
feeing this, and receiuing for her loofe life many
bitter fpeeches, doth clofely kéepe on her old
courfe but now more for fpight then pleafure, for
it is in vaine to thinke ẏ fhe will reclaime her
felfe.   And if he hoping by conftraint to make her
honeft, fall to beating her (though he vfe neuer fo
much feueritie) he fhall but kindle fo much the
more the fire of that lewd loue which fhe beares
vnto others : hereon followes a heape of mifchiefes,
he growes careles of his bufines, letting all things
run to ruine: fhe on the other fide becomes
fhameles, cōuerting into deadly hate the loue that
fhe fhould beare him.   Iudge now what a purga-
torie of perplexities the poore man doth liue in,
and yet for all this he is fo befotted, that he
féemes to take great pleafure in his paines, and to
be fo farre in loue whith Lobs pound, that / were
he not already in, yet he would make all hafte
poffible to be poffeffed of the place, there to confume the refidue of his life, and miferably end his
dayes.

CHAP. III.

The humour of a woman lying in Child-bed.

THere is another humor incident to a woman, when her hufband fées her belly to grow big (though peraduenture by the help of fome other friend) yet he perfwades himfelfe, it is a worke of his owne framing : and this bréedes him new cares & troubles, for then muft he trot vp & down day & night, far, & neere, to get with great coft that his wife longs for : if fhe lets fall but a pin, he is diligent to take it vp, leaft fhe by ftouping fhould hurt her felfe. She on the other fide is fo hard to pleafe, that it is a great hap whē he fits her humor, in bringing home that which likes her, though he fpare no paines nor coft to get it. And oft times through eafe and plentie fhe growes fo queafie ftomackt, that fhe can brooke no common meates, but longs for ftrange and rare thinges, which whether they be to be had or no, yet fhe muft haue them, there is no remedie. She muft haue Cherries, though for a pound he pay ten fhillings, or gréene Pefcods at foure Nobles a peck : yea he muft take a horfe, and ride into the Countrey to get her gréene Codlings, when they are fcarcely fo big as a fcotch button. In this trouble and vexation of mind and body, liues the filly man for

fixe or feuen months, all which time his wife doth
nothing but complaine, and hée poore foule takes
all the care, rifing earely, going late to bed, and to
be fhort, is faine to play both the hufband and the
hufwife. But when the time drawes néere of her
lying downe, then muft he trudge to get Goflips,
fuch as fhée will appoint, or elfe all the fatte is
in the fire. Confider then what coft and trouble
it will bée to him to haue all things fine againft
the Chriftning day, what ftore of Sugar, Bifkets,
Comphets and Carowayes, Marmilade, and /
marchpane, with all kind of fwéete fuckets, and
fuperfluous banquetting ftuffe, with a hundred
other odde and needleffe trifles which at that time
muft fill the pockets of daintie dames : Befides the
charge of the midwife, fhe muft haue her nurfe
to attend and keepe her, who muft make for her
warme broaths, and coftly caudels, enough both
for her felfe and her miftreffe, being of the mind
to fare no worfe then fhe : If her miftreffe be fed
with partridge, plouer, woodcocks, quailes, or any
fuch like, the nurfe muft be partner with her in
all thefe dainties : neither yet will that fuffice, but
during the whole month, fhe priuily pilfers away
the fuger, the nutmegs and ginger, with all other
fpices that comes vnder her keeping, putting the
poore man to fuch expenfe that in a whole yeare
he can fcarcely recouer that one moneths charges.

Then euery day after her lying downe, will fundry
dames vifit her, which are her neighbours, her
kinfwomen, and other her fpeciall acquaintance,
whom the goodman muft welcome with all cheer-
fulneffe, and be fure there be fome dainties in ftore
to fet before them : where they about fome thrée
or four houres (or poffible halfe a day) will fit
chatting with the Child-wife, and by that time the
cups of wine haue merily trold about, and halfe
a dozen times moyfined their lips with the fwéet
iuyce of the purple grape : They begin thus one
with another to difcourfe : Good Lord neighbor,
I maruaile how our goffip *Frees* doth, I haue not
féene the good foule this many a day.

Ah God helpe her, quoth another, for fhe hath
her hands full of worke and her heart full of
heauineffe : While fhe drudges all the wéeke at
home, her hufband, like an vnthrift, neuer leaues
running abroad to the Tennis court, and Dicing
houfes, fpéding all that euer he hath in fuch lewd
fort : yea, & if that were the worft it is well :
But heare you, Goffip, there is another matter
fpoyles all, he cares no more for his wife then for
a dog, but kéepes queanes euen vnder her nofe.
Iefu ! fayth another, who would thinke he were
fuch a man, he behaues himfelfe fo orderly and
ciuilly, to all mens fightes? Tufh, holde your
peace Goffip (faith the other) it is commonly féene

the / ftill fowe eates vp all the draffe, hée carries
a fmooth countenance but a corrupt confcience :
That I knowe F. well enough, I will not fay he
loues miftreffe G., goe-too goffip I drinke to you.
Yea and faith another, there goes foule lies if G.
himfelfe loues not his maid N. I can tell you
their mouthes will not be ftopt with a bufhell of
wheat that fpeake it. Then the third fetching
a great figh, faying by my truth fuch an other old
Bettreffe haue I at home : for neuer giue me credit
goffip, if I tooke her not the other day in clofe
conference with her maifter, but I think I be-
fwaddeld my maid in fuch fort, that fhe will haue
fmall lift to do fo againe. Nay goffip (faith
another) had it bene to me, that fhould not haue
ferued her turne, but I would haue turnd the
queane out of doors to picke a Sallet : for wot ye
what goffip ? it is ill fetting fire and flaxe together :
but I pray you tell me one thing, when faw you
our friend miftreffe C. ? now in good foothe fhe
is a kind creature, and a very gentle Peat : I
promife you I faw her not fince you and I dranke
a pinte of wine with her in the fifh market. (O
goffip faith the other) there is a great change fince
that time, for they haue bene faine to pawne all
that euer they haue, and yet God knowes her
hufband lies ftill in prifon. O the paffion of my
heart (faith another) is all their great and glorious

fhew come to nothing? good Lord what a world
this is. (Why goſſip faith another) it was neuer
like to be otherwiſe, for they loued euer to goe
fine, and fare daintily, and by my faith goſſip, this
is not a world for thoſe matters, and therupon I
drinke to you. This is commonly their communi-
cation, where they find cheare according to their
choice. But if it happen contrary, that they find
not things in ſuch plentie, and good order as they
would wiſh, then one or other of them will talke
to this effect : Truſt me goſſip I maruel much,
and ſo doth alſo our other friends, that your
huſband is not aſhamed to make ſuch ſmall
account of you, and this your ſwéete child. If he
be ſuch a niggard at the firſt, what will hée be by
that time he hath fiue or ſix ? it doth well appeare
he beares but little loue to you ; whereas you
vouchſafing to match with him, hath done him
more / credit then euer had any of his kinred.
Before God, faith another, I had rather ſée my
huſbands eyes out then he ſhould ſerue me ſo :
therefore if you be wiſe vſe him not to it : neither
in this ſort let him tread you vnder foote : I tell
you it is a foule ſhame for him, and you may be
wel aſſured ſith he begins thus, that hereafter he
wil vſe you in the ſame order, if not worſe. In
good ſooth faith the third, it ſéemes very ſtraunge
to me, that a wiſe woman, and one of ſuch

parentage as you are, who as all men knowes is
by blood farre his better, can endure to be thus
vſed by a baſe companion : Blame vs not to
ſpeake good goſſip, for I proteſt the wrong that he
doth you, doth likewiſe touch vs, and all other
good women that are in your caſe.

The Child-wife hearing all this, begins to
wéepe, ſaying ; Alas Goſſip, I know not what
to do, or how to pleaſe him, he is ſo diuerſe
and wayward a man, and beſides, he thinks all
too much that is ſpent. (Goſſip he is ſaith one)
a badde and a naughtie man, and ſo it is well
ſcene by your vſage.   All my Goſſips here preſent
can tell, that when I was marryed to my huſband,
euery one ſaid that hée was ſo haſtie and hard
to pleaſe that he would kill me with greefe : And
indeed I may ſay to you, I found him crabbed
enough : for he began to take vpon him mightily,
and thought to haue wrought wonders, yet I
haue vſed ſuch meanes, that I haue tamed my
young maiſter, and haue at this preſent brought
him to that paſſe, that I dare ſweare hée had
rather looſe one of his ioynts, then Rangle with
me : I will not deny but once or twice hée beate
me ſhrewdly, which I God-wot being young and
tender tooke in gréeuous part, but what he got
by it, let my Goſſip T. report, who is yet a
woman liuing, and can tell the whole ſtorie : to

whom my good man within a while after faide, that I was paft remedie, and that he might fooner kill me, then doo any good by beating me, (and by thefe ten bones fo hée fhould) but in the end I brought the matter fo about, that I got the bridle into my owne handes, fo that I may now fay, I do what I lift : for be it right or wrong, if I fay it, hée will not gainfay it, (for by / this Golde on my finger, let him doo what hée can, I will be fure to haue the laft word :) fo that in very deed, if that women be made vnderlings by their hufbands, the fault is their owne : for there is not any man aliue, be he neuer fo churlifh, but his wife may make him quiet and gentle enough if fhée haue any wit : And therefore your good man ferues you but well enough, fith you will take it fo.

Beléeue me Goffip (faith another) were I in your cafe, I would giue him fuch a welcome at his comming home, and ring fuch a peale of badde words in his eares, that he fhould haue fmall ioy to ftaie the hearing.

Thus is the poore man handled behinde his backe, while they make no fpare to help away with his Wine and Sugar which hée hath prepared, whome they for his kindnes thus requites : yea now and then hauing their braines well heated, they will not fticke to taunt him to his face :

Accusing him of little loue, and great vnkindnesse
to his wife.

Now it doth many times so chaunce, that he
hauing bene to prouide such meates as shée would
haue, he commeth home perhappes at midnight,
and before hée rests himselfe, hath a verie earnest
desire to sée how his wife doth, and perchaunce
being loath to lye abroade because of expence,
trauailes the later, that hée may reache to his
owne house, where when hée is once come, he
asketh the Chamber-maide, or else the Nurse,
how his wife doth; they hauing their errand
before giuen them by their Mistresse, answeres,
she is verie ill at ease, and that since his departure
she tasted not one bit of meat, but that toward
the euening she began to be a little better: all
which be méere-lies.   But the poore man hearing
these words, greeues not a litle, though perhaps
he be all to be moyld, wearie & wet, hauing gone
a long iourny through a badde and filthy way,
vpon some ill paced trotting Iade; and it may
be he is fasting too, yet will hée neither eate nor
drinke, nor so much as sit downe, till he haue
séene his wife.   Then the pratling Idle Nurse,
which is not to learne to exployte suche a péece
of seruice, beginnes to looke verie heauily, / and
to sigh inwardly as though her mistresse had
bene that day at the point of death, which he

ſeeing, is the more earneſt to viſit his wife:
whom at the entrance of the chamber, he heares
her lie groning to her ſelfe, and comming to the
beds ſide, kindly ſits down by her, ſaying how
now my ſwéet heart, how doeſt thou? Ah
huſband (ſaith ſhe) I am very ill, nor was I euer
ſo ſicke in my life as I haue bene this day. Alas
good ſoule (ſaith he) I am the more ſorie to heare
it, I pray thée tell me where lies thy paine? Ah
huſband (quoth ſhe) you know I haue bene
weake a long time, and not able to eate any
thing. But wife (quoth he) why did you not
cauſe the Nurſe to boile you a capon, and make
a meſſe of good broath for you? So ſhe did
(ſaith his wife) as well as ſhe could, but it did
not like me God wot, & by that meanes I haue
eaten nothing, ſince the broath which your ſelfe
made me: Oh me thought that was excellent
good. Marie wife (ſaith he) I will preſently
make you ſome more of the ſame, & you ſhall
eate it for my ſake. With all my heart good
huſband (ſaith ſhe) and I ſhall thinke my ſelfe
highly beholding vnto you: then trudgeth he
into the kitchen, there plaies he the Cooke,
burning and broiling himſelfe ouer the fire,
hauing his eyes readie to be put out with ſmoake,
while he is buſie making the broath: what time
he chides with his maides, calling them beaſtes

and baggages that knowes not how to do any thing, not fo much as make a little broath for a ficke bodie, but he muft be faine to doe it himfelfe. Then comes down miftreffe Nurfe, as fine as a farthing fiddle, in her pettiecoate and kertle, hauing on a white waftcoate, with a flaunting cambricke ruff about her neck, who like a Doctris in facultie comes thus vpon him. Good Lord Sir, what paines you take, here is no bodie can pleafe our miftreffe but your felfe : I will affure you on my credit that I doe what I can, yet for my life I cannot I, any way content her. Moreouer here came in miftreffe *Cot,* and miftreffe *Con.* who did both of them what they could to haue your wife eate fome thing, neuer-theleffe all that they did, could not make her tafte one fpoonefull of any thing all this liuelong day : I know not what fhe / ayles : I haue kept many women in my time, both of worfhip and credit (fimple though I ftand here) but I neuer knew any fo weake as fhe is. I, I (quoth he) you are a companie of cunning cookes, that cannot make a little broath as it fhould be. And by this time the broath being readie, he brings it ftraight to his wife, comforting her with many kind words, praying her to eate it for his fake, or to tafte a fpoonefull or twaine ; which fhe doth, commending it to the heauens, affirming alfo, that

the broath which the others made had no good
tafte in the world, and was nothing worth. The
good man hereof being not a little proud, bids them
make a good fire in his wiues Chamber, charging
them to tend her well. And hauing giuen this
order, he gets himfelfe to fupper, with fome cold
meate fet before him, fuch as the goffips left,
or his Nurfe could fpare, and hauing taken this
fhort pittance he goes to bed full of care. The
next morning he gets him vp betimes, and comes
kindly to know how his wife doth, who prefently
pops him in the mouth with a fmooth lye, faying,
that all night fhe could take no reft till it grew
towards the morning, and then fhe began to
féele a little more eafe, when God knowes fhe
neuer flept more foundly in all her life. Well
wife, faid the good man, you muft remember
that this night is our Goffips fupper, and they
will come hither with many other of our friends,
therefore we muft prouide fomething for them,
efpecially becaufe it is your vpfitting, and a fortnight at the leaft fince you were brought to bed :
but good wife, let vs goe as néere to the world
as we may, féeing that our charge doth euery
day increafe, and money was neuer fo ill to come
by. She hearing him to fay fo, begins to pout,
faying ; would for my part I had dyed in trauell,
and my poore Infant béene ftrangled in the birth,

fo fhould you not be troubled with vs at all, nor
haue caufe to repine fo much at your fpending :
I am fure there is neuer a woman in the world,
that in my cafe hath worfe kéeping, or is leffe
chargeable, yet let me pinch and fpare, and do
what I can, all is thought too much that I haue :
Truft me, I care not a ftraw whether you prouide
me any / thing or no, though the forrow be mine,
the fhame will be yours, as yefterday for example :
I am fure here came in aboue a dozen of our neighbours and friends, of méere kindneffe to fée mée,
and knowe how I did, who by their countenance and
comming did you greater credit then you deferue :
But God knowes what entertainement they had,
hauing nothing in the houfe to fet before thē ;
which made me fo much afhamed, that I knew
not what to fay : Ile tell you what, before God
I may boldly fpeake it (for I haue féene it) that
when any of them lyes in, their very feruants haue
better fare then I my felfe had at your hands ;
which they féeing betwixt themfelues yefterday
when they were héere, did kindly floute both
you and me for their entertainment.   I haue
not (as you know) line in aboue 15. dayes, and
can yet fcant ftand on my legs, & you thinke it
long till I be moyling about the houfe to catch
my bane, as I feare I haue done alreadie.   Beléeue
me wife (quoth he) you miftake me greatly,

for no mã in ỹ world can be more kind to his
wife, thē I haue bin to you. Kind to me (quoth
you) by ỹ maffe ỹ you haue with a murren, no
doubt but I hauc had a fwéete meffe of cherifhing
at your hands, but I fée your drift wel enough,
you gape euery day for my death, and I would
to God it were fo for me: The month indéed is
halfe expired, and I feare the reft wil come before
we be ready for it: My Sifter S. was héere no
longer ago then to day, and afkt if I had euer a
new gown to be Churched in, but God wot I am
far enough frō it, neither do I defire it, though
it be a thing which ought both by reafon &
cuftome to be done : And becaufe it is your
pleafure, I will rife to morrow, what chance foeuer
befall, for the worft is, I can but lofe my life :
full well may I gather by this, how you will vfe
me hereafter, and what account you would make
of me, if I had nine or ten children; but God
forbid it fhould euer come fo to paffe, I defire
rather to be rid of my life, and fo to fhun the
fhame of the world, then long to liue with fuch
an vnkind churle. Now verily wife (faith the
good man) I muft néeds blame your impatience,
for growing fo cholerick without caufe. Without
caufe (quoth fhe?) / Do you thinke I haue no
iuft caufe to complaine ? I will affure you there
is neuer a woman of my degree, that would put

D. I. 24

vp the intollerable iniuries that I haue done, and
dayly doe, by meanes of your hoggifh conditions.
Well wife faith the good man, lye as long as you
lift, and rife when you will, but I pray you tell
me how this new gowne may be had, which
you fo earneftlie afke for? By my
faith (quoth fhe) you fay not well,
for I afke nothing at your hands, neither
would I haue it though I might: I thanke God I
haue gownes enough alreadie, and fufficient to
ferue my turne, and you know I take no delight
in garifh attire, for I am paft a girle, but it makes
me fmile to fee what a fhew of kindnes you would
faine make: Fye on thee diffembler, you can cog
and flatter as well as any man in this towne, and
full little thinke they that fee you abroad, what
a diuell you are at home: for what with your
crooked qualities, with toyling, moyling, carking
and caring, and being befide broken with Child-
bearing, my countenance is quite changed, fo that
I looke alreadie as withered, as the barke of an
Elder bough: There is my Coufen
T. T. who when I was a little girle,
was at womans eftate, and in the end
married Maifter H. with whom fhe leades
a Ladyes life, looking fo young and luftie, that I
may feeme to be her mother: I, I, fuch is the
difference twixt a kind, and an vncourteous huf-

The Fox will eate no grapes.

No more like the woman I was, then an apple is like an oyfter.

band, and who knowes not but he was a futer to
me, and made many a iourney to my fathers houfe
for my fake, & would fo faine haue had me, that
while I was to marry he would not match himfelfe
with any : but fo much was I bewitcht, that after
I had once féene you, I would not haue changed
for the beft Lord in the land ; and this I haue
in recompence of my loue and loyaltie.   Goe too
wife (faith he) I pray you leaue thefe lauifh
fpéeches, and let vs call to minde where we may
beft take vp cloth for your gowne : for you fée,
fuch is our weake eftate, that if we fhould rafhly
lay out that little money which is in the houfe,
we might poffible bée vnprouided of all other
neceffaries :   Therefore whatfoeuer fhould chaunce
hereafter, it is beft to kéepe / fomething againft a
rainy day :   And againe you know within thefe
eight or nine dayes, I haue fiue pounde to pay to
Maifter P. which muft be done, there is no fhift,
otherwife I am like to fuftaine treble dammage.
Tufh (quoth fhe) what talke you to me of thofe
matters : alas I afke you nothing : I would to
God I were once rid of this trouble : I pray you
let me take fome reft, for my head akes (God
helpe me as it would go in pieces) I wis you
féele not my paine, and you take little care for
my griefe :   Therefore I pray you fend my Goffips
word that they may not come, for I feele my felfe

very ill at eafe. Not fo (quoth he) I wil neither
breake cuftome, nor fo much as gainefay their
courteous offer, they fhall come fure, and be entertained in the beft manner I may. Well (quoth
fhe) I would to God you would leaue me, that I
might take a little reft, and then do as you lift.
Vpon thefe fpéeches the Nurfe ftraight fteppes in,
and roundes her maifter in the eare, I pray you
Sir do not force her to many words, for it makes
her head light, and doth great harme to a woman
in her cafe, efpecially her braines being fo light
for want of fléepe : and befides, fhée is God
knowes, a woman of a tender and choyce complexion : and with that fhe drawes the Curtaines
about the bed. Thus is the poore man held in
fufpence till the next day that the Goffips come,
who will play their parts fo kindly, and gaul him
fo to the quick with their quips & taunts, that
his courage wil be wholy quailde, and he alreadie
(if they fhould bid him, like the prodigal childe,
euen to eate draffe with the hogges) rather then
he would difpleafe them. But to procéede, hée in
the meane while is double diligence, to prouide
all things againft their comming, according to
his abilitie, and by reafon of his wiues words, he
buyes more meate, and prepares a great deale better
cheare then he thought to haue done. At their
comming he is readie to welcome them with his

Cap in hand, and all the kindneſſe that may be
ſhewed. Then doth hée trudge bare-headed vp
and downe the houſe, with a cheareful countenance, like a good Aſſe fit to beare the burthen, he
brings the Goſſips vp to his wife, and comming
firſt / to her himſelf, he tels her of their comming.
I wis (quoth ſhe) I had rather they had kept at
home; and ſo they would too, if they knew how
litle pleaſure I tooke in their comming. Nay I
pray you wife (ſaith he) giue them good countenance, ſéeing they be come for good will : with
this they enter, & after mutuall greetings, with
much goſſips ceremonies, downe they ſit and there
ſpend the whole day, in breaking their faſts,
dining, and in making an after-noones repaſt :
beſides their petty ſuppings at her beds ſide, and
at the cradle ; where they diſcharge their parts ſo
well, in helping him away with his good Wine and
Sugar, that the poore man comming oft to cheare
them, doth well perceiue it, and gréeues inwardly
thereat, howſoeuer he couers his diſcontent with a
merrie countenance. But they not caring how the
game goes, take the peniworths of that cheare
that is before them, neuer aſking how it comes
there ; and ſo they merily paſſe the time away,
pratling and tatling of many good matters. Afterward the poore man trots vp and downe anew, to
get his wife the aforeſaid gowne, and all other

things therto futable, whereby he fets himfelf
foundly in debt: fometimes he is troubled with
the childs brawling: fometimes he is brawld at
by the Nurfe: then his wife complaines, that fhe
was neuer well fince fhe was brought to bed,
then muft hée caft his cares anew, deuifing by
what meanes to difcharge his debts and leffen
his expences: then refolues he to diminifh his
owne port and augment his wiues brauerie, he
will go all the yeare in one fute, and make two
paire of fhooes ferue him a twelue-month, kéeping
one paire for holy-dayes, another for working
dayes, and one hat in thrée or four yeares. Thus
according to his owne rafh defire, he is vp to the
eares in Lobs'-pownd, and for all the woe and
wretchednes that he hath felt, he would not yet
be out againe, but doth then willingly confume
himfelfe in continuall care, forrow and trouble, till
death doth fet him frée.

CHAP. / IIII.

The Humour of a woman that hath a charge of children.

THe next Humor that is by nature incident to
a woman, is when the hufband hath bin
married nine or ten yeares hath fiue or fix

children, hath paffed the euill dayes, vnquiet
nights, and troubles aforefaid, hath his _{Being tyred}
luftie youthfulneffe fpent, fo that it is^{with scolding, as a hackney Iade}
now high time for him to repent : But ^{with trauell.}
fuch is his groffe folly that hée cannot, and fuch
his dulneffe, through the continuall vexations,
which haue tamed and wearied him, that he
cares not whatfoeuer his wife faith or doth, but is
hardned like an old Affe, which being vfed to the
whip wil not once mend his pace be he lafhed neuer
fo much : The poore man feeth two or thrée of
his daughters marriage-able, which is foone knowne
by their wanton trickes, their playing, dauncing,
and other youthfull toyes, but he kéepes them
back, hauing perhaps fmall commings in, to keep,
maintain, and furnifh them as they looke for, with
gownes, kertles, linnen, and other ornaments as
they fhould be for three caufes. Firft, that they
may be the fooner fued vnto by lufty gallants:
Secondly, becaufe his denying hereof, fhould nothing auaile : for his wife which knowes her
daughters humors by her owne, when fhe was of
the like yeares, will fée that they fhall want
nothing : Thirdly, they paraduenture, bearing
right womens minds, if their father kéepe them
fhort, will find fome other friends that fhall affoord
it them. The poore man being thus perplexed on
all fides, by reafon of the exceffiue charges which

he muſt bée at, will (as it is likely) be but honeſtly
attyred himſelfe, not caring how he goes ſo he
may rubbe out, be it neuer ſo barely, and would
be glad to ſcape ſo.   But as the Fiſh in the Ponde,
which woulde alſo thinke him ſelfe well, though
wanting former libertie, if he might bée ſuffered
to continue, is cut off before his time :   So is
likewiſe this poore man ſerued, being once /
plunged in the perplexing Ponde, or rather pounde
of wedlocke and houſe-kéeping : for howſoeuer,
when he conſiders the aforeſaid charges and troubles,
he begins to haue no ioy of himſelfe, and is no
more moued then a tyred Iade which forceth not
for the ſpurre, yet for the furniſhing of his wife
and daughters, ſo that he may haue peace at home,
and enioy an eaſie bondage, he muſt trudge vp and
downe early and late about his buſineſſe, in that
courſe of life which he profeſſeth : Sometimes
he iournies thirtie or fortie myles off, about his
affaires :   Another time twice ſo farre to the
Tearme or Aſſiſes, concerning ſome old matter in
lawe, which was begunne by his Graund father,
and not yet towards an ende : he pulls on a pair of
bootes of ſeuen yeares old, which haue bene cobled
ſo oft, that they are now a foote to ſhort for him,
ſo that the toppe of the bootes reaches no farther
then the calfe of his legge : he hath a paire of
ſpurres of the olde making, whereof the one wants

a rowell, and the other for want of leathers, is faftned to his foote with a poynt: he puttes a laced coate on his backe, which he hath had fixe or feuen yeares, which he neuer wore but vppon high dayes, whofe fafhion is growne cleane out of requeft, by reafon of new inuented garments: whatfoeuer fports or pleafures he lights on by the way on his iourney, he takes no ioy in them, bicaufe his mind is altogither on his troubles at home, he fares hard by the way, as alfo his pore horfe, (if he haue any): his man followes him in a turnd fute, with a fword by his fide, which was found vnder a hedge at the fiege of *Bullen*: he hath a coate on his back, which euery man may know was neuer made for him, or he not prefent whē it was cut out, for the wings on his fhoulders comes downe halfe way his arme, and the fkirts as much below his waft : To be fhort, the poore man goeth euery way as neare as may be, for he remembers at what charges he is at home, & knowes not what it will coft him, in féeing his Councellors, Atturnies, & Pettyfoggers, which wil do nothing without prefent pay: he difpatcheth his bufineffe fpéedily, and hies him home with fuch haft, to auoid greater charges that he refts / nowhere by the way. And hereby it chanceth that many times he comes home at fuch an houre, as is as neare morning as to night, and finds nothing to eate, for his wife and

feruants are in bed ; all which he takes patiently,
being now well vfed to fuch entertainment :
Surely for my part that God fends fuch aduerfitie
and diftreffe to thofe only whofe good and mild
nature, he knowes to be fuch, that they will take
al things in good part. But to procéed, it is very
likely that the poore man is very wearie, his heart
heauie by reafon of the care and thought which he
hath of his bufineffe, and it may be he lookes to
be welcome to his owne houfe, and there to refrefh himfelfe, howfoeuer he forgets not his former
vfage. But it falls out otherwife, for his wife
begins to chide ; whofe words caries fuch a fway
with the feruants, that whatfoeuer their maifter
faith, they make fmall account of it : but if their
miftreffe commaund any thing, it is prefently done,
and her humour followed in all things, elfe muft
they pack out of feruice, fo that it bootes not him
to bid them doe any thing, or rebuke them for
not doing it: And his poore man that hath bene
with him, dares not likewife open his mouth to
call for any victuals to comfort himfelfe, or for the
horfes, leaft they fhould fufpect him to be of his
maifters faction, who being wife, of a quiet and
mild nature, is loath to make any ftur, or bréed
any difquietnes in the houfe, and therfore takes all
in good part, and fits him downe farre from the
fire, though he be very cold : But his wife and

children ftand round about it: but all their eyes
arc caft on her, who lookes on her hufband with
an angry countenance, not caring to prouide ought
for his fupper, but contrariwife taunts him with
fharp and fhrewifh fpéeches, whereto for the moft
part, he anfwers not a word, but fometimes perhaps being vrged through hunger, or wearines, or
the vnkindnes of his wife, he doth thus vtter his
mind.   Well wife you can looke well enough to
your felfe, but as for me I am both wearie and
hungry, hauing neither eaten nor drunke all this
day, and being befide wet to the very fkinne, yet
you make no reckoning to prouide any thing for
my fupper.

   Ah / (quoth fhe) you do well to begin firft, leaft
I fhould, which haue moft caufe to fpeake :   Haue
you not done verie well thinke yee, to take your
man with you, and leaue me no body to white
the cloathes?   Now before God, I haue had more
loffe in my linnen, than you will get this twelue-
month.   Moreouer, you fhut the Hen-houfe doore
very well, did you not? when the Fox got in and
eate vp foure of my beft broode Hennes, as you
to your coft will foone finde by the maffe : if you
liue long you will be the pooreft of your kinne.
Well wife (faith the good man) vfe no fuch words
I pray you, God be thanked I haue enough, and
more fhall haue when it pleafeth him ; and I tell

you, I haue good men of my kinne. But quoth
fhe I knowe not where they be, nor what they
are worth. Well (faith he) they are of credit and
abilitie too. But for all that (quoth fhe) they do
you fmall good. As much good (faith he) as any
of yours. As any of mine (faith fhe) and that fhe
fpoke with fuch a high note, that the houfe rung
withall, faying; By cocks foule were it not for my
friends you would do but forily. Well good wife
(faith he) let vs leaue this talke. Nay (faith fhe)
if they heard what you faid, they would anfwere
you well enough. The good man holds his peace,
fearing leaft fhe fhould tell them, being of greater
abillitie then he was, and befides, becaufe he was
loth that they fhould be offended with him. Then
one of the children falls a crying, and he perhaps
which his father loued beft ; wherevpon the mother
prefently tooke a rod, turned vp the childs taile
and whipt him well fauoredly, and the more to
defpight and anger her hufband, then for ought
elfe. The goodman being herewith fomewhat
moued, wills her to leaue beating the childe,
fhewing by his bended browes that he was not a
litle angry at her doings. Now gip with a murrin
(quoth fhe) you are not troubled with them, they
coft you nothing, but it is I that haue all the
paines with them night and day. Then comes in
the Nurfe with her verdit, and thus fhe begins,

ſaying: O ſir, you know not what a hand ſhe hath
with them, and we alſo that tend them. Then
comes in the Chamber-maid with her fine / egges :
In good faith ſir it is a ſhame for you, that at your
comming home, when all the whole houſe ſhould
be glad thereof, that you ſhould contrariwiſe put
it thus out of quiet. Saith he, is it I that makes
this ſtirre? Then is the whole houſhold againſt
him, when he ſeeing him ſelfe thus baited on all
ſides, and the match ſo vnequall, gets him to bed
quietly without his ſupper, all wet and durtie, or
if he do ſup he hath but thin fare : and being in
bed, where he ſhould take his reſt, he is ſo dis-
quieted with the children, whome the nurſe and his
wife doth on purpoſe ſet on crying, to anger him
the more, that for his life he cannot ſléepe one
winke. Thus is he vexed with continuall troubles,
wherewith he ſéemes to be well pleaſed, and would
not though he might be free from them, but doth
therein ſpend his miſerable and vnhappie life.

CHAP. V.

*The humour of a woman that maries her inferior
by birth.*

A Woman is inclined to another kind of humour,
which is when the huſband hath bene married, and hath paſſed ſo many troubles, that he is

wearied therewith ; his lufty youthfull bloud growne
cold, is matched with a wife of better birth then
himfelfe, and perhaps yonger, both which things
are very dangerous; and no wife man fhould feeke
his owne fpoile, by wrapping himfelfe in any of
thofe bonds, becaufe they are fo repugnant, that
it is both againft reafon & nature to accord them.
Sometimes they haue children, fometimes they haue
none, yet this notwithftanding, the wife can take no
paines, yet muft be mainteined according to her
degree, to the hufbands exceeding charges : for
the furnifhing whereof, the poore man is forced to
take extreame toile and paines, and yet for all
this, thanks God, for vouchfafing him fo great a
grace, as to be matcht with her. If now and then
they grow to hot words together (as oft it happens)
then prefently in vpbrading and mena / cing fort
fhe tels him, that her friends did not match her
to him to be his drudge, and that fhe knowes well
enough of what linage fhe is come, and will brag
withall, that when fhee lift to write to her friends
& kinfmen they will prefently fetch her away.
Thus doth fhe keepe him in awe, and in a kind
of feruitude, by telling him of them, who would
perhaps haue matcht her better, & not with him,
but for fome priuy fcape that fhe hath had before,
whereof the poore foule knowes nothing, or if
perhaps he hath heard fome inkling thereof, yet

becaufe he is fimple, the credit that he might giue
thereto is quickly dafht, by a contrary tale of others
fubbornd by them, who perchance will not fticke to
fweare that this is a flaunder raifed by euill toongs,
& forged malitioufly againft her, as the like is
done againft many other good women ; whofe good
names are wronged, & brought in queftiō by bad
perfons on their tipling bench, becaufe themfelues
cannot obtaine their purpofe of them: notwithftanding if her hufband be not able to maintaine
her according to her mind, then will fhe be fure
to haue a friend in ftore, that fhall afford it her
if her hufband deny it : and in ȳ end fhe remembers
that fuch a gentleman at fuch a feaft proffered her
a diamond, or fent her by a meffenger fome 20.
or thirtie crownes, which fhe as then refufed, but
now purpofeth to giue him a kind glance, to renew
his affectiō, who conceiuing fome better hope, and
méeting foone after with her chambermaid, as fhe
is going about fome bufines, cals to her, faying ;
Sifter, I would faine fpeake with you. Sir (quoth
fhe) fay what you pleafe. You know (quoth he)
that I haue long loued your miftres, without ob-
taining any fauour : but tell me I pray you, did
fhe neuer fpeake of me in your hearing ? In faith
fir (faith fhe) neuer but well : I dare fweare fhe
wifhes you no harme. Before God fifter (faith the
Gentleman) if you will fhew mée fome kindnes

herein, and do my commendations to your Miſtres,
aſſuring her of my loue and loyaltie, it ſhall bée
worth a new gowne vnto you, meane while take
this in earneſt: with that he offers her a péece
of gold : She then making a lowe curſie, ſayth :
Sir, I thanke you for your good / will, but I wil.
not take it.   By my faith ſaith he but you ſhall;
and with that he forced it on her, adding theſe
wordes : I pray you let me heare from you to
morrow morning.   She being glad of ſuch a bootie,
hyes her home, and tels her miſtris how ſhe met
with a Gentleman that was in a paſſing good vaine:
and to be ſhort, after ſome queſtions vſed by her
miſtres, it appeares to be the very ſame man whom
ſhe would faine intrap.   I tell thée (ſaith ſhe to
her mayd) if he be as kind as he is proper, he
were worthy to be any womans loue.   Beleeue me
Miſtris (ſaith the maid) his very countenance
A maid fit for ſhewes that he is kind, it ſéemes that he
ſuch a miſtres. was onely made for loue, and withall
he is wealthie, and thereby able to maintaine her
beautie, and her perſon in brauerie whom he
affects.   By this light (ſaith the miſtres) I can get
nothing of my huſband.   The more vnwiſe you,
(ſaith the mayd) to be ſo vſed.   Alas quoth ſhe,
what ſhould I do ?   I haue had him ſo long, that
I cannot now ſet my heart on any other.   Tuſh
(quoth the mayd) it is a folly for any woman to

fet her heart fo on any man, for you know they care not how they vfe vs when they are once Lords ouer vs. Befide, your hufband though hée would, yet cannot mainetaine and kéepe you according to your degrée : but he of whom I fpake will furnifh and maintaine you gallantly, what garments foeuer you will haue : and what colour and fafhion fo euer you like beft, you fhall prefently haue it, fo that there wants nothing elfe, faue only a quaint excufe to my Maifter, making him belćeue you had it by fome other meanes. By my troth (quoth the Miftres) I know not what to fay. Well Miftres (faith the maid) aduife you well, I haue promifed to giue him an anfwere to morrow morning. Alas (faith the other) what fhall we do ? Tufh Miftres (anfwers the maid) let me alone : As I go to morrow to the market, I am fure he will watch to méete with me, that he may know what newes : then I will tell him that you will not agrée to his defire for feare of difcredit : this will giue him a little hope, and fo we fhall fall into further talke, and I doubt not but to handle the matter well enough. According to promife / next morning to market fhe hies, fomewhat more earely then fhe was wont, and by the way fhe méetes with this luftie gallant, who hath waited for her at leaft thrée houres : hée hath no fooner fpyed her, but he prefently makes towards her, and at her

comming, thus falutes her : Sifter, good morrow,
what newes I pray, and how doth your faire
miftreffe?   I-faith fir (faith fhée) fhe is at home
very penfiue, and out of patience ; I thinke that
neuer any woman had fuch a frowarde hufband.
Ah villaine (faith he) the diuell take him.   Amen
(faith the maide) for both my miftreffe and all the
feruants are wearie with tarying with him.   Out
on him flaue (faith hée); but I pray you tell me
what anfwere gaue your miftres touching my fute ?
In faith (quoth fhe) I fpake vnto her, but fhée
woulde not agrée thereunto, for fhe is wonderfully
afraid to purchafe her felfe difcredit, & is befide
plagued with fuch a froward and fufpicious hus-
band, that although fhée were neuer fo willing, yet
could fhe not, being continually watcht by him, his
mother & brethren.   I thinke on my confcience
vnleffe that it were that fhe fpoke to you the other
day, the poore woman talkt not with any man
thefe four months, yet fhee fpeakes very often of
you, and I am well affured that if fhe would bend
her mind to loue, fhe would choofe you before all
men in the world.   He being rauifhed with thefe
words, replies thus :   Swéete fifter, I pray you be
my friend herein, and I will alwaies reft at your
commaund.   In good faith (faith fhe) I haue done
more for you already then euer I did for any man
in my life.   And thinke not (faith he) that I will

be vnmindfull of your kindnes; but what would
you counfell me to do? I-faith fir (faith fhe) I
thinke it beft that you fhould fpeake with her
your felfe; and now you haue an excellent opportunitie, for my maifter hath refufed to giue her a
new gowne; whereat fhe ftormes not a little : you
fhall doe well therefore to be to morrow at the
Church, & there falute her, telling her boldly your
defire : you may alfo offer her what you thinke
good, but I know fhe will take nothing : mary fhe
will thinke the better of you, knowing thereby
your franke & boũtiful nature. Oh (faith he) I
would fhe would gladly take that, / which I would
gladly beftowe on her. Nay, anfwers the maid,
I know fhe will not, for you neuer knewe a more
honeft woman : but Ile tell ye how yee may doe
it afterwards : Looke what ye purpofe to beftow
on her, you fhall deliuer vnto mée; I will doe my
beft to perfwade her to take it, but I cannot affure
you that I fhall preuaile. Surely fifter (faith he)
this is very good counfell : herewithall they part,
and fhee returnes home, laughing to her felfe, which
her miftres feeing, demands of her the caufe therof.
Mary (faith the maid) this lufty gentleman is all
on fire, tomorrow he will be at Church, purpofing
there to fpeake with you : now muft you demeane
your felfe wifely, and make very ftrange of it, but
ftand not off too much leaft you difmay him cleane:

as you wil not wholly graunt, fo muft you feede
him with fome hope.   Shee, hauing her leffon thus
taught her by her maide, gets her vp betimes the
next morning, and to the Church fhee goes, where
this amorous gallãt hath awaited for her comming
euer fince foure a clock.   She being fet in her
pew, makes fhew as if fhe was deuoutly at her
prayers, when (God wot) her deuotion is bent to
the feruice of another Saint : it were worth the
noting to fee how like an image fhee fits : and yet
for all her demurenes, fhe applies all her fiue
fenfes, & that full zealoufly, in this new humor
of religion.   To bee fhort, hee fteales vnto her,
fneaking vnto her, from the belfrey vnto her pew,
and beeing come, greetes her after the amorous
order, and from greeting, he fals to courting ;
wherto fhe doth in no wife yeeld confent, neither
will fhee take ought that he offers, yet anfwers
him after fuch a fort, that he doth thereby affuredly
gather that fhee loues him, and fticks only for fear
of difcredit : whereat he is not a little iocond, &
hauing fpent his time to fo good purpofe, he takes
his leaue, & fhe hafting home to her counfeller,
acquaints her what hath paffed between them,
who thereupon takes occafion to fay thus :
Miftreffe, I know well that now he longs to fpeake
with me, but at our meeting I will tell him that
you will yeelde to nothing ; for which I will faine

my felfe very fory : & I wil adde withal, that my
mafter hath gone out of towne, and will appoint
him / to come hither towards the euening, with
promife that I will let him in, and conuey him
fo fecretly into your chamber, that you fhall know
nothing thereof: At what time you muft feeme
to be highly offended, and if you be wife, you
will make him buy his pleafure with fome coft,
which will caufe him to efteeme the more of you :
tell him that you will cry out, and then do you
call me : by handling him thus, I can affure you,
that you fhall get more of him, then if you had
yeelded at the firft. All this while I will haue in
my keeping that which hee will giue you, for hee
hath appointed to deliuer it me to morrowe, and
I will make him belieue, that you woulde by no
meanes take it. But when the matter is brought
to this paffe, then wil I make fhew to offer you
his gift before him, telling you, that he is willing
to beftow it on you, to buy you a gowne withall ;
then muft you chide, and feeme to be angry with
mee for receiuing it, charging me to deliuer it
back againe to him ; but bee fure I will lay it
vp fafe enough. Well deuifed wench (faith the
miftres) I am content it fhall be fo. This plot
being thus laide, the craftie wench goes prefently
to finde out this iolly gallant, whofe firft word is,
What newes ? Now in good faith fir (faith fhe)

the matter is no further forward then if it were
yet to begin, yet becaufe I haue medled fo farre in
it, I wold be loth I fhould not bring it about, for
I feare that fhe will complaine of me to her hufband and friends, but if I could perfwade her
by any meanes to receiue your gifts, then out of
queftion the matter were difpatcht : and in good
faith ile try once more, I haue one good helpe, and
that is this : my maifter (as I tolde you before)
will not giue her a new gowne, at which vnkind-
neffe, fhee ftormes mightily.   The hot louer
hearing this, giues her prefently twentie crownes
for her good will, whereupon fhee fpeakes

Better then two
yeares wages,
and foone got.

thus :   In good faith fir, I knowe not
how it commeth to paffe, but fure I am,
I neuer did fo much for any man before as I
haue done herein for your fake, for if my maifter
fhoulde haue any inckling of it, I were vtterly
vndone : yet for you I will hazard a little / further:
I know fhe loues you wel, and as good hap is, my
maifter is not now in towne; if you therefore
will bee about the dores towards fix of y̆ clock at
night, I will let you in, and fo conuey you fecretly
into my miftres Chamber ; who doth fleepe very
foundly : for you know fhe is but young : being

Juft as larmäs
lips.

there I could wifh you go to bed to her
and for the reft you neede not (I truft)
any tutor : I proteft that I know no other meanes

for the compaſſing of this matter; perhaps it will
fadge, for it is a great matter, when a louer & his
miſtreſſe are both together naked & in the darke,
which doth help forward a womans conceipt to y̌
which in the day time perhaps ſhe would hardly
graunt. O my ſweet friend (quoth hee) for this
kindneſſe my purſe ſhall be at thy command. To
be ſhort, night comes, he is there according to
promiſe; whom ſhee ſtraight conueyes into her
miſtreſſe chamber: then he preſently vnclothes
himſelf, and ſteps ſoftly into her bed, and beeing
once in, hee begins to imbrace her : hereat ſhe that
ſeemes till then aſleepe, ſtarts vp on a ſodain & with
a fearful voice aſks who is there? It is I ſweete
miſtreſſe (ſaith he) feare nothing. Ah (quoth ſhee)
thinke you to preuaile thus? no, no, and with that
ſhee makes as though ſhee would riſe, & cal her
maid, who anſwers not a word : but alas for pittie
like an vndutifull ſeruant leaues her at her greateſt
need : ſhe therefore gcod woman ſeeing that ſhe
is forſaken, ſaies with a ſigh, ah me, I am betraid :
then begin they a ſtout battel, he vrging his ad-
vantage, ſhee faintly reſiſting, but alas what can a
naked woman doe againſt a reſolute louer? there
is therefore no remedy but that at length (poore
ſoule) being out of breath with ſtriuing ſhe muſt
needes yeeld to the ſtronger: ſhe would faine haue
cryed out (God wot) had it not beene for feare of

difcredit, for therby her name might haue bin
brought in queftion ; therefore all things confidered,
fhe doth vnwillingly God knowes, let him fupply
her hufbands place, garnifhing his temples for pure
good will with *Acteons* badge. Thus hath fhe got a
new gowne, which her good man refufed to giue
her ; to bleare whofe eyes, & to keep him from
fufpition, fhe gets her mother in her hufbands
fight to bring home the cloth & giue it her, / as
though it were her coft : and leaft alfo fhee
fhould fufpect any thing, fhe makes her beleeue
fhe bought it with the money which fhee got by
felling odde commodities which her hufbad knew
not of : But it may be, and oft happens fo, that
the mother is priuie to the whole matter, and a
furtherer thereof : after this gowne fhe muft haue
another, and two or three filke imbrothered girdles,
and other fuch coftly knackes, which the hufband
feeing, wil in the end fmel fomewhat, & begin to
doubt of his wiues honefty, or fhal perhaps receiue
fome aduertifemēt hereof from a friend or kinfman ;
for no fuch matter can be long kept clofe, but in
the end will by fome meanes or other be made
knowne and difcouered. Then fals hee into a
frantick vaine of Iealoufie : watching his wiues
clofe packing : and for the better finding of it
out, hee comes home on a fodaine about midnight,
thinking then to difcouer all, and yet perhaps may

miſſe his purpoſe. Another time comming in at
vnawares hee ſeeth ſomething that he likes not, and
then in a furie falles on railing, but be ſure that
ſhe anſwers him home, not yeelding an inch vnto
him: for beſides the aduantage of the fight which is
waged by her owne truſtie weapon (her tongue I
meane) ſhe knowing withall that ſhe is of better
birth, hits him in the teeth therwith, & threatens
him to tel her friends how hardly he doth vſe her.
To bee ſhort, the poore man ſhall neuer haue
good day with her, but either with thought of her
incontinēce, or if he ſpeake to her, he is borne
downe with ſcolding lies, and deſpiſed of his owne
ſeruants; his ſtate runnes to ruine, his wealth
decaies, his body dryes vp, and weares away with
griefe : he growes deſperate and careleſſe : thus is
he plunged into Lobs pound, wearied in a world
of diſcontents, wherein notwithſtanding he takes
delight, hauing no deſire to change his ſtate, but
rather if he were out, and knewe what would
follow, yet would he neuer reſt till he had gotten
in againe, there to ſpend and end (as now he muſt)
his life in griefe and miſerie.

CHAP. / VI.

The humor of a woman that ſtriues to maſter her huſband.

THe next humor wherevnto a woman is ad-dicted, is, when ẙ huſband hath got a faire young wife, who is proper & fine, in whom he takes great delight, yet perhaps ſhe is bent alto-gither to croſſe, & thwart : ẙ man being of a kind & mild nature louing her intirely, & he maintaines her as well as he can, notwithſtanding her froward-nes : It may be alſo that ſhe hath care of his credit and honeſty, and doth abhorre ſuch lewd-neſſe, as ſhe of whome wee ſpake before did vſe, yet hath ſhee neuertheleſſe an extreame deſire of foueraigntie (which is knowne a common fault amongſt women) and to be her huſbands com-maunder, and a buſie medlar in his matters : be he a Iudge, a Nobleman, or Gentleman, ſhee wil take vpon her to giue ſentence, and anſwere ſuters, and whatſoeuer ſhee doth hee muſt ſtand to it.   This is, I ſay, a generall imperfection of women, bee they neuer ſo honeſt, neuer ſo kindly vſed, and haue neuer ſo much wealth and eaſe, to ſtriue for the breeches, and bee in odde contrarie humours, of purpoſe to keepe her huſband in continuall thought and care how to pleaſe her.   Hee gets

him vp betimes in the morning leauing her in bed
to take her eafe, while he fturres about the houfe
and difpatcheth his bufineffe, lookes to the feruants
that they loyter not, caufeth dinner to be made
readie, the cloath to be laide, and when al thinges are
readie, he fends one to defire her to come downe,
who brings back anfwere that fhe is not difpofed
to dine. No (faith he?) I wil neither fit downe,
nor eate a bit till fhe be here. So receiuing his
fecond meffage by his maide, or perhaps by one of
his children, replyes thus : go tell him again ỹ I
wil not dine to day. He hearing this, is not yet
fatisfied, but fends likewife the third time, and in
the end goes himfelfe, and thus begins. How
now, what ayles you wife, that you will eate no
meate? / hereto fhe anfweres not a word. The
poore man maruels to fee her in this melancholy
dumpe, (although perhaps fhe hath plaid this
pageant many times before) and vfeth all entreatie
he may, to know of her the caufe therof : but in
vaine, for indeed there is no caufe at all, but onely
a meere mockery : Sometimes fhe will perfift fo
obftinately in this humor, that for all the perfwa-
fions and kindneffe that he can vfe, fhee will not
come. Sometimes it may be fhe will, and then hee
muft leade her by the hand like a bride, and fet
her chaire readie for her : meane while it is fo long
before he can get her down, that the meate is colde

when it comes to the table. Being fet, fhe will not eate one bit, and hee feeing that (like a kinde Affe) wil faft likewife: whereat fhee fmiles inwardly, hauing brought him fo to her bowe, firft in croffing him, then in making him to faft from dinner: wherein (to fay the truth) fhe hath reafon, for what needs a woman to feeke his fauoure, who doth alreadie loue her, and fhew her all the kindnes that hee can. Sometimes the good man ryding abroad about his bufineffe, meets with two or three of his friends, with whom perhaps hee hath fome dealings, and hath bene long acquainted with them: It may be also that he inuites them home to his houfe, as one friend will do to another, and fends his man before to his wife to make all things ready in ў beft fort that fhe can for their entertainment: the poore feruing man gallops in fuch haft, that both himfelfe & his horfe is all on a fweate: when he comes home hee doth his arrand to his miftres, telling her withal that the guefts which his mafter brings are men of good account. Now by my faith (faith fhe) I wil not meddle in it, he thinks belike that I haue nothing els to doe, but drudge about to prepare banquets for his companions, he fhould haue come himfelf w[h] a vengeance, & why did he not? Forfooth (faith the feruant) I know not, but thus he bad me tel you. Go too (faith fhe) you are a knaue that medles in more

matters thē you haue thank for. The poore
fellow hearing this holds his peace, ſhee in a fume
flings vp into her chamber, and which is worſe,
ſendes out her ſeruantes, ſome one way, ſome
another: as for her maydes, they haue their / leſſon
taught them well enough, knowing by cuſtome
how to behaue themſelues to wearie their maiſter:
well, hee comes home to his aforeſaid friends, cals
preſently for ſome of his ſeruants: but one of the
maides make anſwere, of whome he demaunds
whether all things bee readie: In good faith ſir
my miſtres is verie ſick, & here is no
body els can do any thing: with that he Oh fetch the aqua vitæ bottle quickly.
being angry, leads his friends into the
hall, or ſome other place according to his eſtate,
where hee findes neither fire made, nor cloath laide.
Iudge then in what a taking he is, although it may
be that his friendes perceiued by the ſending of
his man, that his commaundements were not of
ſuch force as an act of parliament. The good man
being aſhamed cals and gapes, firſt for one man
then for another, & yet for all this there comes
none, except it bee the ſcullion or ſome chare
woman, that doth vſe his houſe, whome his wife
hath left there of purpoſe, becauſe ſhee knewe they
could ſerue to doe nothing. Being herewith not a
little mooued, vp hee goes into his wiues chamber,
and thus ſpeakes vnto her. Gods precious woman,

why haue ye not done as I wild ye? Why (faith
fhee) you appoint fo many things to be done that
I know not what to doe. Before God (faith hee)
& with that fcratches his head, you haue done mee
a greater difpleafure then you think : thefe are
the deareft friends that I haue, and now here is
nothing to fet before them. Why (quoth fhee)
what would you haue me to doe? I wis if you
caft your cards well, you fhall finde that we haue
no neede to make banquets : I would to God you
were wifer, but fith you will needes bee fo lufty,
euen goe through with it your felfe on Gods name,
for Ile not meddle with it. But what the diuell
ment ye (faith he) to fende all the feruants abroad?
Why (quoth fhe) what did I know that you fhould
neede them now: yet did fhee know it well enough,
and had of purpofe fent them forth on fleeueleffe
arrands, the more to anger and defpight him : who
feeing that he can preuaile nothing, giues ouer
talking to her, and gets him downe in a bitter
chafe : for it may bee that his gueftes bee of fuch
account, and he fo much beholding vnto them,
that he had rather haue / fpent a hundred crownes
then it fhould fo haue fallen out. But fhe cares
not a whit, being well affured that howfoeuer fhe
thwarts him, hee will hold his hands, and in fcolding fhe knowes her felfe to be the better. To
bee fhort, the poore man being vexed, with fhame

and anger, runnes vp and downe the houſe, gets
as many of his ſeruants together as hee can : If
his prouiſion be but ſlender at home, hee ſends
preſently abroad ; in the meane while he calles for
a cleane towell, the beſt table cloath, and wrought
napkins. But the maid anſwers him that he can
haue none. Then vp to his wife goes hee againe,
and tels her that his friends doe intreat her to
come downe and beare them companie, ſhewing
her what a ſhame it is, and how diſcourteouſly they
will take it if ſhe come not : And finally he vſeth
all the faireſt ſpeeches that he can to haue her
come, and to welcome and entertaine them for his
credits ſake. Nay in faith (quoth ſhe) I will not
come, they are too great ſtates for my companie,
and no doubt they would ſcorne a poore woman
as I am : It may bee ſhee will goe, but in ſuch
ſort, and with ſuch a countenance, that it had beene
better for him ſhe had not come at all, for his
friends will ſomewhat perceiue by her lookes and
geſture, that howſoeuer they be welcome to the
good-man, ſhe had rather haue their roome then
their company. But if ſhe refuſe to come (as it is
the more likely) then will he aſke her for the beſt
towell, table-cloth and napkins. Napkins (quoth
ſhe) as though thoſe that be abroad alreadie be not
good enough for greater and better men then they
are : when my brother or any of my kinſmen come,

which are I wis their equals in euery refpect, they
can be content to be ferued with them : but were
thefe your gueftes neuer fo great, yet could I not
now fulfill your requeft, though my life fhould lie
on it : for fince morning I haue loft my keyes of
the great cheft where all the linnen lies:

<small>Oh lyer, lyer.</small>

I pray you bid the maid looke for them,
for in good truth I know not what I haue done
with them, and no maruell, for I haue fo much to
doe, that I know not how to beftur my felfe : well
I wote, I haue fpoyled my felfe with continuall
care and trouble.

Now in good faith (quoth he) you haue dreft
me fairely, but it is no matter :   Before God ile
breake open the cheft.   Now furely then (quoth
fhe) you fhall doe a great act, I would faine fee
you doe it, I would for my part you would breake
all the cheftes in the houfe.   The poore man
hearing her in thefe termes, knowes not well what
to doe, but takes that which he next lightes on,
and therefore fhifts as well as he can : he caufeth
his gueftes to fit downe at the table, and becaufe
the beere then a broach is on tilt, & therefore not
verie good, he bids one of the feruants broach a
new barrell, & fil fome frefh drinke, but then there
is neither tap nor fpigget to bee found, for his
wife of purpofe hath hidden them out of the
way.   Towards the end of the dinner, he cals for

cheefe, and fruite, but there is none in the houfe, so that he is faine to fend to the neighbours for the fame, or elfe be vtterly deftitute : meane while his boy being at the table with the gueftes' [feruants], at laft tels them how his miftreffe faines her felfe ficke, becaufe fhe is not pleafed with their mafters cōming. Wel, when bed time comes, he can get no clean fheetes, nor pillow-beers, becaufe forfooth the keyes are loft, fo that they muft be content to lie in thofe that be foule, and haue bene long layne in. The next morning they get them gone betimes, feeing by the good wiues countenance that they are nothing welcome. By the way their lackies tell them what the Gentle mans boy reported ; wherat they laughe hartily, yet find themfelues agreeued, vowing neuer to be his gueft any more. The hufband alfo, getting him vp betimes in the morning, goes prefently to his wife, and thus he begins : By Iefus wife, I mufe what you meane to vfe me thus. I know not how to liue with you. Then fhe replies faying : Now God for his mercie, am I fo troublefome ? God wot I am euery day (poor foule) trobled with keeping your hogs, your geefe, your chickens ; I muft card, I muft fpin, and continually keepe the houfe, looke to the feruants, & neuer fit ftil, but toyling vp & downe to fhorten my daies, and make me die

before my time, and yet I cannot haue one howers
reft, or quietnes with you, but you are alwaies
brawling, & do nothing your felfe, but fpend &
waft your goods and / mine with odde companions.   What odde companions (faith he?)
as though you know not that thefe are fuch men,
as can either much further, or much hinder me.
It is a figne that you deale very well, that you
muft ftand in diftruft of fuch perfons.   Herevpon fhe takes occafion to rayle & fcolde all
the day long, the man being wearied with her
wawardneffe; & age (being hafted with griefe
& forrow) doth vnawares ouertake him.   Briefly
he is in euery refpect wretched: but fuch is
his folly, that he reckons his paines pleafures,
and would not though he might be againe at
liberty, out of Lobs pound, or if he would it
is now too late, for he muft of force côtinue
there in care, thought and mifery, til death make
an end of him and them together.

CHAP. VII.

The humor of a couetous minded woman.

THe next humor belonging to a woman, is,
when the hufband is matched to a modeft
ciuil womã, who is nothing giuen to that thwarting

& crossing humor whereof I spake last. But be
she good or bad, this is a generall rule many
wiues hold and stedfastly beleeue, that their owne
husbands are the worst of al others. It oft
happens that when they match together they
are both young, and entertaine each other with
mutuall delights, so much as may be, for a yeare
or two, or longer, til the vigor of youth grow
cold. But ẙ woman droopes not so soone as
ẙ man, the reason whereof is, becaufe shée takes
no care, thought and griefe, breakes not her
sleepe, and trobles not her head as he doth, but
doth wholly addict her thoughtes to pleasure and
solace. I deny not that when a woman is with
child, she hides many times great paines, and
is oft verie ill at ease, and at the time of her
deliuerance, she is for the most part, not onely
in exceeding paine, but also in no lesse daunger of
death : But all this is nothing to the husbands
troubles, on whose hands alone restes the whole
charge, and waight of main / taining the house,
and dispatching all matters ; which is oftentimes
intangled so with controuersie, and so thwarted
with crosse fortune, that the poore man is tormented with all vexation of mind : Beeing thus
wearied, and as it were worne away with continuall griefe, troublous cogitations, toyle and
trauell, [he can] haue no mind on any other plea-

fure : whereas fhee on the other fide is as luftie as
euer fhee was : meane while his ftock decayes, and
his ftate growes worfe and worfe: and as that
diminifheth, fo muft hee perforce fhorten her
allowance, & maintenance, which is almoft as
great a corfiue to her, as the former. You may
be well affured, that this change in him makes
her alfo change her countenance : frō mirth
and chearefulnes to lowring melancholie, feeking
occafions of difagreements, & [to] vfe them in fuch
fort, that their former loue & kindnes was not
fo great, as are now their brauls, iarres, & dis-
cordes. It doth alfo oftentimes happen, that
the womã by this means waftes and confumes all,
giuing lewdly away her hufbands goods, which
he with great paines & cares hath gotten. The
good man he goes euery way as neere as he can,
and warilie containes him felfe within his bounds,
cafting vp what his yearely reuenues are, or what
his gaine is by his profeffion, be it merchandize
or other, & then what his expenfes be ; which
finding greater then his comming in, he begins
to bite the lip & becomes very penfiue : his wife
& he being afterward priuate together in their
chamber, hee fpeakes thereof vnto her in this
manner : In faith wife, I maruell much how it
comes to paffe that our goods goe away thus,
I know not how : I am fure I am as carefull as

a man can be, I can not finde in my heart to
beſtow a new coate on my ſelfe, and all to ſaue
mony. By my troth huſband (ſaith ſhe) I do
as much maruell at it as you : I am ſure for my
owne part, that I goe as neere in houſekeeping
euery way as I can. To bee ſhort, the poore
man not doubting his wife, nor ſuſpecting her ill
cariage, after long care and thought concludes,
that the cauſe thereof is his owne ill fortune,
which keepes him downe, & croſſeth all his
actions with contrary ſucceſſe, but it may bee
that in proceſſe of time ſome friend / of his being
more cleare-ſighted in the matter, perceiuing all
goes not wel, doth priuily informe him therof;
who being aſtoniſhed at his report, gets him home
with a heauie countenance : which the wife ſeeing,
& knowing herſelf guiltie, begins preſently to
doubt ẙ worſt, & perhaps gueſſeth ſhrewdly at
the authors thereof ; but howſoeuer, ſhe will take
ſuch an order, that ſhe will be ſure to eſcape the
brunt well enough. The good man will not
preſently make any words hereof vnto her, but
defer it awhile, and try in the meane time,
whether he can of himſelfe gather any further
likelyhood, for which purpoſe he will tell her,
that he muſt needes ride ſome ten or twelue miles
out of towne, about ſome earneſt buſines. Good
faith huſband (ſaith ſhe) I had rather you ſhould

fend your man, and ftay at home your felfe. Not
fo wife (faith he) but I will be at home againe
my felfe within thefe three or foure dayes.
Hauing told her this tale, hee makes as though
hee tooke his iourney, but doth priuilie lye in
ambufh in fuch a place, where hee may know
whatfoeuer is done in the houfe: but fhee
fmelling his drift fends word to her fweet heart,
that he do not come in any cafe, and all the time
of his diffembled abfence, fhe carries her felfe
that it giues no likelyhood of fufpition: which
the filly mã feeing, comes out of his ambufh,
enters his houfe, making as if then he were returned from his iourney: and whereas before he
lowred, now he fhewes a cheereful countenance,
beeing verily perfwaded, that his friends report
is a meere lye ; and that he thinks fo much the
rather, becaufe fhe doth at his comming run to
meet him, with fuch fhewe of loue, & doth fo
imbrace and kiffe him, that it feemes impoffible
fo kind a creature fhould play falfe: but long
after being in bed together, he thus fpeaks to
her : Wife, I haue he.rd certaine words that like
mee not. Good faith hufband (faith fhee) I
know not what is the caufe thereof: I haue
noted, this great while, that you haue bene very
penfiue, and was afraid that you had had fome
great loffe, or that fome of your friends had bene

kild, or taken by the Spanyards. No (faith he) that is not the matter, but a thing which greeues me more then any fuch matter can do. Now, God for his / mercy (quoth fhe) I pray you hufband let me know what it is. Mary wife (faith he) a friend of mine told me that you kept company with R. R. the verieft ruffen in all the towne, & a many other matters he told me of you. Hereat fhe croffing her felfe in token of admiration (though fmiling inwardly) replies thus; Deere hufband if this be all, then I pray you giue ouer your penfiuenes : I would to God I were as free from all other fins, as I am from that : then laying one hand on her head, fhe thus proceeds, I will not fweare any thing touching him, but I would the deuil had all that is vnder my hand, if I euer touched any mans mouth fauing yours, or fome of our friends & kinfmen, or fuch at leaft as you haue commanded me. Ha, ha, is this the matter? In troth I am glad you haue told me, I had verily thought it had bin fome greater matter, but I know wel enough whereupon thefe fpeeches grew, & I would that you did likewife know, what moued him to fpeak thē; I know you would not a little maruel, becaufe he hath alwaies Oh braue dif-
profeffed fuch friēdfhip towards you. In   fembler.
good faith I am nothing fory ẙ he hath awaked the fleeping dog. What mean you by that word

(quoth he?) Nay (quoth fhe) be not defirous to
know it, you fhall know it foone enough fome
other time. Birlady (faith he) ile know it now.
By my troth hufband (faith fhe) I was oft wonderfully angry whē you brought him in hither, yet I
forbare to fpeake of it, becaufe I faw you loued
him fo well. But fpeake now (faith he) and tell
me what ẙ matter is? Nay nay (quoth fhe) it
fkils not greatly. Go to wife (faith the good man)
_{Almost as bad} tel me, for I will know it. Then takes
_{as Iudas kisses.} fhe him about the neck, & fweetly kiffing
him, faith thus: Ah my deere hufband, what
villaines are thefe ẙ would feeme to abufe you,
whom I honor & loue aboue al mē in the world.
_{The diuel take} Wel wife (faith he) I pray thee tell me
_{the lyer.}   the man that fo mifvfeth vs. In troth
(quoth fhe) that vile diffembling traitor, that
flattering tell tale, that put this bad report in your
eares, whom you efteeme fo much, repofing fuch
great cōfidēce in him, he is the man, & none but
he that hath earneftly vrged me any time thefe two
years to cōmit folly with him; but God I praife
him hath giuen me grace both to refufe him, and
his offers, / although I were continually troubled
and importuned by him: I wis when you thought
hee came hither fo often for your fake, it was for
this caufe; for neuer a time that hee came, but he
was in hand with me to obtaine his filthy defire,

till in the end I threatned to tell you of it, but I was loath to doe it, fearing to breede a quarrell betweene you, fo long as I was fure to *Thus is he board* keepe him from doing you herein any *throgh the nose with a* iniurie : befide I had ftill a good hope, *cushen.* that he would at length giue ouer : I wis it was no fault of his that he fped not. Gods for my life (faith the good man) being in a great rage, what a treacherous villaine is this? I would neuer haue fufpected any fuch matter in him, for I durft haue put my life in his hands. By this light, hufband (faith fhe) if euer hee come more within the doores, or if euer I may know that you haue any talke with him, ile keepe houfe no longer with you. Ah deere hufband, (and with that fhee clips and cols him againe about *As kind as the* the neck,) fhould I bee fo difloyall as to *Sea-crab sen-zing on a dead* abufe him in this fort? fo fweete, fo *carrion.* amiable, and fo kinde a man, who lets mee haue my will in all things? God forbid I fhould liue fo long to become a ftrumpet now. But for Gods fake hufband forbid him your houfe with whome this knaue hath flaundred mee withall; yet I would the deuill had mee if euer hee made fuch motion to mee, neuertheleffe by Gods grace hee fhall not come henceforth in any place wheere I *Amen.* am : and with that fhee beginnes to weepe, and hee (kind foole) doth appeafe and

D. I. 29

comfort her, promifing and fwearing, that hee will doe as fhee will haue him, faue onely that hee will not forbid him his houfe, with whofe companie the other had charged her, and withall he vowes neuer to beleeue any more of thefe reportes, nor fo much as to harken to any fuch tales againe, notwithftanding hee ftill feeles a fcruple of fufpition in his confcience : Within a while hee begins to fall at defiance with his honeft friende, who informed him of his wiues wantonneffe, and hee feemes to bee fo deepely befotted with her loue, that you woulde fay hee were transformed without inchauntment, into *Acteons* fhape : his / charge of houfhold ftill increafeth, he hath many children, and is perplexed on euery fide : but his wife followes her pleafure farre more then before, for though it be neuer fo openly knowne,

Great reason.

yet will no man tell him thereof, becaufe they know that he will not beleeue them (and which is more ridiculous) he that abufeth him moft, fhall be beft welcome vnto him of any.   To be fhort, age will ouertake him, and perhaps pouertie, from the which he fhall neuer be able to raife himfelfe.   Loe here the great good and pleafure, that he hath gotten by entring into Lobs pound : euery man mockes him, fome faith it is pitty becaufe he is an honeft man : others fay it is not a matter to be forrowed for, fith it is the

common rule of fuch. They of the better fort
will fcorne his company : thus liues he in paine,
griefe and difgrace, which he takes for great
pleafure, and therin wil continue till death cut
him off.

CHAP. VIII.

*The humor of a woman that ftill defires to
be gadding abroad.*

THE next humor of a woman, is, when the
hufband hath bene in Lobs pound fome
fiue or fix yeares, part whereof he hath fpent in
fuch pleafures as wedlock doth at the firft affoord ;
but now the date of thefe delights is out, he hath
perhaps fome three or foure children, but his wife
is now big againe, and a great deale worfe of this
child then fhe was of any other. Whereat the
poore man greeues not a little, who takes great
paines to get her that which fhe longs for : well,
the time of her lying downe drawes neere, & fhe
is wonderfully out of temper, fo that it is greatly
feared that fhe will hardly efcape. Thē fals he
on his knees & praies deuoutly for his wife, who
foone after is brought to bed : wherefore he is not
a little Jocund, making fure account that God hath
hard his praiers. The goffips, kinfwomen, and
neighbours, come in troupes to vifit and reioyce

for her fafe deliuery. She for her part wants no
good cherifhing, whereby fhe recouers her ftrength,
and is as frefh and lufty as euer fhe was.

After / her churching, fhe inuites fome of her
neighbours who alfo inuite fiue or fix others of
her neighbors and friends, who are receiued &
feafted with al kindnes ; which banquet doth
perhaps coft her hufband more then would haue
kept the houfe a whole fortnight : Amongft other
fhe propounds a queftion, & makes a match to
goe altogither to a certaine Faire which will be
within ten daies at fuch a place : to the which
place they fhall haue a moft braue and pleafant
iorney by reafon of the faire weather, for they wil
alwaies conclude fuch an agreement in fome of the
beft feafons of the yeare ; & fhe takes vpon her to
make this motion chiefly in regard of her goffip
which was lately brought abed, that fhe may after
her long pain and trauaile fomewhat recreate &
refrefh her felfe. But fhe anfwers her with thanks
for her good will, faying fhe knowes not how to
get leaue of her hufband. What (faith the other)
that is the leaft matter of a thoufand. Tufh
goffip (faith another) ftand not on that, we will
all goe and be merry, and we will haue with vs
my goffip G. T. my cofin H. S. though perhaps
hee be nothing kind to her : but this is their
ordinary phrafe, & they vndertake this iourney

becaufe they cannot fo wel obtaine their pur-
pofes at home, being too neere their hufbands
nofes. After this agreement, home fhe comes
with a heauie countenance : the good man afketh
what fhe aileth? Marry quoth fhe, the child is
very ill at eafe (though he were neuer in better
health fince he was borne) his flefh burnes as
though it were fire, and as the nurfe tels me, hee
hath refufed the dugge thefe two daies, although
fhe durft not fay fo much till now. He hearing
this, and thinking it true, is not a little fory,
goes prefĕtly to fee his child & weepes for pitty.
Well, night comes, to bed they goe, & then fhe
fetching a figh, begins thus : Hufband, I fee you
haue forgotten me. How meane you that faith
he? Mary (quoth fhe) do you not remember that
when I was in childbed you faid, that if it pleafed
God that I efcaped, I fhould goe to fuch a Fayre
with my goffips & neighbours to make merry, &
cheere vp my felf, but now I heare you not talk
of it. In troth wife (faith he) my head is troubled
with fo many matters, and fuch a deale of bufines,
that I haue no leafure to thinke on any thing els :
but there / is no time paft yet, the faire wil not
be this fortnight. By my truth (quoth fhe) I fhal
not be well vnles I goe. Wel wife (faith he),
content your felfe, for if I can by any meanes get
fo much money ye fhall goe : you know it is not

little that we fhall fpend there : yea more I wis
then will be my eafe to lay out.   Good Chrift
(quoth fhe), is it now come to that? You promift
me abfolutely without either ifs or ands : before
God I will goe whether you will or no : for there
goes my mother, my goffip T. my cofen B. and
my cofen R. and his wife.   If you will not let me
goe with them, I know not with whome you will
let me goe.   He, hearing her thus wilfull, thinkes
it beft for his owne quietnes to let her goe, though
he ftraine his purfe fomwhat the more.   The time
comes, he hyers horfes, buies her a new riding
gowne, & doth furnifh her according to her minde :
peradvēture there goes in their company a luftie
gallant, that will frollick it by the way on her
hufbands coft, for his purfe muft pay for all.   It
may be he will goe him felfe, becaufe hee hath
neuer a man, or els cannot fpare him from his
worke.   But then is the poore man notably perplexed, for fhee will of purpofe trouble him for
euery trifle, more then fhe would doe to another,
becaufe it doth her good to make a drudge of him,
and fo much the rather, that he may not afterward
haue any defire to goe abroad with her againe :
fometimes her ftirrup is too long : fometimes too
fhort, and hee muft ftill light to make it fit :
fometimes fhe will weare her cloake, fometimes
not, and then he muft cary it : then findes fhe

fault with her horſes trotting, which makes her
ficke, and then ſhe will light & walke on foote,
leauing him to lead her horſes : within a while
after they come to a water, then muſt hee be
troubled to helpe her vp againe : Sometimes ſhe
can eate nothing that is in the Inne, then muſt
hee being wearie all day with riding, trudge vp
and downe the towne to find ſomething that will
fit her ſtomack ; all which notwithſtanding, ſhe
will not be quiet : and not ſhe onely, but her
goſſips alſo, will be bobbing and quibbing him,
ſaying that he is not worthy to bee a womans
man; but he is ſo inured to theſe Janglings that
he cares not for all their / words : Well at length
to the Faire they come, and then muſt he play
the ſquier in going before her, making ſo much
roome for them as he can, when there is any
throng or preſſe of people, being very chary of
his wife, leaſt ſhe ſhould be hurt or anoyed by
thruſting.   There moyles he like a horſe, &
ſweates like a bull, yet cannot all this pleaſe her :
Some dames of the company, which are more fluſh
in crownes then her good man, beſtowes money
on gold rings, hats, ſilk girdles, Jewels, or ſome
ſuch toyes, yea coſtly toyes, which ſhe no ſooner
ſees, but preſently ſhe is on fire vntill ſhe haue the
like : Then muſt hee herein content her if he loue
his owne eaſe, and haue he money or not, ſome

fhirt he muft make to fatisfie her humor. Well
now imagine them going homewards, & thinke,
his paine & trouble no leffe, then it was cōming
forth : her horfe perhaps doth foūder much, or
trots too hard, which is peraduenture by reafon
of a naile in his foote, or fome other mifchance.
Then muft hee perforce buy, or hyre another
horfe, and if he haue not money enough to do
fo, then muft he let her ride on his, & he trot
by her fide like a lackey. By the way fhe will
afke for twenty things : for milke, becaufe fhe
cannot away with their drink, for pears, plums, &
cherries : when they come neere a towne, he muft
run before to choofe out the beft Inne: euer and
anon as fhe rides, fhe will of purpofe let fall
her wand, her mafke, her gloues, or fomething els
for him to take vp, becaufe fhe will not haue him
idle : when they are come home, fhe will for a
fortnight together doe nothing els then gad vp
and downe amongft her goffips, to tell them how
many gay and ftrange things fhee hath feene, all
that hath paffed by the way in going and comming,
but efpecially of her good man, whom fhe will be
fure to blame, faying that he did her no pleafure
in the world, & that (fhe poore foule) being ficke
and wearie, could not get him to helpe her, or
to prouide any thing for her that fhe liked : and
finally that he had no more care of her, then if

ſhe had beene a meere ſtranger. But hee poore
ſot finding, at his returne, all thinges out of order
is not a little troubled to ſet them in frame againe,
and toyles exceedingly at his laboure, that he /
may recouer his charges which he hath bene at in
this iourny. But ſhe what for goſſiping, for pride
& idlenes wil not ſet her hands to any thing, and
yet if ought goe well, ſhe wil ſay it was through
her heedfulnes & good huſwiferie : If otherwiſe,
then will ſhe ſcold, and lay the fault thereof on
him, although it be her owne doings. To be
ſhort, hauing thus gotten a vaine of gadding, ſhe
will neuer leaue it, and hereby the poore man will
be vtterly ſpoiled : for both his ſubſtãce ſhall be
waſted, his limbes through labour fild with aches,
his feete with the gout, and age comes on him
before his time: yet as though this were not euil
enough, ſhe wil be continually brawling, ſcolding
and complaining, how ſhe is broken through
child-bearing. Thus is the ſilly man vp to the
ears in Lobs pound, beeing on each ſide beſet with
care and trouble, which he takes for pleaſure, and
therein languiſh[es] whiles he liues.

CHAP. IX.

*The humor of a curſt queane maried
to a froward huſband.*

THe next humor that is incident to a woman,
is when the huſband hauing entred very
young into Lobs pound, and there fettered himſelf
by his too much folly, for a vaine hope of tickliſh
delights which laſted but for a yeere or two, hath
matched himſelfe with a very froward and peruerſe
woman (of which ſort there are too many) whoſe
whole deſire is to be miſtreſſe and to weare the
breeches, or at leaſt to beare as great a ſway as
himſelfe.   But he being craftie, & withal crabbed,
will in no wiſe ſuffer this vſurped ſoueraigntie, but
in ſundrie maners withſtands it.   And there hath
bene great ſtur & arguing about this matter
betweene themſelues, & now and then ſome
battels: but do ſhe what ſhe can either with
her tongue or handes, notwithſtanding their long
controuerſie, which hath perhaps laſted at the leaſt
theſe twenty yeares, he is ſtill victorious, and holds
his right: but you muſt think that his ſtriuing
for / it all this while, hath bin no ſmall trouble &
vexation vnto him, beſide all other aforeſaid euils:
all which, or part therof he hath likewiſe endured:
well, to be ſhort, he hath perchance three or foure

children all maried, and by reafon of the great paines and trauell that hee hath taken in bringing them vp, prouiding them portions, mayntaining his wife, encreafing his ftock, or at leaft keeping it from beeing diminifhed, and liuing with credit amongft his neighbours: At laft it may be hee hath gotten the goute, or fome other daungerous difeafe, and withall is growne old, and thereby feeble, fo that being fet he can hardly rife, through an ache that he hath got in his armes or his legs: Then is their long warre come to an end, and the cafe (as *Ployden* fayth) cleane altered, for his wife beeing younger then hee, and as frolick as euer fhee was, will now bee fure to haue her owne will in defpight of his beard: heereby the poore man, which hath maintained the combate fo long, is now vtterlie put downe: his owne children, which before hee kept in awe well enough, will now take heede to themfelues, and if hee reprooue them for their leudneffe and difobedience, fhee will maintaine them againft him to his teeth, which muft needes bee a great griefe vnto him. But befides all this, he is in doubt of his feruantes, for they likewife neglect their former duetie, and leane altogether to their miftres: fo that hee poore man, which now by reafon of his ficknes, and feeblenes of body, hath more neede of attendance then euer he had, fhall haue very little or none at all, for

though he be as wife and as carefull as euer he
was, yet fith hee cannot ftirre to followe them as
hee was wont, they contemne, and make no more
reckoning of him, then if hee were a meere foole.
Then peraduenture his eldeft fonne thinking that
his father liues too long, will take vpon him to
guide the houfe, and difpofing all things at his
pleafure, as if his father were become an innocent,
and could no longer looke to things as hee was
wont, iudge you whether the good man feeing
himfelfe thus vfed by his wife, children, and
feruantes, be greeued or not. If he purpofe to
make his will, they / will feeke all meanes to
keepe him from doing it, becaufe they heare an
inkling, that he will beftow fomewhat on the
Parifh, or will not bequeath his wife fo much as
fhe would haue.   To be fhort, that they may
make an end of him the fooner, they will many
times leaue him in his chamber halfe a day and
more, without meate, fier, or ought elfe, not one
of them comming to fee what hee wants, or to
do him any feruice : his wife is wearie of him by
reafon of his fpitting, coffing, and groaning. All
the loue and kindneffe, which he had in former
times fhewed vnto her, is quite forgotten : but
his ftrife for fuperioritie, and his crabbedneffe
towards her (when fhe had iuftly mooued him)
this fhe can ftill as well remember, as when it

was firſt doone : neither will ſhe ſpare to prate
thereof to her neighbors, telling them that he hath
bin a bad man, and that ſhe hath led ſuch a life
with him, that if ſhe had not bene a woman of
great patience, ſhe could neuer haue endured to
keepe houſe with ſo crabbed a churle : She will
likewiſe boldly reproach, and twit him in the
teeth with thoſe former matters, for it doth
ſhrewdly ſtick in her ſtomack, that ſhe could not
till now be miſtres : But he that was wont to
charme her tongue, and keepe her vnder, who,
ſeeing him now in his diſtreſſe and weakneſſe,
takes aduantage, and continues his bad vſage,
ſeeing alſo his children, which ſhould feare and
reuerence him, taking part with their mother,
being taught and ſet on by her, ſeeing this (I
ſay) and being no leſſe angry then grieued, hee
cals ſome of them in a rage, and when they are
come before him, thus begins he to his wife.
Wife you are ſhe whome by the lawes both of
God and man, I ſhould loue and eſteeme more
then any thing elſe in the world : and you on the
other ſide ſhould beare the like affection to me :
but whether you doe ſo or not, I referre it to your
owne conſcience, I tell you I am not well pleaſed
with your vſing of me thus : I thinke you take
me ſtill for the Maſter of the houſe as before you
haue done, but whether you thinke ſo or not, bee

fure I will bee Maifter while I liue, yet (you I
thanke you) doe vfe me, and account of me in
very flight maner : I haue alwaies loued you well,
neuer / fuffred you to lack that which was meete :
I haue in like fort loued, and alfo maintained your
children and mine according to my degree, and
now both you and they do very kindly acquite
me.   Why (faith fhe) what would you haue vs
do ? We do the beft that we can, but you can not
tel your felfe what you would haue?   The better
we vfe you, and the more wee tend you, the worfe
you are : But you were neuer other, alwaies brawling, and neuer quiet, neuer pleafed full nor fafting :
I thinke neuer woman was fo long troubled with
a crooked Poftle as I haue bin.   Ah dame (faith
he) leaue thefe wordes I pray you : then turning to
his eldeft fonne, he faide : Sonne, I haue marueld
at your behauiour of late toward me, and I tell
you, I am not wel pleafed therewith : you are my
eldeft, and fhall be mine heire, if you behaue your
felfe as a childe ought to doe ; But you begin
alreadie to take ftate vpon you, and to difpofe of
my goods at your pleafure : I would not wifh you
to be fo forward, but rather while I liue, to ferue
and obey me, as it becomes you to doe : I haue
beene no bad father vnto you, I haue nothing
impaired or diminifhed, but increaft that which
was left mee by my father, which if you doe your

dutie to mee (as I did m[ine] to him) I will leaue
you after my deceafe as hee left to mee : but if
you continue in your ftubbornneffe and difobedience, before God I fweare, I will not beftowe
one penny or croffe vpon thee. Heere his wife
begins againe to thwart him ; Why, what would
you haue him doe ? It is impoffible for any
one to pleafe you : I wis it is high time that you
and I were both in heauen, you know not your
felfe : what would you haue ? I maruell what
you ayle. Well, well, (faith he) I pray you bee
quiet, doe not maintaine him thus againft mee ;
but it is alwaies your order. After this, the
mother and fonne departing, confult together, and
conclude, that hee is become a childe againe, and
becaufe hee hath threatned to difinherite them,
they refolue that no man fhal be fuffered to come
and fpeake with him : his fonne / takes vpon
him more then before, being borne out by his
mother, who together with him, makes euery one
belieue that the poore man is become childifh, and
that he hath loft both his fenfe & memorie. If
any of his honeft friends & former acquaintance,
which were wont to refort to him, come now to
afke for him, his wife wil thus anfwere thē,
Alas he is not to be fpoken with : and when
he demands the caufe thereof, doubting he is
dangeroufly fick, ah good neighbor (quoth fhe)

he is become an innocent, he is euen a child
againe, fo that I poor foule muft guide all the
houfe, & take the whole charge of all things
vpon me, hauing none to help me; but God be
praifed for all.   In good faith faith the other, I
am verie forie to heare this, and doe much
maruaile at it, for it is not long fince I fawe him
and fpoke with him, and then he was in as good
memorie, & fpake with as good fence and reafon
as euer hee did before.   In troth (faith fhee) he
is now as I tell yee.   Thus doth fhe wrong and
and flaunder the poore man, which hath alwaies
liued in good credit, and kept his houfe in very
good order : but you may be well affured, that
hee feeing himfelfe in his age thus defpifed and
iniured, and being not able to remedy himfelfe,
nor ftirre without helpe from the place where
hee is, therby to acquaint his friends therewith,
which might in his behalfe redreffe it, is not a
little grieued, vexed and tormented in his mind
with forow and anger, fo that it is a meruaile
that he falles not into defpaire; for it is enough
to make a Saint impatient to be vfed thus by
thofe which fhould obey, ferue, and honour him :
And in my opinion this is one of the greateft
corrafiues that any man can feele : fuch is the
iffue of his great hafte and extreame defire to
be in Lobs pound, where hee muft now remaine

perforce till death doe end at once both his life and languiſhing.

CHAP. X.

*The humor of a woman giuen to al kind
of pleaſures.*

A N other humor incident to a woman by nature is, when the huſband, thinking that wedlock was of all eſtats the happieſt, and altogether repliniſhed with delight and pleaſure, becauſe he ſaw ſome of his friends, who for a whil after they were maried were very chearefull and iocond, neuer ceaſeth toiling & turmoiling himſelf till he haue gotten into Lobs pound; wherein he is preſently caught faſt like a bird in a net: for this compariſon if we do examine the particulars thereof, doth very fitly reſemble his eſtate. The ſilly birds which flye frō trée to tree & from field to field to ſéeke meat, when they ſée a great deale of corne ſpilt one the grounde, thinke themſelues well apaid, and without any feare come thither to feede there on, picking on the graines of corn; but alas they are deceiued, for on a ſodaine the net is drawne, and they are all faſt tide by the leges, and thence carried in a ſack or panior one vpon another to the fowlers houſe, then coopt vp

in a Cage. Oh howe happy would they thinke
themfelues, if they were againe at their former
liberty to flye whether they lift, but they wifh to
late : yet were this all the euil that they fhould
endure, it were well, but (which is worfe) they
fhal foone after haue their necks wrung off, and
their little bodies fpitted, to be made meat for
men to eate. But they are herein more fimple
then birds, for they being faft in Lobs pound, are
fo befotted with their owne forrowes, that [as] they
haue no power to free themfelues, fo likewife they
haue no wil to doe it. But to proceede, the wife
not louing her hufband, for fome defect which
is in him, that fhe may haue fome collor for that
fhe doth, makes her mother and other friendes,
which blame her for it, belieue, that her hufband
is bewitcht, and by reafon of fome forcery, made
for the moft part impotent : hereupon fhee complaines of her ill fortune, / refembling it to thos,
which hauing the cup at their nofes, cannot
drinke ? Meane while fhe hath a fwéete hart in
a corner, who is not bewitched, who vfeth her
company fo long, and with fo little héed, that in
the end her hufband perceiues it, and falling into
the vaine of iealoufie, beates her wel fauordely,
and kéepes a foule ftirre both with blowes and
words, fo that fhe not liking his vfage, giues him
the flip : but then is he cleane out of patience ; and

ſo huſbands in this taking are ſo mad, that they
neuer lin ſéeking them, and wold giue halfe they
are worth to find her again : who hauing thus
plaid her pagient, and ſéeing her huſbands humor,
compacts with her mother, whoſe good will ſhe
will be ſure to get, by one meanes or other,
(whereas at the firſt ſhe wil perhaps thinke hardly
of her departure from her huſband :) ſhe doth I
ſaye ſo handle the matter with her, that ſhee wil
make the good man belieue her daughter hath
binne all this while at home with her, and that
ſhee came to ſhun his bad vſage, who had ſhee
tarried with him til then, had binne lamed for
euer.   Before God (quoth ſhee) I had rather you
ſhoulde reſtore her againe to mee, then beate her
thus without cauſe, for I knowe that you ſuſpect
her wrongfully, and that ſhee hath neuer offended
you : I wis I haue ſtraightlie examined her about
it, but if ſhe wold haue bin naught, you did
enough to prouoke her : by gods paſſion I think
fewe women could haue borne it.   Wel it maye
bee, that vpon theſe or the like words he takes
her againe : it may bee alſo that they are both
deſirous to be diuorced, each accuſing other, and
ſeekinge to winde themſelues againe out of Lobs
pound, but in vaine ; for either the cauſes that they
alleadge are not thought ſufficient by the Iudge
howe hard ſoeuer they pleade, but muſt of force

continue ftil together, are laughed to fcorne of,
al that heares the caufe; or if they be feperated,
yet will not al this fet them frée, but rather
plunge them in deeper then before, but neither
of them can marry while otheres liues: and their
chaftitie is fo brittle, efpecially heres, that holde it
cannot, nor long endure: fhe who was wont to
be fo frollick muft / néedes continue fo ftil, nay
peraduenture, being now without controwlment,
followes her il life more fréely then before: and
whereas fhee was but earft a priuate queane, is
nowe common in the way of good fellowfhippe,
or elfe fome luftie gallante takes her into his
houfe, and kéepes her by his nofe; which muft
néedes bee vnto him an excéedinge griefe, and
an open fhame to the worlde: and which is worfe,
hee knowes not how in the worlde to remedie
it, but muft perforce endure both while this
miferable life doth laft.

CHAP. XI.

The humor of a woman to get her daughter
a hufband, hauing made a little
wanton fcape.

THE next humor that a woman is addicted
vnto, is, whē a luftie young gallant riding
at pleafure vp and downe the countrye, efpecially

to thofe places of fportes and pleafure where fine
Dames and dainetye Girles meat, whoe can finely
mince their meafures, haue their toongues trained
vpp to amorous chat; in which delightful exercifes
this yonker both by reafon of his youth, his loofe
bringing vpp, and naturall inclination, takes great
felicitie in fuch companie, and fo much the rather,
becaufe hee findes himfelfe alwayes welcome to
fuch places; and the reafon is the comelynes of
his perfon, his amiable countenaunce, and quaint
behauiour, for whoe fo euer hath thefe good helpes,
fhal want no fauour at womens handes : It may
bee alfo : that his parentes are ftil liuinge, and hee
their onely ioye : they haue perhapes noe child but
him, fo that all their delight is in mainetaning him
brauely. It may bee alfo that hee is newly come to
his landes, and loues to fée fafhions, though it coft
his purfe neuer fo largely. If any Gentlewomanne
offer anye kindneffe, hee is readie to requite it :
and at / length through long prancing to many
places, he lights on one that doth exceedingly
plefe his eie, and inflame his hart: fhe is perhaps
daughter to fome Gentleman, fome Citizen, or
fome worthie Farmer. She hath a clean complexion, a fine proportion, and wanton eie, a
daintie toong, and a fharp wit, by reafon of
all which good gifts, fhe is grown very famous.
She hath bin wooed, fued, and courted by the

braueft galants in that contrey, of whom perhaps
fome one being more forward and couragious then
the reft, hath offred her fuch kindnes, as fticks by
her ribs a good while after, and would needs in-
force this curtefie with fuch importunitie, that fhee
had not the power to refift it : for a woman that
hath her fiue wits, if fhe be withal of a cheereful
fanguin complexion, cannot be fo vnkind, or fo
hard-harted, as to deny, or repuls the petition of
an amorous friend, if he do anything earneftly
profecute the fame. And (to be plaine) be fhe
of what complexion foeuer, fhe wil be nothing
flacke to grant fuch a fute. But to returne to our
purpofe, by reafon of her tender compaffion, and
kind acceptance of this proffered feruice, it fo
falls out fhe hath plaide falfe, then is there no
other fhift but to kéepe it clofe, and to take fuch
order as beft they can for the fmoothing vp of ÿ
matter : he that hath don the déed being a poore
yong man, though proper of body, and perhaps
can daunce very well, by which good quallitie he
won her fauour, & within a whil after cropt the
flower of her maydenhead : he (I fay) after a
check or two and no farther matter (leaft this
priuie fcap fhould be openly knowne) is warnd
from comming any more to the houfe, or frequent-
ing her company whatfoeuer. But now you muft
note, that fhe being but a fimple girl betwéene

fourtéene and fifteene yeares of age, nothing ex-
pert, but rather a nouice in fuch matters, and
hauing bin but lately deceiued, knows not her
felfe how it is with her. But her mother which
by long experience hath gotten great iudgment,
doth by her colour, her complayninge of paine
at her hart and ftomack, with other like tokens,
perceiues it wel enough, and hauinge (as before I
faid) caffierd the author of the action, then taks
fhe her / daughter afide, and fchooles her fo, that
in the end fhe confeffeth that he hath bin dallying
with her, but fhe knowes not whether to any
purpofe or not. Yes (fayth her mother) it is to
fuch purpofe (as by thefe fignes I knowe verye
well) that you haue thereby fhamed your felfe and
al your friends, and fpoiled your marriage quite
and cleane. To be fhort, hauinge fomewhat chid
her after the commone order, for hauinge no
more refpect nor care of her honeftie (yet not
chidinge verye extreamely, becaufe fhe knowes the
frailtie of youth by her owne former experience)
fhee concludes thus comfortablye : fith it is done,
and cannot bee altogether remedied, fhee will
féeke to falue the matter as well as fhée can,
charginge her daughter to fet a good countenance
one it, leaft it fhould bee fufpected, and to followe
her counfel and commaundement in al thinges :
whereto the poore wenche willingelye confenteth.

Then her mother proceedes thus: You know maifter T. A. that commeth hither fo often, hee is you feé a proper young Gentleman, and a rich heire; to morrow hee hath appointed to bee heere againe, looke that you giue him good entertainment, and fhewe him good countenaunce. When you fée me & the reft of our good guefts talking together, euer and anon caft your eye on him, in the kindeft and louingeft maner that you can: if he defire to fpeake with you, bee not coy, but heare him willinglie, anfwere him courteouflie. If hee intreate loue of you, tell him that you knowe not what it meanes, and that you haue noe defire at all to knowe it, yet thanke him for his good will; for that woman is too vncourteous and vnciuill, which will not vouchfafe the hearing, or gentlie anfweringe to thofe that loue her, and wifh her wel. If he offer you money, take none in anye cafe, if a ring, or a girdle, or any fuch thing, at the firft refufe it, yet kindely and with thankes: but if hee urge it on you twice or thrice, take it, telling him, fith that he wil néedes beftow it on you, you wil weare it for his fake. Laftly, when hee takes his leaue, afke him when he will come againe? Thefe inftructions being thus giuen, and the plot layd for the fetching in / of this kind foole into Lobs pound, the next day he commeth, and is on alhandes more kindely welcome and entertained: after dinner hauinge had great cheare, the mother falls in talke with the other guefts, and this frolicke nouïce gets him as néere to the daughter as he can, and while the other are hard in chat, hee takes her by the hand, and thus begins to court her: Gentlewoman, I would to God you knew my thoughts. Your thoughts fir (faith fhee) how fhould I kno them except you tell them me? it may be you think fomething that you are loth to tel. Not fo (faith he) yet I wold you knew it without telling. But that (faith fhe fmiling) is vnpoffible. Then quoth he, if I might do it without offence I would aduenture to tell you them. Sir (faith fhe) you may fréely fpeak your plefure, for I do fo much affure me of your honefty, that I know you will fpeake nothinge that may procure offence. Then thus (faith he) I acknowledge without faning, that I am farre vnworthy of fo great a fauour as to be accepted for your feruant, friend, and Louer, which art fo faire, fo gentle, and euery way fo gratious, that I may truly fay that you are replenifhed with all the good giftes that nature can plant in any mortal creature : But if you would vouchfafe mee this vndeferued grace, my good wil, diligence, and continual forwardnes to ferue and pleafe you fhoulde neuer faile. But I woulde therein equal

the moft loyal Louer that euer liued, I would
eftéeme you more then any thing elfe, and tender
more your good name and credit then mine owne.
Good Sir (quoth fhe) I hartily thanke you for
your kinde offer, but I pray you fpeake no more
of fuch matters ; for I neither knowe what loue
is, nor care for knowing it : This is not the leffon
that my mother teacheth mee now-adayes.   Why
(faith he) if you pleafe fhe fhal know nothing of
it, yet the other day I heard her talke of preferring
you in marriag to Maifter G. R.   How fay you to
that (quoth fhee) ? Mary thus (anfweres the Gentle--
man) if you would vouchfafe to entertaine me for
your feruant, I would neuer marry, but relie on
your fauour.

But / that (faith fhe) fhould be no profit to either
of vs both, and befide it would be to my reproch,
which I had not thoght you wold féek.   Nay
(quoth he) I had rather dy then féek your difcredit.
Wel fir (faith fhe) fpeak no more herof, for if my
mother fhould perceiue it, I were vtterly vndone.
And it may be her mother makes her a fign to
giue ouer, fearing that fhe doth not play her part
well.   At the breaking vp of their amourous parley,
he conueis into her hand a gold ring, or fome fuch
toy, defiring her to tak it, and keep it for his fak :
which at the firft (according to her mothers pre-
cepts) fhe doth refus : but vpō his more earneft

vrging of it, fhe is content to take it in ẙ way of
honeftie, and not on any promife or condition of
any farther matter: when it was brought to this
paffe, the mother maks motion of a iourney to be
made the next morning, fome tē or 12. miles off,
to vifit or feaft with fome frind, or to fome fair,
or whatfoeuer other occafion prefents it felf: To
this motiō they al agrée, and afterward fit downe
to fupper, where he is placed next the daughter,
who caries her felfe fo toward him with her pearcing
glances, that the young heire is fet on fire therwith: wel, morning comes, they mount on horfback,
and by the opinion of them al, ther is neuer a hors
in ẙ companie that can carry double but his, fo
that he is appointed to haue the maiden ride behind
him, wherof he is not a little proud; and when hee
féeles her hold faft by the middle, (which fhee doth
to ftaie her felf the better) he is euen rauifhed with
ioy. After their returning home, which wilbee the
fame night, the mother taking her daughter afide,
queftions with her touching all that had paffed
betweene the amourous gallant and her, which
when her daughter hath rehearfed, then procéeds
the wilie Graundame thus: If hée court thée any
more (as I knowe hee will) then anfwere him that
thou haft hearde thy Father and mee talking of
matching thee with Maifter G. R. but that thou
haft noe defire as yet to bee marriede: if hee then

offer to make thee his wife, and vfe comparifones
of his worth and wealth, as if hee were euerye
waye as good as hee, thanke him for good wil
and kindnes, and tell / him that thou wilt fpeake
with me about it, and that for thy owne part
thou couldft find in thy hart to haue him to thy
hufband rather then any man elfe : vpon this
leffon the daughter fleepes, reuoluing it all night
in her mind. The next morning fhe walkes into
the Garden, and this luftic yonker followes, when
hauing giuen her the time of the day, he fals to
his former fute. She wils him to giue ouer fuch
talke or fhee wil leaue his companie : Is this
the loue you beare me (quoth fhe) to feeke my
difhonefty ? You know well enough that my
father and mother is minded to beftow me other
wife. Ah, my fwéete miftres (faith he) I would
they did fo farre fauour me herein, as they do
him : I dare boldly fay and fweare it, and without
vaine glory vtter it, that I am euery way his equal.
Oh fir, anfweres fhe, I would hee were like you.
Ah fwéete miftres, faith he, you deigne to thinke
better of me then I deferue, but if you would
farther vouchfafe me the other fauour, I fhould
efteeme myfelf moft happy. In troth fir, faith fhe,
it is a thinge that I may not do of my felfe, without
the counfell and confent of my parents, to whom I
would gladly moue it, if I thought they woulde not:

bee offended. But it fhould be better if your felfe would breake the matter vnto them, and be fure, if that they referre the matter to mee, you fhal fpeede fo foone as any. He being rauifht with thefe words, and yeelding her infinite thanks, trots prefentlie to the mother to get her good wil: To be fhort, with a little adooe the matter is brought about, euen in fuch fort as hee woulde defire; they are ftraightway contracted, and immediately wedded, both becaufe that her friendes feare that the leaft delaye wil preuent al, and becaufe he is fo hot in the fpurre, that hee thinks euery houre a yeare til it be done. Wel: the wedding night comes, wherein fhe behaues herfelf fo by her mothers counfel, that hee dares fweare on the Bible that hee had her maidenhed, and that himfelf was the firft that trod the path. Within a while after it comes to his friends eares without whofe knowledge he hath maried himfelf, who are exceeding fory, knowing fhe was no meet match for him, and it may be they / haue heard withal of his wiues humor: but now there is no remedie, the knot is knit, and cannot be vndone, they muft therefore haue patience perforce. Well, he bringes his faire Bride home to his owne houfe, where godwot he hath but a fmal time of pleafure, for within three or foure months after their mariag, fhe is brought to bed: iudge then in what taking

the poore man is. If he put her away, his fham
wil be publick, fhe grows common, and he not be
permitted to marry againe while fhe liues, and if
he keepe her ftil, loue her he cannot, fufpect her
he will, and fhe both hate him, and perhapes feeke
his end : finally, all the ioyes, pleafures, and delights
which before time they had, are al turned to brawles
banning, curfing, and fighting : thus is he hampered
in Lobs pound, wher he muft of force remain, til
death end his liues miferies.

CHAP. XII.

*The humor of a woman being matched with
an ouerkind hufband.*

THere is another humor incident to a woman,
which is, when a young man hath tur-
moyld and toffed himfelf fo long, that with much
adoe hee hath gotten into lobes pound, and hath
perhaps met with a wife according to his owne
defire, and perchance fuch a one, that it had bin
better for him to haue lighted on another, yet he
likes her fo well, that he wold not haue mift her
for any golde; for in his opinion there is no
woman aliue like vnto her: hee hath a great
delight to heare her fpeake, is prowde of his
matche, and peraduenture is withal of fo fheepifh

a nature, that hee hath purpofed wholie to gouerne himfelfe by her counfel and direction, fo that if any one fpeake to him about a bargaine, or whatfoeuer other bufines, he tels them that hee will haue his wiues opinion in it, and if fhee bee content, he will go thorough with it, if not then wil he giue it ouer : thus is he as tame and pliable, as a Jack an apes to his keeper. If the Prince fet forth an army, and / fhe be vnwilling that he fhould go, who (you may think) wil afke her leaue, then muft he ftay at home, fight whoe will for the country: But if fhe be at any time defirous to haue his roome (which many times fhe likes better then his company) fhe wants no iourneyes to imploy him in, and he is as ready as a Page to vndertake them: If fhe chide, he anfweres not a word, generally whatfoeuer fhee doth, or howfoeuer, hee thinks it well done. Judge now in what a cafe this filly calfe is : is not he think you finly dreft that is in much fubiection ? The honefteft wooman, and moft modeft of that fexe, if fhee weare the bréeches, is fo out of reafon in taunting and controuling her hufband, for this is their common fault, and be fhe neuer fo wife, yet, becaufe a woman, fcarce able to gouern her felf, much leffe her hufbande, and all his affaires, for were it not fo, God wold haue made her the head ; which fith it is other wife, what can bee

more prepofterous, then that the head fhould be
gouernd by the foote? if then a wife and honeft
womans fuperioritie bee vnfeemely, and breede
great inconuenience, how is he dreft, thinke you,
if hee light on a fond wanton, and malicious
dame? Then doubtles hee is foundly fped: fhe
will kéepe a fweete hart vnder his nofe, yet is he
fo blind ẏ he cannot perceiue nothing: but for
more fecuritie, fhe wil many times fend him
packing beyond fea, about fome odde errand
which fhe wil buzze in his eares, and he will
performe it at her pleafure, though fhee fend
him forth at midnight, in rayne, hayle, or fnow,
for hee muft bee a man for all wetheres: Their
children, if they haue any, muft be brought vp,
apparelled, fed, and taught accordinge to her
pleafure: and one point of their learning is
alwayes to make no account of their father. If
any of their children be daughters, fhee wil marrye
them according to her minde to whom fhee lift,
when fhe lift, and giue with them what dowry
fhe lift, without acquanting him therewith, till
fhee haue concluded the match; and then fhe tels
him, not to haue his confent, but as a maifter
may tell his feruante, to giue him direction howe
to behaue himfelfe to deale therein: finally, /
fhe orders al thinges as fhe thinks beft her felfe,
making no more account of him, efpecially if hee

bee in yeares, then men doe of an old horfe
which is paft labour. Thus is hee mewed vp in
Lobs pound, plunged in a fea of cares, and
corafiues, yet hee (kinde foole) déemes himfelfe
moft happye in his happines wherein hee muft
now perforce remaine while life doth laft; and
pittie it were hee fhoulde wante it, fith he likes it
fo well.

CHAP. XIII.

*The humor of a woman, whofe hufband
is gone ouer the fea vpon
bufines.*

AN other humor of a woman is, when the
hufbande hath binne maried fome feauen
or eight yeares, more or leffe, and as hee thinkes,
hee hath met with as good wife as any man
can haue, with whom he hath continued al ẏ
aforefaide time with great delights and pleafures:
But admit hee bee a Gentleman, and that hee is
defirous to purchace honor by following armes,
and in this humor hee refolues to make a
ftep abroad, and not to tarrye alwayes like a
cowardly drone by the fmoake of his owne
chimney; but when he is ready to depart, fhe

D. I. *33*

bathing her chéekes with tears, falls about his
neck, cols, kiſſeth, and imbraceth him ; thē wéeping, ſighing and ſobbing, ſhee thus begins to him,
Ah ſweet huſbande, will you now leaue me? wil
you thus depart from me and from your children,
whiche knowes not when wee ſhall ſee you againe,
or whether you ſhal euer come home againe or
noe ?   Alas ſweete huſbande, goe not, tarrye
with vs ſtill ; if you leaue vs wee are vtterly
vndone.   Ah ſwéet wife (ſaith he) diſſwade mee
not from this enterpriſe, which concernes both
my credite and alleagiance, for it is our Prince,
commaundement, and I muſt obey : but be you
wel aſſured that I wil not be long from you (if it
pleaſe God.)

Thus / doth he comfort and quiet her in the beſt
ſort that he can, and be ſhe neuer ſo importunate,
be her feares neuer ſo many, her intreaty neuer ſo
forcible, yet go he wil, eſtéeming his renowne and
dutie to his Prince and country more then wife
and children, though next to it he eſtéeme and
loue them chiefeſt of al other.   And at his departure hee recommendes them to the care and
curteſie of his chiefeſt friendes ; yet ſome there be
whoſe tender harts melt ſo eaſely with kind compaſſion, that one of their wiues teares, and the
leaſt of their intreats, wil tie them ſo faſt by
the legge at home, that they wil not ſtir on foote

from her fwéet fide, neither for king nor *Keyfar*, wealth nor honor. Thes are crauens, and vnworthy to be called gentlemen. But to returne to this vallorous and braue minded gentleman, of whom we fpak before, it may be that either by the long continuance of the warres, or by his misfortune in being taken prifoner, or fome other let, hee comes not home in foure or fiue yeares, & al that whil ther is no newes of him : you may be fure that his wife is a forrowful woman, and wholly furchargd with griefe, being thus depriued of her louing mate, and hearing nothing of his eftate. But al things haue an end, and fhe feeing that in fo long a time, fhe can hear no tydinges of him, doth peremtory conclude that he is dead. Then confidering to liue comfortles in widdows eftate, wer an vncouth life, fhe determines to marry her felf to fome one fo foon as conueniently fhe may, which wil be foon inough, for a faire woman, if willing can want no choyce. Thus her former forrow is fomewhat alaid, and within a while after clean extinguifht, by the frefh delights, pleafure, contents and follace which this new choice doth yeeld. So that now hir other hufbande is wholly forgotten, her children which fhe had by him little regarded, and the goods which belong to them, are fpent on others, while the poore wretches want things needfull, but not blowes and hard vfage. To be fhort, the

teares which ſhe beſtowed on her other huſbande
at his departure is dryed vp, her imbraces vaniſhed.
And whoſoeuer ſhoulde ſee her with this ſecond
huſbande, and what kindneſſe ſhee ſhewes / vnto
him, woulde verily thinke that ſhee loues him
farre better then ſhe did the firſt, who in the
meane while is either priſoner, or els fighting in
extreame hazard of his life. But in the end
it chaunceth ſo, that by paying his ranſome, (if
he haue bene priſoner) home hee comes, cleane
chaunged thorough the many troubls he hath
had : And being com ſomwhat néere, failes not
to inquire of his wife and children, for he is in
great feare, that they are either dead or in ſome
great diſtreſſe. And doubtles in the time of his
impriſonment or other daungeres, hee haue oft
thought, ofte dreamed of them, and oft ſorrowed
for them, oft ſought God to preſerue and bleſſe
them. And that perhaps ſometimes, at the very
inſtant when ſhe was in the others armes, toying
and dallying, and in the mideſt of her delights.
Well, inquiring (as before ſaid) [he] heares that ſhe
is married againe : then iudge you with what griefe
he heares it : But his griefe is booteleſſe, for now
the matter is paſt remedy. If he haue any care of his
credite, any regard of his eſtimation, he wil neuer
take her more, though perhaps the other hauing had
his pleſure of her could be wel content either to

reftore her to him, or to leaue her to any one elfe. She on the other fide is vtterly fhamed, and her name ftained with perpetuall reproch, and neither he nor fhe can marry while they liue. Their poore children are likewife griued and fhamed at their mothers infamy. Sometimes likewife it happens, ŷ for the wiues caufe, the hufband being coragious, doth quarrel and perhaps combat with him, who being better then himfelfe, doth either wound or kill him, and the occafion hereof fprung from their wiues prid, becaufe forfooth fhee will take the wall of the others wife, or fit aboue her, whom fhe will in no wife fuffer, nor loofe an inch of her eftate, and hereupon the hufbands muft together by the ears. Thus the fuppofed bleffednes which hee expected by plunging himfelfe in lobs pound, is turned into forrow, truble, danger, and continuall difcontent while life doth laft.

CHAP. / XIIII.

*The humor of a woman that hath bene
twice married.*

THere is another humor belonging to a woman,
which is, when a young man hauing found
the way into Lobbes pound, méetes with a wife
of like years, fresh, lusty, fair, kind and gracious,
with whom he hath liued two or thrée years, in al
delights, ioys and pleasure that any married couple
could haue : neuer did the one displeafe the other,
neuer foule word past betwixt them, but they are
almost stil kissing and colling each other, like a
couple of doues.   And nature hath framed such
sympathy betwéene them, that if the one be il at
eafe or difcontented, the other is fo likewife.   But
in the midst of this their mutuall loue and follace,
it chanceth that she dies ; wherat he gréeues fo
extreamely, that he is almost beside himselfe with
forrow : he mournes, not only in his apparel for a
shew, but vnfainedly, in his very heart, and that fo
much, that hee shunnes al places of pleafure, and
al company, liues follitary and spends the time in
daily complaints & mones, and bitterly bewaling
the losse of fo good a wife, wherein no man can
iustly blame him, for it is a losse worthy to be

lamented. And a iewel which whoſoere hath is happy (but this happines is very rare). To be ſhort, his thoughts are al on her, and ſhe ſo firmely printed in his mind, that whether he ſléepe or wake, ſhe ſéemes alwaies to bee in ſight ; but as all thinges hath an end, ſo here had ſorrowe. After awhile ſome of his friendes hauing ſpied out a ſecond match, which as they think is very fit for him, do preuaile ſo much with him, through her perſwaſions, that hee accepts it, and marries him-ſelfe againe, but not as before, with a yong maid, but with a luſty widow, of a middle age and much experience ; who by the trial which ſhe had of her firſt huſband, knowes how to handle the ſecōd : but that ſhe may do it the better, ſhe doth not preſently diſcouer / her humor, til ſhe haue thoroughly markt how he is inclined, what his cōditions are, & what his nature is : which finding milde, and kind, and very flexible (the fiteſt mould to caſt a foole in) hauing now the full length of his foot, then ſhewes ſhe herſelfe what ſhe is, vnmaſking her diſſembling malice. Her firſt attempt is to vſurpe ſuperioritie, and to become his head, and this ſhee obtaines without any great difficultye, for there is nothing ſo lauiſh as a ſimple & wel natured young man being in ſubiečtion, that is married, to a widow, eſpecially if ſhe be, as the moſt of them are, of a peruers and crabed nature. I may very wel com-

pare him to an vnfortũat wretch whofe il happe is
to bee caft into a ftrong prifon, vnder the kéeping
of a cruel and pittileffe Jaylor, that is not moued
to compaffion, but rather to great rigor, in the
beholdinge the miferies of this poore wretch ; whofe
onely refuge in this diftreffe, is to pray vnto God
to giue him patience to endure this croffe, for if
hee complaine of his hard vfage, it will afterwards
proue worfe.

But to proceede : This iolly widdow wil within
a while grow Jealous, feare and fufpect that fome
other dame hath part of that which fhe fo mightily
defireth, and wherewith fhee could neuer bee fatisfied, fo that if hee glut not her infatiable humor,
ftraighteway fhee conceiueth this opinion if hee
doe but talke, nay, which is worfe, looke on any
other woman ; for fhee by her good wil woulde
bee alwayes in his armes, or at the leaft in his
companye : For as the fifh whiche hauinge
beene in water, that through the heate of the
fommer is halfe dryed vpp, beginnes to fticke
full of mudde, féekes for frefh water, and hauinge
founde it, doth willingly remayn therin and wil in
no wife return to his former place : euen fo an
olde woman, hauinge gottenne a younge man, will
cling to him, like an Iuy to an Elme. But on
the other fide, a young man cannot loue an olde
woman, howfoeuer hee doth diffemble, neither is

there any, that more endaungers his death : for it is with him, as with one that drinketh mufty wine, who if he be thirftye feeles / nothinge whiles hee is drinking, but at the ende of his draught, he feeles fuch a difpleafing tafte, that it doth almoft turne his ftomack. But if yong men can in no wife fancy old women, what loue think you yong women can beare to old men, whē befid the fundry imperfections of their age, which are fo loathfome, that it is impoffible for a frefh yong tender damfell, be fhee neuer fo vertuous, to endure the companye, much leffe the kiffes and imbraces of the perfone which hath them, all the lufty gallantes there-abouts will not faile to vfe whatfoeuer deuifes and meanes poffible for the horninge of the olde dotard, hoping that fhee wil bee eafily woon to wantonnes : and furely they grond this hope on great likelihood, for fith it is no difficult exploit to graft the like kindnes on a yong mans forhead, who is able in far better meafure to féede his wiues appetite, and fhee hath therefore more caufe to be true to him, it may furely feeme no great matter to per-forme the like piece of feruice with this other infortunate dame, who is almoft hunger ftarued for lacke of the due beneuolence of wedlocke. But now to returne to our young man, yoakt (as before I faide) to this olde widdow, I conclude that his eftate is moft miferable : for befides the

daunger of his health, and befide the fubiection,
nay rather feruitude which hee liues in, this third
euill, I meane his wiues iealoufie, is alone an
intollerable torment vnto him, fo that be he neuer
fo quiet, neuer fo defirous to content her, neuer fo
feareful to difpleafe her, yet cannot he auoyd her
brawles, obiections and falce accufations of lewdnes
and difloyaltie, for an olde woman infected with
iealoufie, is like a hellifh furie: If he go to any of
her friends about any bufines, yea to the Church
to ferue God, yet will fhee alwayes thinke the
worft, and affure her felfe, that he playes falce,
though indeede he be neuer fo continent, who
whatfoeuer he pleadeth in his owne defence, yea
though he proue himfelfe blameles by fuch reafons
as fhe can by noe reafon confute, yet will not all
this fatisfie her, fuch is the peruerfenes of her
ftubborne, crabbed, and mali[ti]ous nature, made
worfe by dotage and raiginge Iealoufie ; / for being
priuie to her owne defectes, and knowing that he,
by reafon of his youth and hafomnes may perchance
fal in fauour with a yong dame, thinking withall
that a yong man, whē he may haue fuch a match,
wil be loth to leaue it for a worfe, or prefer four
veriuce before fweete wine, She cōcluds peremptory
in thefe fugeftions as before. Lo here the iffue of
this affes turning into Lobs pound, and intangling
of himfelf again, when he had once gotten out to

his former liberty ; which if he once more looke for, he is mad, for he muſt now perforce continue there while life doth laſt, which [by] this meanes will be farre ſhorter, and hee looke farre older, hauing beene but two yeares married with this olde crib, then if he had liued ten yeeares with a young wife.

CHAP. XV.

The humor of a young woman giuen ouer to al kind of wantonneſſe.

THer is yet another humor that a woman is ſubiect to, which is, when an vnfortunat yong man, hauing long laboured to get into Lobs pound, & hauing in the end obtained his deſires, doth match him-ſelfe with a luſty wanton young wench, which without fear of him, or care of her own credit, takes her pleaſure freely, and withal ſo ouer boldly, and vnaduiſedly, that within a whil her huſband perceius it; who there vpon being not a little inraged, doth in the heate of his impatience, after much brawling on both ſides, roughly and deſperatly threaten her, thinking therby to terrifie her, & mak her honeſt by compulſion : But that makes her worſe, for whereas before ſhe did it for wantoneſs, now will ſhe do it for deſpight : and what with the

on and the other, be fo inflamed that were fhe
fure to be killed for it, yet would fhe not leaue
it :   Which he perceiuing, watcheth her doings
fo narrowly, that in the end he fées her fwéet
hart com clofely to his hous; then / being on
fire with furie, runnes haftily to furprize him,
and enters his wiues chamber with full purpofe
to kill him, though he had ten thoufand liues :
But iudge you in what a taking the poore yong
man is, in feeing himfelfe thus furprized, and
looking for nothing els but prefent death, becaufe
hee hath nothinge to defende himfelfe.   But
fhee for whofe fake hee hath incurred this
daungere, doth kindely frée him by this ftratagem,
for as her hufbande is ready to ftrike or ftabe
him, fhee catcheth him haftiely aboute the middle,
cryinge out, Alaffe man what dooe you meane ?
While fhee thus ftaies her hufband, the younkere
betakes him to his heeles, running downe the
ftaiers amayne, and out of the doores, as if the
diuell were at his tayle, and after him the good
man as fafte as hee can driue.   But when hee
fees that he cannot ouertake him, hee turnes
backe in a like rage, to wreake his angere one
his wife.   But fhee dreadinge as much, getes her
haftielye (before his returne) to her mothere, to
whome fhee complaines of his caufeleffe fufpition and deuillifh furie, iuftifying her felfe, as

if ſhe wer not the woman, that would commit
ſo leaud a part : But her mother ſifting the
matter narrowely, her daughter confeſſeth her
faulte ; but to make it ſéeme the leſſe ſhe teles
her a large tale of the younge manes importunity,
whoe for ſo longe time together did continually
trouble her, and whether ſoeuer ſhee wente hee
woulde bee ſure to folow her, begging pitifully
her loue and fauour ; that ſhe had often ſharply
anſwered him, & flatly denied his ſute, yet could
ſhe not for all that be rid of him : ſo that in
the end, ſhe was inforct for her own quietnes to
graunt his requeſt. She repeats withall, how
kindly & intierly he loues her, how much he
hath beſtoed on her, how many foule iournies
he hath had for her ſake in rayne and ſnowe, as
well by night as daye, in danger of théeues, in
perrill of his life, and how narroly he eſcaped
her huſband the laſt time, ſo that for verye pittie
and compaſion, ſhe was moued to fauour him, &
no woman could be ſo hard harted, as to ſuffer ſo
true and kind a yong man to lan/guiſh for her
loue, and die vnregarded : for on my life, mother
(ſaith ſhe) if I had not yéelded, he woulde haue
dyed for thought.

The mother hearing her daughter to ſaye thus,
acceptes her anſwere for currant, and thinkes that
ſhee hath ſufficiently iuſtified her ſelfe, but to

preuent further fcandal, and to appeafe her angry
fonn in law, & reconcile her daughter vnto him
by cafting a mift before his eyes, fhe takes this
cours, fhe fends for her efpeciall goffip & companions, whos counfels in like cafes fhe doth vfe:
they comming at the firft cal, & being al affembled
either before a good fier (if it bee winter) or in a
greene arbor (if it be fomer) one of the noting her
daughters heauy countenance demandes ƒ caufe
therof: Mary, faith fhe, fhe hath had a mifchance
about which I haue made bold to trouble you,
& craue your aduice: with that fhe recounts the
whole matter vnto them, but fhewing the true
caufe of her hufbands anger: to be fhort, fhe hath
ready two or three pottles of wine, & a few iunkets,
which they prefently fal aboord, that they may the
better giue their feuerall verdits afterwards; mean
whil they cofort the young woman, bidding her
affure her felf, that hir hufband is more perplexed then fhe: and that I know by min own
experience, for my hufband and I wer onc at
variance, but he could neuer be quiet til we wer
made friĕds. In good faith goffip (faith another)
and fo ferued I min. Another makes a motion
to fĕd for the yong gallant that is fo true a louer
to her goffipes daughter, that his prefence may
cheer her, & rid away her melancholly. This
motion doth hir mother faintly cotradict, but in

the end moſt voices preuails, he is ſent for, and
comes with a trice; then ther is much good chat,
many a reproche and kinde ſcoffe giuen the poore
huſband: And to mend the matter comes in the
chambermayd, who was priuie to all the former
cloſe packing between her miſtres and her ſweete
hart, and for her ſilence and imployment in
furthering both their contents, ſhe hath goten a
new gowne, and ſomwhat els : it may be her
maiſter hath ſent her abroad about ſome buſines,
or perhaps ſhe coines an excuſe of / her ſelfe,
thereby to make a ſtep abroad to ſee her miſtreſſe,
and to bring her newes how al things go at home :
She hath no ſooner ſet a foote within the roome
wher they are, then one of them aſkes how her
maiſter doth?   My maiſter (ſaith ſhe) I neuer ſaw
a man in that taking : I dar ſay that ſinc yeſterday
morning when this misfortune happened, he hath
not eaten one crum, dranke one drop, or ſlept one
winke al yeſter night.   To day he ſat down to
dinner, and put one bit in his mouth but could not
ſwallow it, for he ſpit it out preſently, and ſat a
good while after in a dumpe: In the end ſtriking
his knif on the table, he roſe haſtily, and went into
the garden, and immediatly cam in again : To be
ſhort, he is altogether out of temper, and can reſt
no where; he doth nothing but ſigh and ſob, and
he looks like a dead man : hereat they laugh apace,

and to be fhort, they determine that two of the
chiefe of them, fhall goe and fpeak with him the
next morning, & that when they are in the midft
of their talk the reft fhal come in afterward.
The mother with her two goffips, according to
this plot, doe procéede in the matter.   And next
morning finding him in his dumpes, one of them
gentilly afkes him what he ayles? herto he anfweres
onely with a figh : whereupon fhe takes occafion
thus to fpeak.   In good faith goffip I muft chid
you, my goffip your wiues mother told mee I
know not what of a difagréement betweene your
wife and you, and a certain fond humor that you
are fallen into : I wis I am forry to hear it : And
before God you are not fo wife as I had thought
you had ben, to wrong your wife thus without a
caufe, for I durft lay my life ther is no fuch matter.
By this good day (faith another) I haue knowne her
euer fince fhe was a little one, both maide and wif,
and I neuer faw but wel by the womã : And in
good footh it griues me to the very hart, that her
name fhold now come in queftion without caufe :
Before God you haue don the poore woman that dis-
grac, and fo ftained her good name, that you [will]
neuer be able to make her amendes.   Then ftepes
in the chamber-maid with her fine eggs.   In good
faith (faith fhe) I know not what my maifter hath
feene, or whereon hce doth / ground his fufpition,

but I take God to my witnes that I neuer faw any fuch matter by my miftreffe, and yet I am fure that if there were any fuch thing, I fhould fee it as foone as another. Gods body drab, faith he al inragd, wilt thou face me downe of that which my felf faw? Oh goffip, quoth on of the dams, God-forbid, that euery man and woman which is alone together fhould do euill. I deny not, faith the chamber-maide, that the villan knaue hath long fued vnto my miftrefs for fuch a matter, but by my honefty mafter, I know ў there is neuer a man aliue whom fhe hates more : and rather thē fhe would comit any fuch folly with him, fhe would fe him hãgd and be burned her felf : I maruel how the diuel hee got into the houfe. Here the other goffips com in on after another, and each giues her verdit : In good faith goffip, faith one, I think that next your wif, ther is not a woman in the world ў loues you beter then I do : and if I knew or thoght any fuch mater as you fufpect, be fure I wold not let to tel you of it. Surely faith another, this is but the diuels worke to fet them at variance, for he cannot abide that hufband and wif fhold liue wel together. In good faith faith the third, the poore woman doth nothing but weep. By Chrift quoth the fourth I fear it wil coft her her life, fhe griues and takes on in fuch fort. Then comes the mother weeping & crying out, making as thogh

D. I. *35*

fhe would fcratch out his eies with her nails,
exclaiming in this fort. Ah curfed catiffe, woe
worth the hower that euer my daughter matcht
with thee, to be thus fhamed & flandered, & haue
her name fpotted without caus. But fhe is well
enough ferued, that would take fuch a bafe churle,
when fhee might haue had fundry good gentlemen.
Ah good goffip, faith another, be not out of
patience, Ah goffip, faith fhee, if my daughter
were in fault, by our good lord I would kill her
my felf. But think ye I haue no caus to be
moued, when I fee my child, being giltles thus
vfed? with that fhe flinges out of doores in a
rage, and all the goffips comes vpon him thicke &
threefold, who is fo full of fundrie thoughts, & fo
grieued and troubled, that he knowes not whereon
to refolue, nor what to fay. In the / end they
growing fomwhat calmer, promife if he wil, to
vndertake the recōciling of him and his wife,
which he moft erneftly defireth them to do. They
accordingly performe it, fo that al controuerfies
are ended, all ftrife ceafed, the matter hufhed vp,
and his wife taken home again ; who taking greater
courage by the fucceffe hereof, and being now
cleane paft fhame, will grow farr bolder in her
villany then before. And the poore meacock on
the other fide, hauing his courage thus quailed, wil
neuer afterward fal at ods with her, for feare of

the like ſtorme, but wil ſuffer her to haue her own
ſaying in al things, and be in a manner ſubiect to
her, ſpending the remnant of his life, in
care, feare, diſcontent, and griefe,
his goods waſting he knowes
not how, and himſelfe a
laughing ſtock to al
that knowes
him.

FINIS.

www.ingramcontent.com/pod-product-compliance
Lightning Source LLC
Chambersburg PA
CBHW031345070726
47496CB00017B/1787